Occult specialist Kathy Ryan returns in this thrilling novel of paranormal horror from Mary SanGiovanni, the author of Chills . . .

Some doors should never be opened . . .

In the rural town of Zarepath, deep in the woods on the border of New Jersey and Pennsylvania, stands the Door. No one knows where it came from, and no one knows where it leads. For generations, folks have come to the Door seeking solace or forgiveness. They deliver a handwritten letter asking for some emotional burden to be lifted, sealed with a mixture of wax and their own blood, and slide it beneath the Door. Three days later, their wish is answered—for better or worse.

Kari is a single mother, grieving over the suicide of her teenage daughter. She made a terrible mistake, asking the powers beyond the Door to erase the memories of her lost child. And when she opened the Door to retrieve her letter, she unleashed every sin, secret, and spirit ever trapped on the other side.

Now, it falls to occultist Kathy Ryan to seal the door before Zarepath becomes hell on earth . . .

Book by Mary SanGiovanni

Behind the Door

Also Featuring Kathy Ryan
Chills

Also by Mary SanGiovanni
Savage Woods

Published by Kensington Publishing Corporation

Behind the Door

Mary SanGiovanni

LYRICAL UNDERGROUND
Kensington Publishing Corp.
www.kensingtonbooks.com

LYRICAL UNDERGROUND BOOKS are published by
Kensington Publishing Corp.
119 West 40th Street
New York, NY 10018

All Kensington titles, imprints, and distributed lines are available at special quantity discounts for bulk purchases for sales promotion, premiums, fund-raising, educational, or institutional use.

Special book excerpts or customized printings can also be created to fit specific needs. For details, write or phone the office of the Kensington Sales Manager: Kensington Publishing Corp., 119 West 40th Street, New York, NY 10018. Attn. Sales Department. Phone: 1-800-221-2647.

Lyrical Underground and Lyrical Underground logo Reg. US Pat. & TM Off.

First Electronic Edition: August 2018
eISBN-13: 978-1-5161-0682-0
eISBN-10: 1-5161-0682-2

First Print Edition: August 2018
ISBN-13: 978-1-5161-0685-1
ISBN-10: 1-5161-0685-7
Printed in the United States of America

To Charles L. Grant—sometimes the loudest screams echo in the whispers.

Acknowledgments

Thanks to Mike, Suzanne, and Christy SanGiovanni, Michele and Mike Serra, Sprout and Seedling, Brian Keene, Martin Biro, James Abbate, and Becky Spratford, and to loyal readers. Your support keeps me going.

Chapter 1

In the town of Zarephath, Pennsylvania, just past the Pennsylvania-New Jersey border and northwest of Dingmans Ferry out by the Delaware Water Gap, there is a Door.

Many stories about it form a particularly colorful subset of the local lore of the town and its surrounding woods, streams, and lakes. Most of them relate the same essential series of events, beginning with a burden of no small psychological impact, progressing to a twilight trip through the southwestern corner of the woods near Zarephath, and arriving at a door. Numerous variations detail what, exactly, must be presented at the door and how, but ultimately, these stories end with an unburdening of the soul and, more or less, happy endings. It is said "more or less" because such endings are arbitrarily more or less agreeable to the individuals involved than the situations prior to their visit to the Door of Zarephath. More times than not, the "less" wins out.

There are some old folks in town, snow- and storm cloud–haired sept- and octogenarians who sip coffee and people-watch from the local diner or gather on front porches at dusk or over the counter at Ed's Hardware to trade stories of Korea and Vietnam, and in one venerable case, World War II, and it's said they know a thing or two about that door. The old-timers remember the desperation of postwar addictions and nightmares and what they used to call shell shock, of families they couldn't help wearing down or beating up or tearing apart, despite their best efforts to hold things together. They remember carrying burdens, often buried but never very deeply, beneath their conscious thoughts, burdens that crawled their way up from oblivion and into nightmares and flashbacks when the darkness of booze or even just the night took over men who had once been children and who were expected to be men. They remember late-night pilgrimages through the forest on the outskirts of town, trekking miles in through rain or dark or frost-laced wind to find that door, and lay their sins and sorrows at its feet. And they remember that sometimes, forgetting proved to be worse.

The old women too remember bruises and battered faces and blackouts. They remember cheating husbands and cancers and unwanted pregnancies and miscarriages and daughters being touched where they shouldn't by men who should have protected them. The old women remember the Door in Zarephath being a secret, almost sacred equalizer that older women imparted to younger women, a means of power passed from one group whose hands were socially and conventionally tied to another. And they remember watching strong women fall apart under the weight of that power.

And these old folks remember trying once to burn the door down, but of course, that hadn't worked. The Door in Zarephath won't burn because it isn't made of any wood of this earth, anything beholden to the voracious appetite of fire. It had an appetite of its own that night, and no one has tried to burn it down since. Rather, the old-timers have learned to stay away from it, for the most part, to relegate the knowledge of its location and its promises to the same dusty old chests in the mind that the worst of their war stories are kept. There's an unspoken agreement that as far as the Door in Zarephath goes, the young people can fend for themselves. While the folks in Zarephath won't stop a person from using the Door, they aren't usually inclined to help anyone use it. Not in the open, and not just anyone who asks about it. Behind some doors are rooms hidden for good cause in places human beings were probably never meant to know about—rooms meant never to be entered—and the old folks of Zarephath understand that for reasons they may never know, they were given a skeleton key to one such room. There's a responsibility in that, the kind whose true gravity is maybe only recognized by those with enough years and experience and mistakes left behind to really grasp it.

People often say the old-folks' generation were stoic, used to getting by with very little and largely of a mind frame not prone to histrionic anxiety or useless worry. People say it has to do with surviving the Depression and growing up in a simpler, more rugged time. But for the old folks in Zarephath, the strength of their fiber comes from what they remember— and from what they have come to accept forgetting. It comes from what they no longer choose to lay before the Door.

* * * *

To say the loss of Kari's daughter, Jessica, had left a hole in her heart significantly understated the situation. It was more of a gaping maw in the center of her being, a hungry vortex that swallowed light and love, vibrancy and memory.

It had swallowed her friendships early on. People, even the most well-meaning of them, rarely knew what to say when someone's child died. Telling her time would heal all wounds sounded trite. Telling her everything would be okay sounded patronizing. How could such an inescapable hollowness ever be okay? And telling her Jessica was in a better place might come across as the biggest bullshit of all. There was no way anyone could possibly know what lay beyond the walls of mortality, and given the circumstances, the suggestion came across as being rather insensitive anyway. There was nothing even the most eloquent and empathetic could say to take away a hurt like that.

"How are you holding up?" they'd ask with that look on their faces, part discomfort and part superiority in being somehow removed from such a horrible thing. Maybe the urge to slap that look off their faces showed through in her weak smiles and tired eyes. Or maybe her attempts to speak of banalities that went nowhere were just the kind of nothing-words that stalled relationships or even moved them backward. It was easier for people to drop away, couple by couple, then one by one. Eventually, those awkward meetings became fewer and farther between. The calls stopped coming, followed by the emails, and then eventually the texts petered off too. There were no further attempts to get her out of the house and reconnected with the world. She was a sinking ship and they were bailing before they got sucked into her currents. It was clear in their eyes, in their voices. It was in the distance they put between her and them. She had been relegated to a kind of camp or colony for people who had undergone an Awful Tragedy, a thing they were thankfully unable to relate to in any meaningful way.

That gaping maw had swallowed her job, as well. Her boss had been gracious in granting her time off from the office. He'd given her weeks, a month, and then another. She had dipped into and then run dry her long-term disability time. And when she'd come back to the office, the Mondays and Fridays when she couldn't find a reason good enough to get out of bed looked bad. Her zoning out during production meetings looked bad. Her stacks of unfinished paperwork looked bad. She'd quit after enough "please close the door" conversations led her to believe she was on the verge of being fired.

It had swallowed her marriage, certainly. Steven hadn't managed more than a few months in the house, the two of them passing each other like solemn ghosts from different eras, unseeing, unhearing, and unable to comfort each other in the grief that had overwhelmed them both. When he finally drifted away for good, out of the house and into an apartment in another state, he became no more than a name on divorce paperwork and a face in old pictures she tucked away in a box.

She hadn't lasted much longer there in the house amid the dust and empty picture frames. If Jessica's spirit had haunted the old house instead of her memory haunting Kari, then it might have been more bearable. At least she'd be able to feel some presence of and closeness to her daughter. But the girl wasn't there, at least not so far as Kari could tell. The girl had fled that house and that life, and wherever her soul was, it seemed far beyond Kari's reach. So Kari had fled that old house and life too. The problem was, although the new house in Zarephath was the only thing that had gone well in a long time, it didn't feel like home, not like the one with Jessica's room, plastered as it was with posters of smiling, clean-cut objects of innocent preteen crushes. Not like the one with Steven's clothes on his side of the closet and his keys on the table by the front door. She supposed her sense of security and family had been engulfed by that gaping maw too.

Finally, it had swallowed her sense of self. Her sleep was shot to hell, and the depression and anxiety had become so bad that who she was no longer existed without the meds. Kari hated what the meds did to her; rather, she hated what the lack of meds in her system did. First, there was the headache, a storm of pain that gusted not just around her head, but up her nose and through her sinuses, behind her eyes and down her throat. There was the heavy weight of heat that made her sweat, a sour kind of sweat that turned her stomach if she lifted an arm or turned her head toward her shoulder. Then came the dizziness, an offshoot of the headache whose roots seemed to reach down into her arms, hands, and fingers, sucking the strength out of them and making them shake. Her eyes would narrow to a glare from the pain and fog. Within her chest, a growing sense of unease would turn into a panic whose edges fluttered far from and untethered to any rational ground.

It was during those times that the memories of Jessica hurt worst. In fact, there were so many memories that she was starting to forget what it was like not to hurt.

She felt all those things the night before she found out about the Door in Zarephath. It coincided with the one-month mark in the new house, and perhaps more importantly, the eve of the third anniversary of Jessica's passing. If it were possible, the pain was sharper and deeper and more all-consuming now than it had been in those nightmare-blur first weeks right after finding Jessica's body. Losing someone, she thought, was like quitting an addiction. First there came the withdrawal pangs of the mental and physical sort, the ache of not being able to hear her laughter or footsteps on the stairs, see her smile or hug her, smell the child-hair smell. But in a way, the routine, the comfortable familiarity, was a much tougher part of the habit to break. Kari found she still looked out for the school bus at five minutes to three, still made sure the door was unlocked and checked the sidewalk for Jessica's approach from the bus stop. She still found herself sometimes at the bottom of the stairs to call her daughter down for dinner or call up to tell her to brush her teeth and that Kari would be up in a minute to tuck her little girl in. She still made lists of toys to buy her daughter for Christmas, still perused the Halloween costumes for something Jessica might like. She wasn't sure if those rote actions were her way of proving she was still there, still Mom, or if they meant she herself had become a shade stuck in an endless loop of repeating the past.

That night before, as she bent over the dishwasher, she grabbed a handful of serrated knives by their blades. They pressed into the skin of her palms, cold but not hard enough to cut her. Her hand shook and she dropped them to the counter with a clatter.

She was due to have lunch the next afternoon with Cicely, the nice old lady next door and one of her only acquaintances in Zarephath, or anywhere at all anymore. They had planned on the Alexia Diner on Dingmans Turnpike, and over what had become their weekly coffee and hot open-faced turkey sandwiches, she intended to tell Cicely she was finished—with life, with everything, with trying to fight the current to be normal, functional, and in the process of healing. She wasn't any of those things, and she couldn't pretend anymore. She was cocooned in her personal world of grief and simply saw no other ways to break free. And no amount of friends' well-meaning attentiveness or love or understanding, and no amount of her own swallowing of pain and indignation and unfairness could make up for it.

The loss of Jessica felt like a fist crushing what was left of her heart in her chest. And she was simply finished. The guilt and the sadness were too much to carry alone.

She had hidden the note from Steven. She'd hidden it from everyone. It felt like the last thing, the only thing, she could do to protect her precious daughter. She'd found it crumpled into a tight little ball in Jessica's fist. The girl's reasoning was suggested in a few neat lines of looping girlish script. She couldn't keep secrets anymore; there were so many and she felt so guilty and embarrassed and even afraid, but mostly, she was exhausted.

Kari knew how she felt.

She picked up one of the knives again, entertaining the kind of thought that had come to fill in those tight little end spaces where her mind let memories of Jessica trail off. End-cap thoughts, was how she'd come to think of them. This one was less refined than some of the others; it involved a lot of blood—a tubful, maybe—and the indignity of being found naked or maybe just in her underwear. Messy and embarrassing and probably painful, if cutting her legs while shaving and letting them slip back under the warm water was any indication.

Her almost-twelve-year-old daughter had done something and gone somewhere she never had been and could never have imagined, had lived a part of her life and ended it without her mother and father, and that seemed wrong. It seemed wrong that children that age should ever feel the need to take on adult things like that, especially alone. Kari didn't want Jessica to be alone. And if Jessica could open that door to another plane of existence, then how could Kari call herself a decent mother and yet not have the guts to follow?

Kari put down the knife.

She'd talk to Cicely. Then she'd decide.

* * * *

People like Toby Vernon built entire lives and whole senses of self around lies. Lies were the brick and mortar that built cities, even empires, of good faith, goodwill, and human connection. Among the sharply honed senses of the predator was a toolbox of excuses and fabrications based on body language, expressions in the eyes, and tones of voice, wielded quickly and efficiently to achieve a result. Lies allayed fears or manipulated them, soothed guilt or exacerbated it. Of all the talents to protect and develop as a primary survival skill, lying was at the top of the list.

And people like Toby were good at it.

He was turning forty that year, which meant he had spent the last twenty-four years since his conviction, incarceration, and release perfecting his ability to lie. He had learned to change like a chameleon. He could be charming, unassuming, unworthy of notice or comment. He was also selective and, at times, ruthless. And it had been almost two and a half decades gone by since he had been arrested or convicted of anything that had to do with children.

However, his confidence, and with it some of his skill, had waned after the girl in Dingmans Ferry. It wasn't that he didn't know deep down, deeper than his lies and justifications could reach, that he hurt children. He had, in the past, tried to justify it as a necessary evil, a means of pain management or sedation or simply an inexorable addiction. He was not so deluded as to think the children were unaffected by his...attentions. It had never been so clear to him, though, nor had it ever inspired such self-loathing, as it had with that girl. Something changed after that. Toby had taken a good look at his life the last four decades or so and realized that all that perfected lying had never been perfect at all. He had never escaped his mother's belief that he was a monster, pure and simple, the kind that most of the rest of the world would see put down sooner than a rabid dog.

It made him afraid of others, as if he were somehow suddenly exposed. Mostly, it made him afraid of himself, a notion he wasn't used to and didn't like at all.

Toby had always wanted to be normal, to date regular adult women, to get married. When he'd realized, much to his disappointment, that his sexual attraction to preadolescent girls wasn't something he could outgrow or ignore, he'd resigned himself to what he was. In fact, he'd suppressed instead that sad, self-pitying hope of ever getting better. After the Dingmans Ferry girl, though, that need to feel normal reemerged, and it was almost—not quite, but almost—as strong as the urges themselves. He didn't want to feel self-loathing every time he drove past a playground or worry that the hawk-eyes of watchful mothers in grocery stores were judging him with disapproval and hostility. He no longer wanted to feel that old familiar tension and discomfort throughout his body at the birthday parties of family's and friends' children.

There were only so many times one could park a half-block or so from the middle school during recess and come to a boil of lust and shame, only so many uncomfortable drives home with a hard-on in his pants and the echoes of his mother's disgusted words in his head, before it came time to admit to being at a crossroads. Down one way lay peace; there might never be redemption, but there might be some cosmic credit for and solace in having overcome the basest part of himself. Down the other way meant the risk that one day, those little bloodied flower-print panties were going to end up shoved down some slender, pretty little throat or some fragile set of growing bones was going to break. He didn't want that. Lord knows, he didn't want it to come to that.

He asked the gods behind the Door to take the urges away.

Edward Richter had told him about the Door. He knew Ed from the hardware store, where the old man had been working stocking shelves and ringing up purchases for the last seventeen years. Ed was more than a familiar face around town, though Toby wasn't sure he could quite classify Ed as a friend. Ed shared the same affliction, a predilection for children, though his preference was for little boys. Toby had seen it right away: the familiar mannerisms and expressions and the wolfish look in the eyes, just as he supposed Ed had recognized the same in him. It was a tenuous bond between them, for hunting is a lone pastime, and a lonely one.

He and Ed got together once a month, usually at Ed's house, a small, pale-yellow bi-level on the edge of town out by the woods. They drank beers and vented about work or politics or debated the merits of the Mets vs. the Pirates. Sometimes they talked about their respective stints in jail. Sometimes they talked about children. But until that one night three weeks prior, Ed had never mentioned the Door. No one had, in all the years Toby had lived in Zarephath.

"Well, Ed," Toby had said that night in response to Ed's asking after his well-being, "I've hit a wall, I think."

"In what way?" Ed cocked an eyebrow at him and sipped his beer.

Toby shook his head. "I drove past the park yesterday—you know the one out on Miller Road, by the firehouse?"

Ed nodded. The flash in his eyes, imperceptible to anyone but a fellow predator, told Toby that Ed knew it well.

"There was this little girl. She was sitting on top of the monkey bars, with her feet dangling over and the wind moving little blond strands of her hair across her cheek…She was beautiful, Ed. I mean stunning. I wanted her. But…it was more than just wanting her. It wasn't enough, just watching her."

A small, uncomfortable smile passed over Ed's lips. "It seldom is."

"I wanted to hurt her, Ed."

The older man looked up in surprise. "Oh?"

"I don't know, it was…not like the other times. It was more intense a feeling, more…primal. Savage. I never felt that before…at least, not to that extent, you know?"

"Can't say that I do," Ed said, shifting in the chair. "Not that I'm judging, mind. Just not familiar with what you're describing." Something in his eyes and the tone of his voice led Toby to believe Ed was lying. It was the subtlest shift to survival mode through denial and diminishing. Toby wasn't going to argue, though.

"I can't keep on like this. I need to do something before I…hurt someone. Jesus." He rose, stalking to the far corner of the den with his beer. Suddenly that little room seemed incredibly stifling to him, with its dim, seventies color scheme and old furniture that clung to its ghosts like a dust shroud. "I can't take it anymore. I wish I could carve this whole part of me away, make these feelings just dry up."

"And therapy…?"

Toby groaned. "It's useless, man, especially in the short-term. You know that. And I'm frankly terrified a shrink will suggest the surgery. I guess maybe I could do the drugs, but the guys on the forum who are taking them seem so miserable, or just numb to everything. I don't want to be like that, either. Plus, there are all these possible side effects—serious ones." He sighed. "I don't know what to do. I just want to be normal. I want the urges to go away. I'd do anything at this point. Christ, maybe I should be on those damn drugs…" He shook his head. He felt lost.

"Well, uh…there is another way. No drugs, no surgery, and no therapy. But you have to be really sure, really clear in your own head about what you want. Is that what you really want?"

Toby turned to the old man. "Yeah, yeah, of course. Wouldn't you, I mean, if you could get rid of that part of you that feels what we feel for kids, wouldn't you cut it out of you? It's like a tumor, Ed. I'd just as soon be rid of it."

Ed cleared his throat. His gaze was fixed on his beer bottle, but Toby knew he had something to say, hanging there just behind that unsmiling mouth.

"What?" Toby prompted.

"Well…there's the, uh…the Door."

"What? What door?"

"The Door…you know." Ed gestured toward the window and beyond it, the edge of the forest. "The one out in the woods. The Door."

"I don't know what you're talking about, Ed. The door to what? And what does it have to do with me?"

"Ain't no one ever told you about the Door? For fuck's sake, how long have you lived in this town?"

"Ed, what door?"

Ed gazed at his beer for several seconds before answering. "It's a Door that…gives you stuff. Or takes stuff away that you don't want anymore. Like suppose your old lady is cheating on you with the guy down the street, right? Well, you go to the Door—you have to go alone, see, at night—with a letter. You fold the letter and seal it with wax that has drops of your blood in it. And inside, the letter asks for your wife not to see the guy anymore, or for the guy to just go away, right? Just up and disappear. And in three days—never heard of it taking no longer or shorter—you get what you want. Like, the guy gets hit by a bus, maybe. Or he just vanishes, no trace, just gone. You get your old lady back. Maybe."

"You're kidding me." But Toby could tell that the older man wasn't, just as he could see the predator behind Ed's grandfatherly eyes. Ed was serious; he believed what he was saying whole cloth.

Ed shook his head slowly. "You ask any of the old folks around here. They'll tell you. The Door is real. Go out, see for yourself. It's standing out there, plain as day. One of Zarephath's great unkept secrets. And it does work, just like I told you. You ask for something to be taken away, like, like your attraction to little girls there, and you *will* get what you want. Though I gotta say, it may not be like you think…and you can't take it back. You can't undo what you asked. And you sure as hell can't open the Door no matter what, no sir."

"So you think a magic door is going to solve my problems? Is that what you're telling me?"

Ed shrugged. "Poke fun all you want, but you go see if I'm telling tales. Go see."

"If it's so great and powerful, then why haven't you ever used the Door?"

Ed gave him a faint smile. "I'm an old man. Not much of a sex drive anymore. No real need. Besides, I guess when I was a younger man, I was… selfish. Selfish, and a little afraid of giving up the only thing I knew, only thing I was sure about. And of course, the old folks at the time made sure I knew about the drawbacks, just as I guess I ought to make sure you know."

"Drawbacks?"

"You don't get nothing for free, Toe. You know that. Like I been tryin' to say, there's risk, using that Door. Always risk." He sipped his beer thoughtfully. "Of course, it sounds like there's a mighty big risk in your not using it at this point too. Guess it's up to you."

Toby sat, rolling the beer bottle between his hands as he considered what Ed had said. "So what, I just write a letter? Like to Santa Claus? Tell this Door what I want? Then what?"

"Then you seal it, like I said. Melt some wax, mix a little of your blood in, then seal it, like those old-fashioned letters, you know?"

Toby nodded.

"Then you go out at night—has to be full dark—and you make your way to the Door—"

"How do I find it? What if I get lost?" Toby broke in.

"Well, you can bring a flashlight and a compass, or one of them app things on your phone, if you got it."

"Okay, so assuming I find the door, then what?"

"Then you slip the letter under the Door. That's how I had always heard it done. No words necessary. Just slip it under, then walk away. Go home, keep your mouth shut. Deed is done."

Toby frowned. The whole thing was crazy. Magic doors, wishes granted. Fairy tales were for kids, not for men who exploited them. He shook his head. He wanted a solution to his problem more than anything, but…this? Was Ed fucking with him?

Ed seemed to read the doubt on his face and leaned forward, tipping the mouth of his beer at Toby like a pointer finger. "Look, I know how it sounds, believe me. I know. You don't have to take my word for it. If you want to consider using the Door, I'll take you out there tomorrow afternoon. You can see it for yourself. If not, we can forget we ever had this conversation. You just said you was looking for a solution that wouldn't involve drugs or surgery or hurting one of them pretty little girls in the park. This…well, this might be the only option you got, buddy."

Chapter 2

"And that's it? Three days and then—"

"Then, the Door gives you what you want." Cicely stirred the Splenda into her coffee, dwarfed by the high-backed brown booth seats of the Alexia Diner. She wasn't looking at Kari, which was not like the older woman at all. As long as Kari had known her, Cicely looked everyone and everything in the eye. She was a small woman of firm curves and sure words and smooth, dark brown skin that made her look much younger than she was. The wisdom of her years, though, was in her eyes.

"But…what? What's the catch?"

Cicely finally looked at her. "You don't always get it how you want it. And there's no way to take it back, sugar, because rule number one is that you absolutely, under no circumstances ever, open that Door. Once you deliver your letter, it is out of your hands."

Kari considered it. She had tried therapy, she'd tried drugs, she'd tried hypnosis and support groups and self-help. And there was the more recent contemplation about joining her daughter. She'd have given anything to have the pain taken away from her, even if only for a little while. A few years ago, she would have thought the things Cicely was telling her were crazy. A lot can happen in a few years, though—a lot of nightmares that seem too real, a lot of nights working hope that there was an afterlife into belief. People putting their faith in things far less concrete than Cicely's Door. If there was even the slightest chance, even the vaguest possibility that what Kari was hearing was true, even in part, then wasn't it worth a try?

"Where is this Door?" she finally asked.

Cicely glanced around the diner to make sure no one else was listening. She'd done it a few times during the conversation so far, as if the subject of the Door might lead to trouble from some other patron of the diner. Seemingly satisfied that the conversation had still gone unnoticed, Cicely said, "I can show you, but if you do choose to use the Door, you'll have to go back alone with your letter. What you ask the Door, you gotta ask alone." She met Kari's gaze and suddenly placed her hand on top of Kari's. "Now, listen. I'm only telling you about all this because I see the pain in you—you're drowning in it. It's in every outward part of you, much as it is on the inside...and I understand that desperation. But because I understand it, I wouldn't be a good friend if I didn't warn you—you gotta be careful. You gotta make sure you word your letter carefully, hear? You don't wanna give them behind the Door any reason to give you anything other than what you want."

Kari was quiet for a moment, mulling over how to word the question in her mind. She didn't dare hope for a positive answer, but she had to ask. "Has anyone ever...." Losing her nerve, she let the unfinished question hang there between them.

"Ever what?"

Kari took a deep breath and continued in a hushed voice. "Asked for someone who died to, you know, come back?"

Cicely stared at her for a moment, and then a deeper understanding dawned on her face. "Oh, oh no, no, no. Don't you go thinking like that," she said, shaking her head and wagging a finger at Kari. "Absolutely not. I won't show you if that's what you're thinking—"

"No, not really. No. I was just curious how...well, how that would work."

"It doesn't," Cicely replied with a curt little frown. Her features momentarily darkened as some memory passed over them. "You ain't the first one to think of such a thing, but I can tell you, it ain't never been nothing but disaster."

"What happened?"

Cicely sipped her coffee before explaining. "First time was back in '42, I think. Boy killed overseas, during the war. His parents, Joe and Marlie Thumer, were devastated. They'd already lost another son to a fire the year before. Well, the poor fools asked for their sons back from the dead, alive and well. The grief was overwhelming them, just like you. But Kari, what they got back were stinking, rotting corpses, shambling up along the country road." She shivered. "We all remember. I was little, only four then. My mama scooped me up and ran me into the house when she saw them boys. Tried to cover my eyes, but I saw—I remember to this day. I guess their brains still worked—I suppose that was what was 'alive and well' about them—but you could see it in their eyes, the pain, the misery of being trapped in bodies still falling apart…." She shook her head. "Their mama kept them in the house about a week, and it wasn't 'til she found what them boys had done to the family dog…. Their papa took them out to the barn and ended their suffering for them. Single bullet each to the back of the skull."

"My God," Kari said. It was horrible, to be sure, but…maybe it was how they worded things in the letter. Maybe, if she could be more careful….

Cicely seemed to read her lingering hope in her eyes and continued. "That ain't the only case, sugar. Just the first one. Another woman, Annalie, asked for her dead daughter to return to her, to be alive again and like she was before the accident. Worded *her* letter better than the Thumers, she thought. What Annalie got was to relive the day her daughter's car smashed into a tree. She had her baby back a few hours, maybe, and went through the pain of her death and funeral all over again." Cicely sighed. "You want another story? I got plenty. No, you ain't the only one to want her baby back, but for the love of the good Lord above, if you got any common sense, ask for something else, anything else. Ask for the pain to be taken away. Ask for only the happy memories. Do *not* ask for your daughter to come back to you. When you ask for things that defy the laws of God and nature, it never, never works out. Look, I know I said you can ask for anything and you *can*, sure, but we learned quick 'round here that you *don't*. We come to learn there are some things you just don't ask for without it biting you in the ass."

"Okay, okay, I get it. I'll be…more careful. Ask, like you said, to be done with the pain."

Cicely's features softened, as did her voice. "I know the temptation is there, sugar. I know. But you have to trust me on this. The magic doesn't work that way, and folks, they don't get too many chances to use the Door."

"Oh?" Kari was still mulling over all the older woman had said.

"No one uses the Door twice. It isn't done."

"So, it's never been done, or isn't done anymore?"

"In every case I can think of, the person who used the Door again had his or her request backfire, and the person died. Every case. No one asks anything of the Door twice."

Kari nodded slowly. "This is a lot to take in," she finally said.

Cicely nodded. "I know, sugar. And as far as I'm concerned, if you think the risks are too much, I sure would understand that. I wouldn't blame you if you chose not to believe a word I'm saying, just wanted to chalk it all up to the folk ramblings of some crazy old lady. I'll consider the whole matter dropped. As I mentioned, I have some mixed feelings about the whole thing. But if you do choose to…to go ahead with asking the Door for some peace of mind, I'll back you. You're a good woman, Kari. You deserve to have that tragedy taken away from your heart and mind. But ask for that, sugar. For the love of God, just ask for it to be taken away."

* * * *

Carl "Deets" Dietrich made his way through the woods by memory. He'd brought a flashlight, but it hung by its key ring clip from the belt loop of his faded jeans. He couldn't quite bring himself to turn it on—that would have made the surreal too real, too much like conscious action and not like sleepwalking. Plus, he didn't want anyone to see or know, if possible, that he was out there using the Door. He didn't want to answer questions and he certainly didn't want to spark rumors. As he saw it, he was in enough trouble already.

It didn't matter if the flashlight was on or not—Deets knew the way. The moon was unusually bright that night, and he'd scouted the area a few times before under the guise of hunting. No one had asked why he never bagged anything. People seldom questioned his failures anymore.

He clutched the letter tightly as he tromped through the underbrush, worrying about how loud his footsteps sounded, worrying about the sweat from his palm somehow seeping through the letter and blurring the ink, worrying about the wax on the seal breaking. Mostly, though, he was still worried about the cops finding evidence linking him to that hit and run on Derber Avenue. He was so tired of worrying. So tired…

His uncle was the one who had suggested the Door without even realizing it, shortly after reading about the accident in the paper. It *was* an accident, but Deets had panicked. God, how he'd panicked. He hadn't been drunk, but he'd been drinking and it had been dark and a little foggy and—

He'd gotten out to try to help the boy, but he looked…crumpled, like a wadded-up piece of paper that someone had splattered red paint on, then left in a puddle of it. He was twitching a little, but then he stopped and seemed to somehow sink even further into himself. As Deets stared in wide-eyed horror, his breath hitched over and over and over until he was sure he was hyperventilating. A moment's flash of surety that he would pass out from fright right next to the body in the road came almost like a physical shove, causing him to stumble backward, then flee for his car.

He managed not to have to pull over to vomit until he'd put a good five miles between himself and the scene of the accident. *The crime scene.*

He doubled over again and dry-heaved at the thought of it, half-blinded by his own headlights. The cops would find him, would check cars on the road for dented, bloody bumpers. Maybe they could even find his vomit and test it for DNA. *Stupid, stupid, stupid.* He stumbled back to his car. What was he going to do?

It was well after three-thirty in the morning when he let himself into his boss's service garage and a quarter after five by the time he'd managed to wash off all the blood and hammer out the dents. The boy had left only two: one on Deets's bumper and one on the hood of his car. The windshield was still intact. He thought the boy must have been light, a fragile little thing to do so little damage to his car, and he fought the urge to throw up again.

He was home in bed by six, with no one the wiser, so far as he could tell. No witnesses, no evidence—just nearly overwhelming guilt and fear. Despite those feelings, though, exhaustion overtook him and he fell asleep. Saturdays were his day off, so no one woke him—no police banging on the door or angry family members, the boy's or his.

When he stopped by his mom's for a late breakfast, his uncle was reading about the hit and run of an unidentified teenaged boy on Derber Avenue. It took every fiber of Deets's being not to snatch the paper out of his uncle's hand.

"No leads, it says. They don't know who the bastard is that hit him. Damn savage, is what I say. Probably drunk too." His uncle sipped his coffee, oblivious to his nephew blanching behind him.

"That poor boy's parents," his mom murmured over her frying pan of eggs. Deets felt the color leave his face. The boy hadn't even really looked like a person when he'd hit him, so the idea of him having a family, people who would miss him, hadn't really occurred to Deets.

"And you want to bet they never catch the guy? Not if he knows about the Door. Guy can fix it so they never find out."

His mother gave her brother a sharp look—she'd always been superstitious and never let such talk, particularly about the Door, happen in her house, not after what happened to Deets's grandfather. She noticed her son then and smiled at him. "Hi, honey. Want some eggs?"

Deets wasn't remotely hungry, but returned a weak smile and nodded. His head had begun to pound.

The Door. He could go to the Door.

He wrote the letter that afternoon, wording it as carefully as he could. The next part was a little tough; Deets was squeamish when it came to blood. However, he managed after the second try to run his fingers close enough to the blades on his razor to open up a small wound across the tip.

Quickly, he cupped the blood and moved to the candle he'd "borrowed" from his mother's collection. He lit the candle and as soon as the wax on top near the wick liquefied, he let the blood patter down on top of the candle. Then, blotting his finger with a tissue, he folded up his letter in thirds. He wasn't sure how to seal it, but decided on tipping the candle so that some of the liquid wax with swirls of his blood landed on the edge of the paper. He then pressed it to the fold.

There. It was done. Now he just had to deliver it.

He managed to find the Door in the daytime about a week later. It had been a very long week. He flinched every time the phone rang and felt his stomach curl into a tight ball of terror every time there was a knock on his front door. He wasn't sleeping and his nerves were wearing thinner and thinner. Every "hunting" trip out to the woods had been a failure, and he'd been on the verge of screaming like a madman at the trees when he turned and... there it was. He sucked in a breath. He'd found it.

It was nothing like he'd imagined; somehow he'd pictured an ornate gothic door of polished mahogany with gold filigree and intricate carvings, or maybe something glowing and swirling within a shining frame of silvery branches, like a fantasy portal in a video game. There was nothing fancy or unique about it, though, other than the fact that it was a freestanding, rectangular door and frame in the middle of the woods. The Door itself had been constructed of heavy wooden planks, weathered to a pale gray and held together with thin crossbeams ostensibly nailed to the planks at eye- and knee-level. The doorknob was a burnished bronze, simple and round, but there was no plate or keyhole. The frame, which flanked and crowned the Door, was composed of big, heavy-looking cobblestones arranged two and three wide, and the Door was set a half-inch or so above the threshold, allowing just enough room for something like a letter to be slipped beneath. As Deets stepped closer to it, he thought he heard a low, distant hum.

Awed, Deets reached out a hand, hesitated, then lightly touched the wood and then the stone. Both felt worn smooth, but intensely solid and strong—so strong that it was as much a mental impression as a physical sensation. It was almost as if the Door vibrated with strength, and the sensation was enough to make him draw his fingers back quickly.

He circled the Door slowly, but the far side of it looked more or less like the front, minus the doorknob. He even tried peering under it, but of course, there was nothing to see. Whatever was really on the other side of the Door, whatever his mother was so afraid of, was not going to show itself now in broad daylight. He'd have to come back at night.

And he did. As an hour and then half of another passed while he still navigated the woods in the dark, a new worry emerged—that he wouldn't be able to find the Door again, or if he did, that something would go terribly wrong. It made him think of his grandfather. He didn't know the whole story—his mother was unwilling to tell him and his uncle was evidently unable—but he knew it involved his gramps's own nightly trek out to the Door, and how something had gone wrong some time after he'd slipped his letter under the Door. Deets could only imagine what his gramps had asked for that left him a half-charred thing with a rictus smile, contorted, almost curled in on itself, which the police had found later the following day.

He shivered, noticing only in the periphery of his thoughts that there was no breeze to chill him; the leaves on the trees remained still, waiting, holding tiny breaths, watching him.

Deets had spooked himself just to the point of turning around and going home when the mists parted and he once more stood face-to-face with the Door, now illuminated by a shaft of moonlight.

He approached it slowly. Somehow, standing before the Door at night held a different kind of gravity in his mind. The nebulous stories about his grandfather seemed more substantial, and the full weight of the terrible thing he did hung between him and the Door like a palpable, miasmic thing. It was hard to breathe, and he was vaguely aware that the hand clutching the letter was shaking.

He approached the Door slowly, his mouth dry. All around him, the forest was dead silent and it was only when he got close enough to the Door to touch it that he heard even the faintest suggestion of the hum, and that was something he felt more than heard. He swallowed and the air moved stickily down his throat. He peered around the side of the frame to see if anything behind the Door had changed. It hadn't; there was no alternate dimension, no other world. Only darkness there, and the far side of the Door, and the forest decaying into darkness beyond.

He faced the Door again and for a moment, had the crazy notion to turn the knob and open the Door right up, to gaze into whatever was on the other side, humming faintly and dispensing benevolence and malevolence at will. His hand, in fact, had managed to close half the distance between him and the knob before that voice in his head, the one who didn't talk nearly often enough, screamed at him to stop. He jerked his hand back, horrified. Had that happened to his grandfather? Had it been opening the Door that had killed him? And how had he come so close to opening it himself without even realizing?

He took a step back and sank to his knees. The humming seemed to be louder, though that could have been his imagination. He tried looking under the Door again, but saw nothing but black.

Then he thought he heard voices, whispering from under the Door. His heart pounded. The hair on his arms stood on end. His breath stuck in his chest.

He shoved the letter under the Door and fell backward, scuttling away from it.

At first, nothing happened. Then small indentations formed in the rock of the frame, filling with a glowing blue liquid to illuminate a series of runic characters the likes of which he'd never seen. They cast an eerie glow on the Door as well as the trees and ground nearest by. Deets wanted to scream, but couldn't. He couldn't move, couldn't even really think. All he could do was watch the glowing symbols in the Door and the flash of blue light that swept the under-space beneath into which he'd shoved his letter.

Then, all at once, the lights went out. The moon, perhaps behind a cloud now, lit nothing, and Deets was left alone in pure darkness with the Door.

He did cry out then, a sound that could easily have been mistaken for a bird or some other night animal. Fumbling with the flashlight, he switched it on and with shaking hands, pointed it at the Door.

It stood as it had in the daylight; silent, unmoving, unyielding, and indifferent.

Deets got to his feet and backed away until his shoulder bumped a nearby tree. He was afraid of taking his eyes off the Door, afraid of turning his back on it even for a moment. He edged around the tree in his way and when the Door was finally out of his line of sight, he ran.

* * * *

Kari thought about the letter for days. After her lunch with Cicely, the older woman had taken her out to the woods and shown her the Door. It was a simple, unostentatious slab of wood, hardly something she could imagine being capable of granting wishes, as Cicely had said. Door and frame stood with no visible means of support amid a grove of oak trees, which seemed to know better than to grow too close. Kari could chalk that up to optical illusion and the power of suggestion. The low hum she felt, rather than heard, when she got close enough to touch the Door might have had something to do with it. She wasn't quite ready, after all she'd tried in order to get better, to put her faith in magic.

Over the rest of that week, though, the Door and its promise of peace of mind kept returning to her thoughts. She could be whole again, if it worked. She could have a life again.

The only thing that kept her from asking for her daughter back from the dead was the mental image of her dead but animated child lumbering back from the cemetery, like some terrible ghoul. Despite her initial incredulousness at Cicely's story, there was something so…haunted, she felt, about Cicely's eyes when she told Kari about the boys who'd come back falling apart, rotting right off their own frames, that it had stuck with her, a shiver beneath the surface of her conscious thoughts. The old woman wasn't making something up; rather, she was remembering something that had informed her nightmares for decades. And Kari was desperate, but not stupid and not insensitive. She wanted her daughter back, but not if it meant subjecting the poor girl to even more pain and horror than she had already experienced. She couldn't do that to Jessica. She needed to believe her daughter rested in peace, and she could never forgive herself if that peace was interrupted or worse, taken away permanently.

No, Kari had decided the best thing to ask the Door for was what Cicely had suggested: to have the painful memories and thoughts taken away from her head and heart. There would come a time, God willing, that she would see her daughter again, but until that time, she just wanted to forget the pain, to put it aside some place where it couldn't drive her into the ground. She worded her letter thus:

> *Please take away my painful thoughts and feelings regarding Jessica.*
> *Please give me peace in my mind and in my heart.*
> *Also, please let her rest in peace knowing, wherever she is, that she is very much loved by her mother and father.*

It had taken four drafts, but she was finally satisfied. She'd kept it succinct and as specific as possible and thought it covered everything she needed to have happen in order to move on with her life. She couldn't see a way that it could possibly backfire on her. To ease her friend's mind, she'd shown Cicely her letter that next week at the diner. Cicely approved with a grim nod of the head. That night, Kari had sealed it with wax and blood, as instructed, but due to the thunderstorm raging outside, delivery would have to wait. That was okay. The hard part was done. She could hold off one more night.

That night when she slept, with the letter on the night table next to her bed, she did not dream.

Chapter 3

Retired Monroe County sheriff Bill Grainger had been sober for a long time. To anyone who asked, including his grandson, who was a state trooper himself down near the Pine Barrens in Jersey, he said it was the best thing he'd ever done for himself and that he only wished he'd done it sooner, when he could have salvaged his relationships with his wife and sons.

Inwardly, though, it was a challenge not to drink. He missed having a cold beer after mowing the lawn. He missed the warm, sleepy feeling that a fifth of vodka gave him every night while he watched old black-and-white westerns or whatever football game was on. He missed drinking at the pub on Oak Street with the boys after work on Thursday and Sunday nights. He missed sleeping without dreaming of his army buddies getting their legs blown off in 'Nam.

What he did *not* miss were the fights with Helen over how much he'd had to drink, and as a result, what other woman he'd been too friendly with at the bar or what inappropriate story he'd related with boozy guffaws at a dinner party. In fact, he'd gone to some lengths to delude himself that he hadn't been as rough and clumsy with her on those nights she gave in and let him have sex with her, despite the fact that with the amount of booze in his system and the fragmented war horrors in his head, it was a fifty-fifty chance that he'd even be able to get it up. He didn't miss how disappointed his children looked when he was too hungover on a Saturday morning to play catch in the backyard, go to their Little League games, or take them to Dorney Park. He skipped out on more than one Sunday-morning Mass at St. Catherine's as well, which embarrassed Helen immensely. He did not miss those early and sporadic AA meetings where he felt he was sitting under the shadow of his own thoughts, haunted by his guilt and anger.

People say alcoholics don't stop drinking until they hit their own personal rock-bottom. Bill wanted to believe it wouldn't have to come to that. He kept trying to stop drinking; he even managed to long enough to begin convincing Helen that he'd changed. He hadn't really wanted to change, though. That, he realized, had been the problem. He didn't want to stop drinking, but only curb it a bit, now that he was in control.

When he lost his family, he realized he wasn't in control and never had been.

Bill had never been a violent drunk or even a nasty one, but he was a careless one, and that had been just a little too much for Helen. One morning in 1978, when his head pounded hard enough, it felt, to crack his skull and his stomach was a rotting hull, she had quietly packed bags for herself and the kids and left. She'd left him there in a haze of bright light and miserable pain, and he couldn't say he blamed her one bit.

At the time, that had seemed like rock-bottom. He couldn't imagine screwing up his life any worse. Of course, if that had been the case, he might have asked the Door to give him his family back. He was superstitious, a trait magnified by the jungles of Vietnam, but he might have gotten past the fear of inadvertently harming his loved ones just for a chance to redeem himself in their eyes.

However, one can only use the Door once (folks knew that even back in the seventies), and as it turned out, his move from Newark, New Jersey to Zarephath, Pennsylvania gave him another, more pressing reason to use the Door.

She had been hitchhiking in the rain. What he noticed first were her legs, pale and shapely beneath a pair of denim shorts. When she turned and hooked a thumb in his direction, he saw a naturally lovely face whose turned-up nose dripped water off the tip. The girl had blond hair, parted in the middle and currently plastered across her forehead and down her arm. He had stopped his van alongside her and rolled the passenger window down. It was really coming down out there, as evidenced by her soaked-through tie-dyed tank top; the slopes of her breasts and nipples protruding under the thin, wet fabric drew his attention. He had been a little drunk (which, he'd come to find in those days was sort of like saying someone was "a little pregnant"), but he thought she knew exactly what he was looking at and was hoping it was enough to get her a ride.

It was. She hopped in, bringing a scent of water and pine with her, as if she'd been sleeping outside. It was a pleasantly earthy, even sexy kind of scent, and he breathed it in. He missed the scents of women.

"Where to, beautiful?" he slurred.

"Anywhere you're going is good with me," she said. "Can I have one of those beers?"

He nodded at the half-gone six-pack at her feet. It was his third of the night. "Help yourself. Heading to Zarephath, over the border there."

The girl cracked open one of the beers and took a sip before answering. "Going to see the Door?"

"The what?"

She smiled at him. "Never mind, honey. Zarephath is fine."

"Good. Hand me that vodka in the glove compartment, will you?"

"I got something better," she said, and shoved a pill in his mouth. She handed him the vodka from the glove compartment and he used it to wash the pill down. So many years later, he couldn't remember much about the pill itself, not even the color, but after it slid down his throat, things slowly began to change.

Bill was a talker when he was drinking, and that night was no exception. He told her all about Helen and the kids, spinning it in a way that might garner him sympathy and maybe a little more. She seemed like the kind of girl fully willing to pay in trade for rides. He remembered that part.

The girl listened semi-sympathetically, finishing off the remaining two beers as he navigated the rain-slicked back roads toward the PA border. When she crushed the last can and tossed it into the backseat, her eyes took on a kind of dreamy, hungry look, and turning to him, she began stroking his crotch. He remembered that part too. It felt good; it was the first warm, nonjudgmental touch he'd experienced since he first returned from 'Nam. He felt himself grow hard under her touch and shifted in his seat. She undid his pants and lowered his zipper, freeing his hard-on so she could grasp and stroke it. She ended up giving him road head until he couldn't take it anymore and pulled the van over.

Bill had never been a violent drunk or even an angry one, but he'd been a mean son of a bitch when he was high. He took whatever the other GIs handed him and let it take him over. He was fearless then, a berserker. He'd destroyed the enemy, saved the salvageable from among his fellow soldiers, and put others, begging for mercy, out of their misery, and when he was high, none of it mattered. His platoon liked fighting high. How else could they have mowed down so many Vietcong in that village?

Yeah, he was someone else when he was high, and he didn't want or need to bring that someone home. For Helen's sake, he'd left the drugs behind when he'd stepped on American soil. The drink would have to be enough. And it was, until the night he'd picked up the girl.

What came after his pulling the van over, he remembered in hazy, jagged pieces. He remembered her under him, grinding her hips against him, and he vaguely remembered entering her, but he couldn't recall the things she was saying that had made him so angry and ashamed. He could see in his mind her blue eyes getting big, her mouth a shrieking, silent O. He might have had a hand on her neck or chest—that was lost to the fog of drugs and time. He thought maybe he might have called her Helen. When he dreamed of that night, he dreamed of punching her, over and over, everywhere.

He remembered her screaming in the rain and running beyond the beam of the headlights into the night. Whatever happened then was lost to the darkness, as well.

At some point he must have passed out, because he woke up in the back of the van where he'd been with the girl. His mouth was dry, his dick was limp, and his body ached all over. His head felt like metal was folding its sharp edges into his soft tissue. He sat up and looked in the rearview mirror. The burning on his cheek emanated from three angry red scratches just below his eye and his lip was split. He examined himself and found he had more scratches on his left shoulder, his chest, his neck....

He didn't notice the blood where the girl had been lying until several minutes later. There was a small puddle where her ass would have been, and little smears against the rear window and the back of the passenger seat. He had a bright, painful flash of a naked girl running and screaming, the rain streaking the blood on her body. He looked around for her clothes but couldn't find them; she must have taken them with her.

But what had happened? What made her run away like that? What had he done?

Bill had found that sometimes when he blacked out, pieces came back to him over the course of the next few days. That didn't happen, though, as he made the long last leg of the trip to Zarephath. He couldn't remember—in fact, never did.

He half-expected to be picked up by the police upon his arrival in Zarephath. He figured the girl would make her way to town, likely on foot as he couldn't imagine her trusting any other motorists for a while. She'd go to the police and file a report on her attack and the cops would be looking for his van. He had told her that was where he was going, after all, and at the time, he'd seen no reason to lie about it. The self-loathing he felt eclipsed his fear of arrest. If the cops cuffed him and brought him to jail, he'd go quietly. He had nothing, was nothing—well, that wasn't true. He was, evidently, a monster, a werewolf unleashed by some unidentified pill popped into his mouth by a girl whose name he'd possibly never know. And monsters were dangerous; a cage seemed like a reasonable place to put him.

He discovered upon arriving in town, however, that the police were not looking for him at all. One gave him a curt wave when Bill's van passed the patrol car on the road, but otherwise, there was no sign in the light of morning, waning to evening, of anyone looking for him.

He expected the police to come for him all that week, and the next, and for the first few months after. He even went and got a job at the Monroe County Sheriff's Department, though he wasn't sure himself if it was to keep closer tabs on a possible investigation or to build up enough guts to confess. He thought a hundred, maybe a thousand times over the next few years of going to his fellow officers and telling them about that night, but he'd long since cleaned the blood out of the van and his minor injuries had healed. He didn't even have the victim's name. The girl apparently wasn't a local; Bill got to know nearly everyone in Zarephath, as it was one of Monroe County's municipalities, but neither she nor anyone like her showed up anywhere. She wasn't anyone's daughter or granddaughter, at least no one's in town. He wondered a few times if he'd hurt her so badly that she bled out somewhere and died in the woods, but scans of local newspapers showed nothing. He'd even driven a couple of times to the town that encompassed that particular stretch of road and read *their* newspapers, and still he found nothing.

He still felt guilt, despite his ardent attempts to protect and serve. He felt self-hate, even though he'd responded to rape calls and had even prevented a couple in the line of duty. He often took out his police-issued .38 and considered blowing away what was left of his alcohol-sodden brain. As he sat on the bed, holding that gun more gently and longingly than he'd ever held Helen, he realized he'd found his own personal rock-bottom and it was hell.

Then Ed, the local hardware-store guy, told him about the Door. They were both fairly young men then, not friends but friendly, and although Bill had never taken to the way that Ed sometimes eyed the young boys that came into the store with their fathers, he'd never gotten any police complaints about Ed and figured him to be a decent enough guy. He'd heard Ed mention the Door in passing, as a bit of local color, and Ed had seemed genuinely surprised that Bill knew nothing about it. He'd been happy enough to fill Bill in on the details; back then, people weren't as tight-lipped about the Door as they were today. And desperate as he was to get out from under the weight of whatever indistinct, but awful thing he'd done, he'd written a letter and slipped it under that damned Door.

He didn't ask for his family back. He asked for that girl, whoever she was, to be okay.

He never told anyone, not even Ed and certainly not his grandson, the only family member willing to speak with him, that he'd used the Door.

Bill had plans that afternoon to go with Ed to show some young guy Ed hung around with where the Door was. He had mused in the past that for someone who claimed to have never used the Door, Ed knew an awful lot about it. This new guy, as well as a few others over the years, all had learned about the Door from Ed, and it was Ed who instructed them in what to do if they chose to use it. Sometimes Bill wondered, though never out loud, if the reason Ed was so involved in other people's using the Door was because it made him feel superior, or at least equal, to those with secrets bad enough to bury. Bill had his own reasons for tagging along; he didn't want anyone misusing the thing. Lord only knew what the reckless could bring down on Zarephath. He supposed, though, that if he were honest with himself, there was some meager sense of comfort in the idea that everybody sinned, and by each man's estimation, at least one of those sins was too much to carry to the grave. It didn't leave him with much faith in humanity in general, but it kept him sober.

The late-August sun would be setting in a few hours; they'd have to hurry. It might screw up this guy's chances of using the Door if they were all still there after dark. He wanted a drink; even after all those years, he couldn't help wanting something to calm his nerves. As he picked up his keys to his truck and headed out the door to meet Ed and this guy Toby, he thought maybe staying sober was the least he could do.

* * * *

Kari reached the Door a good hour after full dark, almost a week later. She'd left her purse in the car but had her keys tucked into her jeans pocket. She used her cell phone's flashlight to navigate her way. In her free hand, she clutched the letter.

She thought a bunch of times about shoving the letter in a drawer and just forgetting the whole thing. If the Door even worked the way Cicely said—and she still had some doubts about that—she couldn't be sure what that would mean. Was she being some kind of coward for asking that the pain be taken away from her? Was there some psychological repercussion she wasn't thinking of, in choosing avoidance rather than processing her feelings?

In the end, though, two things made her bite the bullet and trek out into the Zarephath woods after nightfall. The first was the unflagging realization that she had done everything else she was supposed to do in order to supposedly process the death of her daughter, and nothing had worked. She had known people in her life, old men who'd lost a wife of forty years or younger teens who'd lost a parent, who *never* recovered from it, despite time and the patience and understanding and support of loved ones and the best intentions of the sufferers themselves. Some people didn't heal, because some wounds to the heart and soul were too deep, too jagged. Some cracks never knitted together again. And those people didn't just soldier on until they passed from this life to the next; rather, they faded away until they died. And Kari couldn't bear to be one of those people. It might have been selfish or psychologically damaging or whatever else to decide she needed help in being pulled out from under her sorrow, but she was reaching a point where if she didn't receive that help, it would bury her indefinitely. Her soul was too tired, too choked as it was, to fight for any kind of air.

The second thing that confirmed her decision was a dream which she chose to take as Jessica giving her blessing. In it, Kari was at a carnival. There were roller coasters and a Ferris wheel that seemed to graze the clouds, a pirate ship that rocked back and forth, lined with lights, a fun house with an overzealous clown mouth serving as an entrance. There were no ticket takers, though, nor ticket booths that she could see. There were carnival games as well, like the whack-a-mole, balloons and darts, and the Duck Pond, but no one overseeing these, either, other than the slightly bedraggled and mangy stuffed prizes that hung from their gallows frame around the booths.

It occurred to Kari as she wandered, lost in the dreamscape crowd, that the people were what was really off about the place. For one thing, no one seemed to walk, but rather glided around the carnival, even though their legs were moving. Their faces were pale and blurred in a way that made them seem remote and alien. No one held anyone's hand or took much more than a passing notice of others. Parents (she knew them to be parents) moved blithely without their children, and children ran independent of a guardian, regardless of age. Neither noticed or cared about finding one another. It gave Kari the distinct and uneasy feeling that the children had been left or were otherwise unaware of a number of predators circling the crowd like vultures, looking to hurt the children.

In the dream, Kari panicked, sure that Jessica was lost somewhere and only moments from seduction and violence at the hands of one of these blurred people—one with rows of jagged teeth and a mouth as big as the fun-house entrance.

At the moment of this realization, the scene about her drained of color. The prizes in the game booths looked haunted by childhood horrors and the blurred faces took on sinister distortions. Ominous gray thunderheads raced across the sky above, crashing soundlessly together to cast a dark pall over the deteriorating scene below. Kari ran, desperately searching the booths and rides for Jessica's face.

Then she saw the carousel.

From the top of the brass center pole, a canopy rose in an uneven peak, a twirling smear of red and blue arabesques outlined with lights, supported by thinner poles that warped and curved at grotesque angles. It was difficult for her mind to process the substance of the platform floor. It was at times a rotting metal disc whose wounds bled rust, and at other times was a mere blur, like the faces of the people she'd passed, regardless of the alternately fast and almost painfully slow rotations the carousel made. The seats of this monstrosity were not horses in any traditional sense, but things only vaguely equine, with too many or too few legs and eyes in all the wrong places and tentacles reaching for and nearly blending one into another.

There were no people on or near that particular ride, except one. One beast of mottled black and white had powerful forelegs frozen in mid-gallop, while its rear half resembled a scorpion's back legs and tail. Its head was a thick half-braid of tentacles whose ends wavered toward the back end of the creature before it, as if looking to catch and devour it in some as-yet undisclosed mouth.

On its back, Jessica rode serene, unfazed by the coming storm or the unnatural wrongness of the place. She sailed by and was out of sight as she passed around back of the carousel, then emerged again from the other side. Round and round, she was in view one moment and gone the next, then back again, and it looked to Kari like the creature she rode was stamping and pawing and writhing beneath her.

"Jessica!" Kari screamed, but the girl simply looked at her and smiled. Around them, the winds were gathering and grumbling, not quite a roar, but close.

"Take the letter, Mom," Jessica said through her smile. "Take it to the door." And she and her beast continued on in their rotation, on to the far side of the carousel. Kari waited for her to reemerge, and when she did, Kari called out to her. Jessica waved, like she'd done so many times on so many rides when she was little.

"Do it," she said, and then she slipped away, back to the far side of the carousel. Again, Kari waited for her to pop back around. The ride slowed and then sped up again, but as it came full circle, both Jessica and the monster she'd been riding were gone. Kari eyed every beast that came around, calling and then screaming Jessica's name, then hopped up on the platform to search the whole thing at once, but her daughter was nowhere to be seen. The empty space where she and her horse-thing had been was steadily closing as the tendrils and appendages of the other creatures reached for each other to close the gap.

She leaped back off the ride, sure somehow that it would only be a moment before whatever had swallowed Jessica would take her too, and as dream-tears blurred her vision, she woke herself up.

Remnants of that dream, mostly the unease she'd felt, returned to her and rested like a shroud as she approached the Door. Funny, the walk alone through the woods hadn't spooked her, but her proximity to the Door filled her with a kind of ill-defined dread. Dread of what? Delivery of the letter was supposed to be a good thing, or at least, the doorway, so to speak, to a brighter future. Cicely had warned her one last time about not opening the Door and about wording her request carefully, and had eyed the letter with unsubtle suspicion, as if Kari might have switched it for a letter with different contents, but in the end, Cicely had wished her well and just before Kari left, squeezed her arm almost maternally.

"Now you be careful, sugar," she'd said with a warm and encouraging smile. "I'll be praying for you."

So she had that going for her: Cicely and the God she put so much faith in were on her side. She kept that thought firmly in place as she approached the Door.

She could hear, or rather feel, its faint hum, a sense of life or maybe sentience from beneath or beyond the Door. Perhaps it was what Cicely called "them behind the Door."

She approached it cautiously, suddenly and irrationally afraid it might open and suck her in, or maybe shoot lightning from the small crack beneath, or—

It was just a door, not a wild animal. It wasn't alive, right? Just a few slabs of wood in a stone frame.

It wasn't just a door, though. Even the most devoted skeptic would have had difficulty in maintaining his or her resolve of logic and the physical laws of the universe when standing so close to that Door. Kari's remaining doubts had fallen away. There was something to those slabs of wood and stones—be it magic or electromagnetic pulses or whatever, there was something that could be felt on a primal, gut level that erased all doubt.

She shut off the flashlight app and then her phone, and tucked the latter into the jeans pocket opposite her keys. Slowly, she lowered herself to her knees. She half-expected some glowing light to seep out from around and especially beneath the Door, or maybe fingers reaching for it, but none did. The moment was, were she to really stop and think about it, somewhat unceremonious. Whether that was a relief or a source of further unease was hard to say.

She kissed the wax seal as if kissing Jessica's cheek one last time, and slid the letter under the Door. Then she peered underneath to see if it was simply sitting in the dirt on the other side.

It wasn't. The letter was gone.

For a moment, the humming grew louder, and in that moment, she had the near-hysterical notion to stretch her fingers under the Door after the letter and see what would happen. Then the humming faded and so did the thought.

She rose, wondering what, if anything, would happen next. The Door was silent, cold, and dark as she backed away from it, but she watched it like it *was* a kind of wild animal.

Then small indentations that filled with a glowing blue liquid formed in the frame. She saw that the glow took the forms of runic characters, though none that she could recognize. Both the Door and the nearby foliage and trees took up that glow until a flash of blue light swept the space where her letter (and almost her fingers) had been.

For several seconds after the Door went dark, she stood frozen to the spot. That uneasiness from her dream had washed over her. It was not quite regret, but a sense of disappointment that she didn't feel better. In fact, she wasn't quite okay with what she had done. The feeling ebbed, eventually, but it took a long time, or seemed to. With hands she couldn't entirely feel, she dug her phone out of her pocket, switched on the flashlight app, and made her way back through the woods to her car.

The night—and the Door—had swallowed up her secret and her sorrow, and would remain mute.

Chapter 4

Toby whistled as he drove to the office the next morning. It was a Wednesday, the sun was shining, and for the first time in his life, he felt genuinely free. He hadn't thought of little girls in days. He hadn't driven past the park in a week—hadn't even wanted to. In fact, driving home from work the other evening, he'd seen a woman—a grown woman—on the street, a leggy brunette in a tank top and shorts, and he'd checked her out. And it wasn't because he was trying to practice keeping up the ploy of being attracted to adult women. It was because he was genuinely attracted to her. He'd felt a stirring in his pants hitherto reserved for young girls, and he'd gleefully gone home and jerked off to his mental pictures of the woman. When he came, he laughed and cried at the same time, a wellspring of emotion. He'd never felt so…normal.

He spent the rest of that night deleting porn files from his computer and pictures off his phone. He didn't keep a single one, not even for nostalgic reasons. He removed browser cookies and shut down his nearly-anonymous memberships to certain forums. He didn't feel tempted to look at the new posts or respond to conversations in progress. Lastly, he got rid of the shoebox with the Polaroids and pictures printed from film from the old days. He burned those in the sink, and it felt like the shame was being burned out of his soul along with the photos.

He got rid of everything in the house that he had ever used to pick up children, ply them into complacency, or otherwise memorialize his time with them, and it felt really, really good. It was like he'd developed an allergy, and in removing all trace of and every path to those allergens that he could, he could finally breathe again.

It occurred to him that he could have taken his letter a step further and asked that all his victims (he hated to use that word, but there it was, and it was true) be healed from what he had done to them, or to have their memories of the time they'd spent with him be erased. He hadn't really thought of that when he was writing the letter; it had been more of an exercise in removing his own feelings and the impending threat they brought. He didn't dare write another letter, though. Ed had said one could only use the Door once. Still, he hoped that even if he couldn't make up for what he'd done, at least he could now keep it from happening to anyone else.

He could maybe have a normal life, with a wife and—

Well, with a wife, at least. Maybe not with kids. One couldn't look a preternatural (or was it supernatural?) event in the face and not be just the slightest bit leery of cosmic karma.

Regardless, he could finally move on. He couldn't wait to tell Ed all about it that night after work. They were getting together for their usual crushing of the beers at Ed's place. In a way, he was apprehensive about seeing Ed. What could they really have in common now? And would it negatively impact his new lifestyle to pal around with Ed? Didn't alcoholics have to cut off their drinking friends and their alcohol-related patterns of behavior if they had any hope of staying sober?

Then again, Ed was really the only friend he had. Sure, he had acquaintances, maybe some he could let in a little now that he wasn't so worried about preying on their kids, but Ed knew him in a way no one else did. Didn't that deserve some loyalty?

Toby supposed he'd just have to see how he felt when he got there. Late summer nights, with their crickets and fireflies and heavy, quiet air, had a way of swallowing anxiety, especially in Ed's little dimly-lit den. Maybe everything would be okay there too.

His eyes followed a big-breasted blonde until his car had passed, and he felt good. He felt unbroken.

Yeah, everything would work out now. Life was changing for the better.

* * * *

"So it went smoothly the other night, then, sugar? You got to the Door and got your letter delivered?"

Cicely and Kari sat at their usual booth at the Alexia Diner. It was quiet that afternoon; many of the regulars were absent—Bill, Ed,

Grant, Edna, Flora, even that shiftless Dietrich kid—and the waitstaff seemed preoccupied.

Kari considered the questions for a moment as if she couldn't quite recall the context, finally nodded, then took a sip of her coffee.

"Good. Good, I'm glad to hear it. I hope it all goes well for you. And I certainly believe Jessica would understand." Cicely patted Kari's free hand.

"Who?" Kari looked confused.

Cicely frowned. "Your daughter, sugar."

"Oh…oh, right, of course. Sorry." Kari gave her an embarrassed smile and a little dismissive wave. "Sorry. Haven't been sleeping well. Been having weird dreams and I think it's making me a little flighty."

Cicely palmed her coffee mug with unease, feeling its warmth in her hands. "Anything you want to talk about?"

Kari shook her head. "I don't really remember much about them. I guess it's more the feelings they leave behind when I wake up, but even those…I don't know quite how to explain it."

"Well, it's understandable, I'd say," Cicely replied. "After all you've been through, all the recent changes, maybe your body and soul just need time to adjust."

"Yeah, maybe you're right." Kari sipped her coffee again and gazed out the window, though it seemed to Cicely that she was looking at something farther off, out of view, a time or place from before she ever had need of the Door. Then she seemed to remember Cicely and said, "I'm sorry, you were saying?"

"Well, just that I hope the days will be brighter for you, that things will start looking up now, and that I certainly believe Jessica would understand why you did what you did."

"Who?"

* * * *

Deets had to read the newspaper article three times before his brain would process the words or accept them as real. It was an article about the boy he'd hit with his car…which, according to the paper, had not actually been hit with a car, but had been crushed under the limb of a tree that had cracked in the rainstorm that night:

Initial findings, which at first mistook the boy's death to be a vehicular homicide, were then amended by the coroner's report to death by

*accident. A combination of wind and the force of the rain on the night
of the accident caused a massive tree branch to break free and strike
the boy, Noah Thomas, 18, of Monroe County, killing him almost
instantly. Officers report that the rain, which had washed a good
portion of the victim's blood off the limb and the road, obfuscated the
scene, creating some confusion....*

Deets felt hot tears well up in his eyes, blurring the text. He mashed
them away with a fist and read through the article again.

The Door...his letter had worked. His wish that the car accident had
never happened had been granted. He was free and off the hook. The tears
came again and this time he let them spill down his cheeks. It was okay.
Everything was going to be okay.

He tore the article out of the paper and stuffed it in his pocket. He
needed to hold on to some proof, to keep some record of the change until
his mind accepted the new reality.

On his way to work that morning, the article still in the pocket of his work
overalls, he began to laugh and laugh hard. His stomach muscles knotted
from the exertion, and fresh tears rolled down his cheeks. He laughed so
hard he had trouble focusing on the road. It was a thin, hysterical laugh,
he knew, but it felt good nonetheless. He was no longer a murderer forced
to get behind the wheel of his killing machine every morning. He could
take the *FOR SALE* sign out of the rear window now. He was free, free,
and it felt so good.

When he arrived at the garage, his boss's wife, Flora, was at the front
desk. A woman of about sixty with a wild jumble of gray-streaked red
curls piled on top of her head, she looked up from her *Better Homes and
Gardens* magazine and smiled at him. She was pretty good-looking for her
age—a fit little figure and a pretty face only just showing the first signs
of crow's-feet, and when she smiled, Deets felt warm.

"How ya doing this morning, sweetie?" she asked. She had a bit of a
West Virginian drawl, having given up her ties to the lands south of the
Mason-Dixon Line, but not her flavor, to be with her husband.

"I'm...I'm great," Deets said in earnest. "Better than I've been
in a long time."

She winked at him. "Glad to hear it, hon. You're a good guy. It's nice
to see you happy." Then she went back to her magazine.

Deets went back to his locker to get his tools, a bit of that warmth from
talking to Ms. Flora diminishing. She'd called him a good guy. Was he?

His karmic slate was wiped clean, but did that make him a good guy? And if not, what would?

With the shine a little off his mood, he got his tools and got ready for the day.

* * * *

When Kari woke up that morning, she knew she'd been dreaming, but some of the details were hazy and growing fainter as more of the morning pressed itself into her bedroom and her awareness. She could remember a beautiful little girl, at least, with long, chocolate-colored hair and blue eyes and a soft, shy smile. The girl was someone she had loved very much in the dream, as a mother loves a child. She also knew that in the dream, the girl was in danger, but she couldn't remember what from or why. As she slid out of bed, a cloud of anxiety followed after her like a scent. It wasn't the dream that perturbed her so much as the fact that it was fading, and as it did so, it was taking with it something from her that she desperately wanted to keep. But what was it that she wanted to hold onto? What was she forgetting?

She made coffee in the kitchen and when she realized she was humming to herself, she giggled. When was the last time she'd hummed or giggled? It had been years. *Three* years, as a matter of fact…which struck her as accurate, but oddly specific. Something had happened three years ago; it was on the tip of her tongue, just beneath the surface in her mind, but…but what?

The anxiety came wafting back, nebulous and nagging. The thing that happened was related to the dream and thing she was forgetting. The girl in the dream—

Jessica.

That was it. Jessica, her daughter.

Kari felt a tight fist of anger and shame in her gut. How was it even possible that she'd forgotten her own daughter's death? How could she not have recognized the dream images of Jessica herself? She tried to conjure up in her mind a specific milestone—a birthday, a special occasion, even her daughter's birth—and felt oblivion tugging at it like a tide, pushing and pulling at the details and trying to carry them away. How could—

Then she remembered the requests she made by letter—and the Door.

Oh no. No no no, not like this….

She realized with horror where the anxiety was coming from. She wasn't just losing the sad memories about her daughter's death. She was losing all of them.

"This can't be happening," she muttered to herself.

Her mug of coffee forgotten, she returned to her bedroom, went to her closet, and pulled a large shoebox off the shelf. It contained an album of Jessica's baby pictures, a pacifier, and her favorite stuffed animal, a brightly colored, fuzzy fish her dad had won her on the boardwalk during a family vacation at the beach. It also contained the admittance hospital bracelet Kari had worn when she'd given birth, Jessica's birth certificate, some drawings and school papers, and Mother's Day cards (which her father had helped her pick out, of course). Steven had kept some things, as well—Jessica's first onesie, the birth announcement, a cigar with a pink ribbon around it, that sort of thing. But Kari had insisted on keeping the shoebox when they'd gotten divorced. It wasn't just that she wanted it; she needed it, and although she could rarely bear to look at it nowadays, it had been a mainline to the past, when life had been full of promise and giggles, birthday parties and school lunches. There had been a girl named Jessica in her life once, a child who lit her up from the inside and had made Kari a mother. She wasn't sure if she was allowed by the laws of the universe to maintain that title, but it meant everything to her to know it had once been the most important she had ever had.

Now it might be the only tie to that past, the only tether to a reality that was being eaten away by her own request to the things behind the Door.

She took a deep breath as her trembling hand grazed the lid. What if… what if the parameters put forth by the letter extended to physical objects and not just mental ones? She pulled off the lid.

The contents were still there—the pictures, the little mementos, all of it. She exhaled in relief. So far, nothing on the outside seemed different. Still….

She thought she understood now that vague disquiet that something was missing, that she was misplacing things in her mind. Over the last three days, her mind had been letting go of her memories of Jessica—her daughter, her little girl—like so many balloons released into the sky. She'd felt lighter, more at peace, sure, but this…this wasn't what she wanted. She didn't want to forget her baby entirely; she only wanted to lessen the burden of pain that Jessica's death had put on her.

It was the letter. The Door had worked, just like Cicely said it would. Actually, it had backfired, like Cicely had implied it could. She had gotten what she asked for, and the realization that forgetting was even worse than remembering blindsided her.

She'd made a terrible mistake. And she'd have to try to undo it before it got any worse.

Worse? a new voice in her head asked somewhat coyly. *Is it really so much worse not to have to be saddled with memories of a child's suicide? With the accusing looks behind veils of superficial sympathy? With all the destruction losing a child has wrought on your life? Wouldn't forgetting entirely be better?*

She told herself no, and could almost imagine invisible shoulders shrugging in her mind.

You wouldn't even know the difference. It would be like it never happened.

She didn't like this new way of thinking, this antithetical approach to Jessica's memory, and wondered if it was a side effect of having used the Door. It certainly didn't feel like her own way of thinking, though she refused to entertain the thoughts having an outside source.

She also refused to listen to those thoughts. She would *not* forget her daughter. She wouldn't let it happen, even if it meant....

"Rule number one is that you absolutely, under no circumstances ever, open that Door. Once you deliver your letter, it is out of your hands." That was what Cicely had said, but what if someone wanted to take back a wish? Such finality seemed overly dramatic. People made mistakes. Maybe there was still time to get the letter back and undo her request.

Despite her resolve, she decided not to ask Cicely about it. It had been made clear that asking more than once from the Door invariably resulted in death, but there had been no such discussion about the consequences of opening the Door. Cicely had said nothing about that, other than never to do it. Maybe no one was left alive who remembered what was on the other side, or what happened to people who tried to find out. Or maybe it was something that the old folks wanted sole propriety over, a thing just for them to have shared. Either way, Kari would not be deterred. She suspected Cicely would strongly disagree with her plans, but Kari just wouldn't tell her. Maybe Cicely did have stories, but Kari didn't want to know if others had tried to take back their letters and failed. She didn't want to be put off of her mission. She couldn't be.

Kari couldn't forget Jessica entirely. Memories both good and sad, she now understood, were all she had left.

So she'd just take the letter back. There had to be a way. Under the best and perhaps most miraculous of circumstances, maybe she could dig it out from under the Door, just slide it out with a stick or something. Something. And in a worst-case scenario, she would plead with "them behind the Door" or trade something to get her letter rescinded. Surely she couldn't be the first person who had ever tried to take back a letter, even if it meant breaking the rules. And wouldn't the law of averages indicate sometimes people succeeded?

Probably not, the new voice in her mind told her. *In fact, likely not. Why do you think the number-one rule is never to open the Door?*

She swept the voice from her mind.

As she rushed around the house looking for her purse and keys (they were never where she thought she'd left them), she recognized that she probably wasn't thinking clearly. Cicely had been very specific about the letter and its contents being out of one's hands once delivered. And she'd been just as clear about not using the Door twice. What was done was done, by Cicely's estimation. But fear overrode logic in Kari's mind. She never wanted to open that shoebox and have absolutely no recollection of the significance of the items within. Nothing seemed like a greater betrayal to her daughter than to forget her. She hadn't been able to protect her little girl, but she'd be damned—literally, if it came to that—if she'd let all maternal bonds just go up like wisps of smoke.

Kari would get that letter back if it meant opening that damned Door herself and taking it out of the hands (or talons) of whatever was on the other side.

She opted to go back at night. She considered going while there was still light out, but ultimately discarded the idea. During the daytime, the Door had been so much wooden planks. Whatever magic in it seemed to come out at night, or at least appeared to be much stronger then. While it might be safer to open the Door when its magic was ebbing low, the likelihood that she would have access to her letter, wherever it had gone, would be lower too. No, if she was going to stand a chance of success, she'd have to go when there was enough of the magic to allow her access to wherever her letter really was. Besides, she didn't want to wait another day. By tomorrow morning, it was possible she would have forgotten all about Jessica.

That night, she retraced her steps through the woods, this time with just her keys and her phone with its flashlight app. It seemed to take less time to find the Door than it had on her first trip. It loomed up out of the dark before she was quite ready for it, hovering still and silent, surrounded by its oaken sentinels. Those oaks seemed so much smarter than the people of Zarephath, as far as Kari was concerned. They sensed the unnatural aspect of the Door and shrank away from it, but people...well, they had poked and prodded at it and only accepted its somehow sinister apathy when shown just how alien a thing the Door was.

And what was she here to do? Really, if the Door was some kind of wild alien beast, then she was essentially planning on opening its mouth and sticking her hand in.

She glanced around the shadowed woods as if she might get caught, then took a deep breath and knelt down in front of the Door. She peered under but saw nothing. The hum was electric, though, setting her stomach atilt with its reverberation. Her hands in the dirt felt nothing coming up from the ground; the hum was most definitely coming from the Door. This close, she didn't have much hope of it working, but she grabbed a nearby stick and swung it in the space between dirt and wood on the off chance that she might catch the corner of the letter and drag it out. She had no such luck, though. Her stick did little more than kick up puffs of dry earth.

Sitting back on her haunches, she huffed, then tossed the stick. Okay, so it was going to have to be the hard way, then. She looked up at the Door. It hummed, uninterested in her.

Slowly, she got to her feet, backing off a foot or two so she could knock on the door. The sound was swallowed by the hum. She knocked again, harder, but that sound too was muted and without echo.

"Uh, hello?" Kari leaned in again so that her forehead was almost touching the wood. "Hello? Is anyone, uh, there?"

She thought she heard something like a squawk and a hiccup from the other side, but it could have been wishful imagination.

"Hello," she tried again. "I'd like to please speak to the… um, the gods behind the Door. If you're there, I mean. I hope. I delivered a letter about memories of my daughter almost a week ago, and I was wondering if I could please have it back? Please?" Kari began to cry. "Please. I made a mistake and I just…just want to undo it. I miss my daughter, but I don't want to forget her."

When she received nothing in the way of response or even recognition, she began to cry harder, pounding on the Door. "Please! Please, I'm begging you! I don't want to lose the only thing I have left of her! I want to take it back! Please! Just undo this and I'll do anything! I promise! Please!"

She could barely hear her own desperate cries, devoured as they were by the hum from beyond the Door. She rested her forehead against the wood then and let it all out—the pain, the loneliness, the guilt, the shame—all of it in a flood of hot tears against the rough surface of indifference.

"Please," she whispered, and it was then that she heard a low grumble, a sound that was almost words. It was very faint, but she knew it was no trick of the imagination that time. Something *was* behind the Door, maybe listening.

She renewed her pleas, pounding on the Door until the heels of her fists hurt, but no further reply made its way across to her side.

"Fuck!" she shouted, and the oaks seemed to cringe, equating her with the unnatural thing in their midst. To herself, she muttered, "Fuck this" and grabbed the doorknob, turning and yanking with all of her strength.

The Door swung open slowly but with force and—startled—Kari fell backward onto her rear. She'd figured deep down that no one ever opened the Door because it was locked, but clearly, that was not the case.

Kari could feel the change in the air before anything else. The humming had stopped as if the movement of the Door had flipped a switch.

She shuddered, but crawled closer to take it all in.

Beyond the crisp edges of this world was a rectangular opening onto another. Through it, Kari could see a silent, raging ocean in shades of silver and gray, extending for miles in all directions as far as visibility allowed. An eighth of a mile or so out from the place directly below the Door, with waves crashing violently against it and occasionally obscuring it from view, was a rocky island. A large slate tower of intricately carved arabesques rose up from the island, slanted slightly to the right. The structure reminded her of mausoleums, with its facade so impervious to everything but death.

Above the tower and the sea was a midnight sky, utterly starless. That, maybe, terrified her most of all; it meant the world on which she was looking was no known place in her universe, but rather, some place far beyond where even the seemingly endless stars could reach.

Then Kari saw the creatures. She tried to breathe, but couldn't draw the air into her lungs.

What she noticed first was the movement, the emergence of misshapen heads and long, jointed appendages from the savage surf, dark shapes clawing onto the rocky shore and then darting between the large, heavy boulders. She couldn't make out much detail, other than that their body parts seemed disconnected beneath the skin, as if parts of their skeletons worked independently of each other. They had to have been terribly large for her to make out any detail at all. Occasionally she caught an eye, shark-like and casting its own yellowish glow, which seemed to flow over the back of one of the creatures or sink into the skin to reappear someplace else. She also saw mouths; many, many mouths that opened onto other mouths both ringed and lined with teeth, and from those inner mouths flailed—what? Tongues? Tentacles?

They were looking up at her.

It took her a moment to realize it as she teetered dizzily on her knees at the edge of the Door, but a number of them had paused in their scrambling and were clawing up at the sky in her direction. Eyes opened in the grasping palms, then closed and were replaced by mouths. They were calling to her. *Oh God, oh God, oh God* They were calling to her....

The shore was teeming with the creatures now, and what were they? The town's sins and secrets, their ugliness and hate and jealousy and perversion in physical form? Or some terrible gods who fed on such things?

When the first one sprouted leather wings, Kari screamed and threw herself away from the opening. She sat there, trying to catch her breath, when she realized the starless world beyond was no longer silent but droned, like the bass buzz of sawteeth, and she realized what was coming.

"Shit! Shit!" She scrambled to her feet and ran to the door, yanking on it with all of her strength.

It wouldn't budge.

"No! *No no no*, this can't be happening, this can't—" she pulled with all her strength, then went around to the other side and threw her weight into the Door. It skittered a few inches, then seemed to catch in the dirt. She screamed into the night and the forest around her shuddered in reply. She threw herself against the Door again and was relieved to find it moved with her. She gave it one last shove and as she did so, she happened to look up on the world being closed off—right into the glowing eye of one of those things, not more than five feet from her face. She screamed again, the full tank of adrenaline in her body providing just enough strength to slam it shut, cutting off the glow of that hateful, glowing eye and that awful buzzing that had almost vibrated itself into words.

She was left with silence, a cold darkness that had grown unseasonably colder due to a breeze picking up around her, and a little swirling dervish of leaves at her feet. The door itself stood as it always had: silent, immobile, ageless. Cicely had told her the old-timers loathed what it could do, what it held beyond, what it could give and what it could take away. Now, she understood. She hadn't before, not really; blind and deaf as she was in her grief, but she finally understood why Cicely had seemed so reluctant to tell her about it. There had never been a chance of getting her letter back, never an opportunity to undo what she'd so hastily done, and now, she was going to forget about her precious little girl forever.

Tears blotted out the world and she felt her hands ball into fists and pound the thick wood of the door without much conscious thought. She hated it too. And she hated herself for using it.

Chapter 5

The day after the opening of the Door, the wind blew differently through the town of Zarephath. It worked its way into crevices in homes and stores and flew up under layers of late summer clothes to draw goose bumps across the skin. It tangled wind chimes instead of running its fingers playfully through them. It knocked over garbage cans. In the afternoon, it sighed as if it carried the weight of the world's sadness on its back, and that night, its banshee wail caused the citizens of the town to shiver and mutter and overthink things.

It could have been the coming of the fall, the turnover of heat and sun and substance to long shadows, chills, and uncertainty. It could have been, but Toby didn't think so.

Toby had never been particularly sensitive or in tune with subtle signs of the universe. He was certainly not religious or even very spiritual, being largely unable to follow even the Golden Rule of doing unto others. He often thought that the disconnect of empathy in his character was what had allowed him to develop the sexual tastes that he had. Perhaps it was the other way around. Nevertheless, he couldn't quite ignore the sense that something was off-kilter in the very fabric of his daily grind.

Toby left work early that evening and let himself into his little apartment. Reheating the leftovers for dinner could wait. What Toby wanted was a nap.

For most of his life, he had found sleep (and as an extension, the art of lucid dreaming) something of a refuge, in that he could be himself in dreams, free of judgment and safe from retaliation. No one would know. No one would care. No one could stop him from peeling off the heavy, restricting layers of polite society and just engaging the world as the savage thing he believed himself to be. After the delivery of his letter, though, his dreams, when he could remember having any at all, were mostly benign. He hadn't needed to hide there, really. He'd dreamed of work meetings and grocery shopping and talking baseball with Ed.

That evening he dreamed of fire. That was how it started: a fire in some kind of warehouse. He never saw the flames, but could feel their heat, and the smoke blinded his eyes and stuck to his nose and throat. A tiny hand with amazing strength took his and pulled him to his feet, leading him through the smoke to a wooden door just starting to warp under the intensity of the heat. Then the little hand was gone. He'd opened the door and stepped through, and in the next instant, he was on a silent, rock-strewn island with a bruise-colored, starless sky above. Surrounding the island was an ocean in mixed shades of silver and charcoal-gray, with black, shapeless things moving through the rough waves. The pounding of that water against the shoreline forced him back, the spray of the brine and surf abrading his skin with tiny welts.

There was a tower at the center of the island, its pinnacle reaching upward much higher than he could see. Another door stood at the base of the tower. Unlike the warehouse door, this door was big, bigger than any human being would ever need, and incredibly ornate. A gorgeous gold-veined marble the color of ivory, it had an unusually asymmetrical Gothic arch shape that almost seemed to keep slipping away from the eyes, as if either they or the brain couldn't quite process such a formation by the normal laws of physics. Around the doorframe was a series of bas-relief faces alternating with the kind of runic writing Toby had seen on the frame of the Door in the woods.

In the dream, Toby approached the tower door. It didn't appear to have a knob, knocker, or any other such ornamentation, so he just pushed on it. He felt a momentary hum in his hand and wrist and then the door swung open on silent hinges.

Inside the tower was a single room with a polished floor of beautiful inlaid wood, dark mahogany and light pine. The floor seemed to be lit from some great light over his head, though when Toby looked up, the illumination fell off fifteen or twenty feet above into darkness. Likewise, the light faded outward so that Toby had no real guess as to the nature of the walls or the size of the room.

He became aware by degrees of harpsichord music, which was growing louder. He turned, trying to make out the source, but could see nothing that might have produced the sound. As he turned back to the center of the room, he gasped.

From the shadows on the far end of the room, gorgeous masquerade ball dresses began to emerge, convening in the spotlit center of the floor. At once, they began to dance. Toby was no expert on historical fashion, but he thought from their shape and ornamentation that they might have been early 1700s-style French gowns. As if to affirm this, the rather foppish embroidered and stockinged men's fashions of the same era came out of the shadows as well, with jackets taking the gowns by the sleeve and parading with them in a minuet across the floor. None of these clothes was tenanted by any visible being, but as he watched, he saw a Venetian masquerade mask appear a few inches above the necklines of the various dresses and jackets. Often these were full face masks of exquisite colors and glittering designs, with feathers and gems adorning them. When they turned away from him, Toby could see that the concave interiors of the masks were empty.

Toby shuddered. Something about the scene struck him as intensely haunting and almost sad, despite the bemused way in which the masks tilted and turned, engaged in some silent, intimate conversations with their partners. Toby even saw one pair of masks kiss. He backed away toward the edge of shadow, intent on escaping the tower room by the same door through which he'd entered, when he felt the tiny hand grasp his again. He looked down and felt a wave of sick fear.

There was no hand per se actually touching his, but only the little sleeve of a child's dress of the same period. Above it hovered a small mask decorated to resemble the sweet, cherubic innocence of a child and above that, a little lace cap.

Before he could pull his arm back, the strength of the little sleeve had yanked him forward onto the dance floor. Even in the dream, he had no real idea how to do the minuet, so he shuffled forward, his hand caught in the iron grip of the invisible hand beside him. When they reached the end of the promenading space, the hand let go of his and he bolted to the far edge of the dance floor, away from the demanding little dress, but found himself fenced in by a circle of the costumes, their sleeves touching. The masks were watching him expectantly and although their expressions hadn't changed, there was something of malice in the sightless eyes and coy mouths. He wanted to be away from them, to change the tenor of the dream to anything else, but found his ability to influence had left him. He backed toward the center of the circle, his gaze darting from mask to mask to make sure none of them were closing in on him, but they remained statue-still, watching and waiting.

The light in the center of the circle seemed brighter and somehow hotter. The music had begun to wind down to the point of becoming off-key, a minuet train come off the rails. He had a moment to hope that the slowing of the music meant the dance was over when that same tiny invisible hand grabbed his forearm and whirled him around.

The little dress stood opposite him in the center of the circle. The sleeves reached down toward the front hem and began to lift it slowly, revealing silky little stockings. The hem pulled farther back and Toby could see the lacy beginnings of underthings. He found himself wondering if little girls had worn underthings in the 1700s, and was dismayed to realize the sight before him was giving him an erection.

"You're a child," he told the dress-thing, but it only hiked the hem farther. The flickering outline of a whole child shimmered within that dress, with a lovely little powdered face and blond curls beneath the bonnet.

Toby turned away from it and tried to break through the ranks of clothes, but for fabric, their resolve was strong. He couldn't budge a single dress or jacket. He turned back to the little dress, his dance partner trying to seduce him in front of all the other expectant masks.

"Please," he said softly. "I don't want to." He had heard that phrase many times before. He had heard it last with the girl from Dingmans Ferry. *Please, I don't want to do this. You're hurting me.* He had found ways around the protests, though. Softer touches and sweet-tasting drinks had been his go-to methods. But he had been the one in control, and it had been about the girls and not their empty clothes.

The little sleeve reached out to touch him.

"Please," he whispered to the dress. "Please don't."

It was only when he came that he woke up. There were tears on his cheeks he hadn't realized he'd shed and the front of his pajama pants felt wet and sticky. Ashamed, he tumbled off the couch and into the bathroom.

What the hell was going on? He'd believed those thoughts and dreams about little girls were gone forever. Ed had said nothing about time limits or reversions to the way things had been before. He had said that if one requested something of the Door, that person got what he or she asked for… given that the wording was right. And his wording had been impeccable, hadn't it? He'd rewritten and revised it until it was. So…what had that dream been about?

He stood at the bathroom sink, staring at himself in the mirror. He'd been lucky enough to retain a boyish kind of handsomeness, an honest and almost vulnerable youthfulness that put children at ease. Although physically that face was the same, the reflection in the mirror looked haunted and the expression in the eyes worn down.

"I'm sorry," he told the face in the mirror as he stripped off his pants and washed up. "I'm sorry. I'm sorry. I'm sorry."

He wasn't apologizing to himself, though. He was apologizing to the girl from Dingmans Ferry. He'd hurt her even though he tried not to. She was scared and she let him do things and then after that last time she went home and....

The desire for little girls had been taken away, but not the guilt.

If she'd only told someone, and that someone told the police, he'd be in jail right now instead of trying to wash away the aftereffects of hell.

He tossed his pajama pants in the hamper and put on a clean pair from the drawer. What had the girl's name been? Something with a J, he thought. Janie. Jessie. Something like that. His mind wouldn't let him remember. He couldn't explain why the feelings he so often associated with her had come back, and yet not the girl's identity. There was still a big, gaping hole where the recollection of her name should have been.

It was dark now. His stomach lurched at the thought of eating dinner and he didn't much like the idea of trying to go back to sleep, so he went into the den to put on the TV. He supposed he could lose himself in some mindless show for a while.

He stopped short halfway across the room, when the TV screen came into his view. It was a flat-screen, though not mounted to the wall. Rather, it stood on a cabinet in which he had kept his DVDs, before burning the lot of them. One of those DVDs, not burned or even very charred, leaned against the TV with its case, black as a void and missing a title, standing out to him even against the dark screen.

Someone had written a message in white across the surface of the DVD cover. Was it chalk? Paint? It was a child's scrawl, to be sure, round and neat like the kids were taught in school. It read *WATCH ME*.

Toby didn't want to. He charged across the room and swept up the box, then crossed back to the kitchen to dump it in the trash. Whatever the contents were, he didn't want to see them.

Except...part of him did. And that scared him more than even the impossible presence of the DVD.

He tied up the trash bag and took it out to the curb. There. He was done with it. It was out of the house.

When he went back inside, though, he half-expected to see it propped up again against the TV screen like some *Twilight Zone* episode. He was almost afraid to look in the den. When he did, he saw no sign of the DVD case and allowed himself a small sigh of relief.

It was a small victory, though. It wasn't just the changing of the seasons that had made him uneasy. There was something else, something very off. In the morning, he'd have to call Ed and see if he could figure out just what had gone wrong with his letter to the Door.

* * * *

It never ceased to amaze Cicely how subjective time could be. Seven years, for example, seemed to her both a terribly long time and a blink of an eye, depending on how one looked at it. Seven years of childhood passed like an ice age, slow and momentous, while the same amount of time in the prime of one's youth, strength, and vitality passed in a night. Seven years in prison no doubt felt like an eternity to an average law-abiding citizen and an easy stint to a hardened criminal.

Her marriage to Reggie had been *seven times* seven years, a literal lifetime's worth of hell, and way too long by any standard. Too many years of eyes that could look right through her and big feet on the coffee table next to the beer bottles whose condensation left rings on the wood. Too many times when they were scrambling to pay bills because he couldn't get along with others at job after job. So many vicious ways of making sure she'd never get pregnant or if she did, that she'd never carry the baby to term. So many long years of his drinking and carousing with other women, his temper, his cruel little jabs, his rough, clumsy foreplay that sometimes resulted in his passing out, but more often than not led to a dozen brutish and bruising violations. Indeed, forty-nine years was such a long, long stretch of time—one she thought would never end.

And then she had learned about the Door, and shortly after delivering her letter, he had gone missing. After that, it had been seven years of wearing what she wanted and watching what she wanted and sleeping in peace and making meals she liked, only for herself. Those seven years, which had flown by so much faster than the seven before them, were drawing to a close, and the lawyer she had spoken to last week informed her she could now get the process going to declare Reggie dead in absentia. She found a deep satisfaction in that. She'd never liked loose ends, and after all those years of Reggie's cruelty hanging over her, she felt it was about time to see him put to rest for good.

Not that she didn't appreciate how events had unfolded. The Door had done right by her and she knew she was lucky in that regard. The gods behind it were capricious, and while they always granted requests slipped under the Door, the manifestations of those requests took arbitrary shape sometimes. She'd known plenty of people who were displeased, to say the least, if not outright horrified by their results.

She was lucky; Reggie was gone. No mess, no fuss, just…gone.

If Cicely had known that her friend had opened the Door in the Zarephath woods, she might have been worried. As it was, she set about her schedule that first night after as she did every other night, cooking dinner that was not perfect and that was okay—because *she* liked it—then choosing to read because she preferred it to watching TV. Sometimes she read from her Bible, finger-worn from flipping to passages that gave her comfort or inspiration. Sometimes she read cozy little mysteries. Tonight, the chill outside put her in the frame of mind for the latter.

She had just gotten to a part in her book describing a break-in at an abandoned motel when she heard a door slam.

She looked up from her book, mentally ticking off her locking of each door and closing of each window. A car door outside, perhaps? She couldn't imagine anyone visiting, though, at that time of night. Putting her book down, she peered out the bedroom window. No cars were parked in front of her house. Maybe it had been—

"Ci-Ci, I'm home. Did you miss me?" The booming voice echoed through the darkness downstairs. Cicely's heart froze. She recognized the voice immediately, although it had been seven years since she'd heard it. It was followed by footsteps moving down the hall.

She closed her eyes, a hand pressed against her chest, against the scream lodged there that threatened to give away her location. With her breath held, she listened as the sounds moved toward the kitchen, then backtracked toward the den.

"Where are you, Ci-Ci? Let me lay my eyes on you," Reggie called from below. His voice boomed. It was tinged with the faintest trace of anger. Even on his best days, his voice always had that tinge of anger. She'd grown particularly sensitive to it in the later years, coming to loathe the deep bass tone she had once found so sexy.

"Woman, where the hell are you?"

The voice was at the bottom of the stairs. Cicely made her way to the bedroom door as the heavy tread began to climb the stairs.

Reggie had been a big man, and powerful. She had once believed he didn't realize his own strength, which was sort of endearing. That strength had once made her feel safe and secure. Now it scared her. Over the years, Reggie had wielded it, or sometimes just the threat of it, the merest suggestion of it, as a weapon.

She eased the door closed as quickly and quietly as she could and locked it. The little turn of metal didn't seem like nearly enough to keep him out.

"Don't you want to see me, Ci-Ci?"

She hated that nickname. She always had.

"Cicely." Now the voice was right outside the bedroom door. "Don't you want to know where I've been for seven years? What them behind the Door did to me?"

Cicely felt that stuck breath grow cold and sink to her stomach. He knew. He knew she'd wished him away. Oh God, he knew.

"Get out of my house," she whispered.

"Your house? *Your* house?" There was that tinge of anger again, a little sharper now. There was a touch of something else too in that voice, something liquid and unfamiliar. "You mean, the one I bought and paid for? Quit foolin' around, woman, and open the door. I want to see you."

"I—I thought you were dead."

His laugh made her skin prickle. "Dead? Is that what you asked for in your letter? That what you slipped under the Door in the woods?"

This was wrong. This was all wrong. Her head had begun to buzz, or at least it felt that way. The buzz might have been an undercurrent in that voice that was like Reggie's, but not entirely. "Reggie, no, I—"

"I can slip things under doors too. Wanna see?"

Cicely took a step back. Now her heart pounded and her breath came fast, as if all her inner systems, shocked into inactivity while she watched and waited, were exploding back into life again. She felt the blood pumping through her, filling her with heat and a horrible certainty that was further confirmed by the things slithering toward her under the door.

She screamed. Thin, slimy black tendrils that reminded her of the trailing tentacles and arms of a jellyfish were whipping back and forth across the hardwood floor, splattering some clear, viscous substance that hissed and smoked when it touched the wooden boards or the wall.

Cicely hadn't realized she was moving until the backs of her legs bumped the foot of the bed. She flinched, then sat, her gaze focused on the horror that was definitely not Reggie, not on his worst day, which was snapping and smacking back and forth, searching for her.

"Cicely." The voice on the other side of the bedroom door came again, and this time there was only the faintest likeness to Reggie's. "Open the door."

"No!" she screamed. "Go away! Go away!" She squeezed her eyes shut and covered her ears, but she could still hear the wet slapping and slurping of the tendrils against the floor. The underlying buzz of the thing's voice had taken on a timbre of its own, separate from what the Reggie-ish voice on the other side of the door was saying. She tried to tune it all out.

What she'd asked of the Door had come back to bite her after all.

"No matter, Ci-Ci. You can't wish me away again. I'm back and I'm not…going…anywhere…."

"Go away!" she screamed even louder, her voice on the verge of cracking from hysteria.

Suddenly the voice and the slapping and splattering sounds stopped. She opened her eyes. The tentacles were gone from under the door, as was any trace of the smoking substance it had splattered on the walls and floor. Her heart sounded very loud in her ears, but otherwise, she couldn't hear anything, voice or movement, from the hall. Afraid to move, she sat while the minutes on her digital nightstand clock ticked by. Her legs felt numb, but she forced them to move, forced her whole cold body to rise off the bed. Slowly, she crossed the room to the door. A few more minutes passed before she could get her shaking hand to reach for the knob, unlock the door, and open it.

The hallway was dark and empty, as it had been a mere half hour ago. She chanced a step out into the hallway to peer over the stair railing, but no one waited on the steps.

What had just happened? Had she imagined it all? She might have been getting old, but she knew she wasn't senile, not yet. She didn't believe she'd nodded off and dreamed it or hallucinated Reggie's voice and those terrible tendrils. So had it been a ghost? An aftereffect of the anniversary of his disappearance and all the memories it had dredged up? Nah. She was a tough old bird and had processed those feelings long ago. So what had just happened to her?

The nagging thought returned that what she experienced most likely had to do with the Door, but why? Why now? She'd been specific in her letter about him disappearing and never coming back, alive or dead. She'd thought it all through. In fact, she'd secretly prided herself in how careful, how meticulous she had been in constructing the letter, and had attributed that to her better-than-average results.

She stood at the top of the stairs and sighed. She knew she'd never sleep that night if she didn't check the whole house to make sure he was actually gone. She descended the stairs, flipping on the lights as she moved from room to room, looking for any of the old familiar signs of his presence, and any possible new ones too. She checked for Marlboro cigarette butts on the windowsills; he used to leave them there because he was too lazy to use the ashtrays she left for him on the coffee and kitchen tables and even the bathroom sink. She glanced by the front door for his work boots or his car keys hanging on the little hook above the front hall table. She looked for beer bottles on the coffee table in the den.

There was nothing of him in the house—no sign that he had ever been there at all. The tightness in her chest began to finally loosen. Whatever had happened, he was gone, hopefully for good. Maybe it had been some weird cosmic hiccup, some—

She stopped short in the front hall. She'd been systematically checking the windows and doors to make sure they were all fully closed and locked, then shutting the light of each room when she was satisfied there was no trace of Reggie there. She'd been about to climb the stairs back to the bedroom when she saw the little note on the front door. It was a Post-it note, the kind she'd often left to-do items or even little love notes for him when they were first married. He'd never used the notes, but the handwriting on this one was unmistakably his. She went to it and yanked it off the door, her hand beginning to tremble again. It read:

See you soon, Ci-Ci. Can't wait to get my hands on you again. —Reg

She felt angry then, as angry as she was scared. She crumpled the note into a tight little ball, unlocked and opened the front door, and tossed the paper out into the night. Then she quickly shut the door and locked it. She couldn't help peering out the side window to see if some Reggie-form came to reclaim the note, either in anger or amusement, but she saw no one, no movement outside.

Finally, she climbed the stairs to her bedroom. She closed and locked the bedroom door as well, just in case. She tried to read for a bit to calm her nerves, but she kept seeing his tight, jagged script in her mind. *Can't wait to get my hands on you again.* She felt sick.

Eventually, she gave up and turned out the light, lying in the cool dark of her room. A respectable time after Reggie had gone missing, she'd stripped that room bare, repainted it, got a new bed and new bedding, moved around the furniture, and had thrown away his clothes and effects and anything else that reminded her of her life with Reggie. It was her safe place now, a sanctuary for her, a place of serenity and rest. She'd felt safe there.

She closed her eyes to the shadows and thought about was how thin a barrier that bedroom door really was.

Chapter 6

Bill Grainger finally knew it was time to call his old friend, Kathy Ryan, when some of his dead army buddies showed up on his front lawn.

He had known Kathy, as several police officers on the east coast did, in her capacity as a freelance consultant for crimes with occult elements, particularly obscure ones. She specialized in cult activity of the more esoteric variety, and although she could not be induced to talk about it, he suspected she'd seen some wild stuff in her career, stuff like the Door that simply defied explanation. She had been called in by Bill as a matter of protocol regarding certain difficult-to-explain deaths likely involving the Door of Zarephath, and she had impressed him with her work ethic, her extensive knowledge, her attention to detail, and most of all, her sense of humor. She was very good at providing truths for his own personal benefit and reasonable lies for his files, and had helped him definitively close a number of Zarephath's unsolved deaths.

Bill very much enjoyed Kathy's company and thought that, despite the scar, she was still a looker. Had he been a couple of decades younger, he might have tried to sleep with her, but word was that was a wild ride in itself, perhaps too much so for him, and so he was content to keep their relationship business. Over the years, he'd come to think of her as a friend, and while he hadn't ever worked up the nerve to give her details, he had confided in her that he'd once used the Door himself. She never asked why, nor had she ever made him feel judged for it in any way, and for that, he was both grateful and immensely respectful of her. He thought she saw him as someone vaguely paternal and seemed to appreciate his concern in a way she never could quite express, and it made him feel good to be useful in that way to her.

He'd always feared, somewhere in the back of his mind where all long-term fears are eventually relegated, that someday, someone actually would open that damned Door. He had hoped it wouldn't be in his lifetime, but the "what if?" had been enough to keep Kathy apprised for her comprehensive file. He knew some day he might have to make the phone call to her about how to safely open or close the Door or otherwise undo something it had done. He'd held off, even when people's requests went horribly sideways, because he had come to find his place among others in the town. That usually meant letting certain things stand, even if they left more questions than answers. No one knew the full capability of that Door out in the woods, and no one wanted to push to find out. It was not their Door. It simply existed in their space, and it had no loyalty to them as reluctant caretakers and sentinels.

The Door wasn't his first thought—not just then—upon seeing the figures on the lawn, because they hadn't looked like people at first. They hadn't looked like anything recognizable, really, just things without shape that quickly scattered to the shadows or took on the suggestion of forms and half-forms before melding into other shadows.

What they looked like to Bill were the products of a brain whose gears were beginning to slip and send faulty messages to his eyes. Despite some hard living, Bill thought he was in pretty good health. He'd worked out much of the PTSD from Vietnam and since retiring as sheriff, he'd made sure to eat reasonably well and get out on nice evenings for walks. But hard living had a way of catching up to people, and so he ticked off those figures as some kind of hallucination. He'd heard old folks talk about sundowning as an early symptom of dementia and the thought crossed his mind that maybe a life of nightmares was finally running him down. He didn't feel disoriented, though. He knew who and where he was. He knew the name of the President of the United States and the year it was. He also knew that no kind of wild animal native to the region ever got that big.

And yet a pack of them, whatever they were, were darting back and forth across his property.

He went to get his gun, a .38 to replace the one he'd been issued as a sheriff, and some ammo, and by the time he came back, one of the closest shapes to the front door—close enough to catch the porch light—was morphing itself into a girl that struck him as somewhat familiar. Though it was a clear and cloudless night, he saw the girl was soaked. Water dripped off the upturned nose of the naturally lovely face. The blond hair, parted in the middle, hung plastered across her forehead and down her arm. She wore a soaked-through tie-dyed tank top in which her nipples protruded under the thin, wet fabric, and very short jean shorts that hung low on her hips. From her open-legged stance on the lawn, she was staring at him with fearless blue eyes and hitching a thumb as if looking to bum a ride.

A subconscious part of him recognized her long before that understanding broke through the surface. She was the hitchhiker he'd picked up decades ago...but she hadn't aged at all. She was still a girl, the same one who'd given him drugs and clawed her way out from under him and run screaming into the rain-choked darkness.

After all those years, it appeared that the request he'd made by letter to whatever dwelled behind the Door had not been answered, at least not in the way he had hoped. That girl out there didn't look okay at all. She looked pissed.

Bill had to breathe slowly several times, in and out, in and out, to keep from throwing up.

She marched toward the front door, but stopped short of the walkway to the porch. With the porch light fully shining on her, he could see unnerving signs of deterioration—rotted flesh along her hairline, pronounced veins, filmy cataracts beginning to cloud the blue of her eyes, and a black decay along the beds of her fingernails that had begun to spread up her fingers.

When her mouth formed that silent O he could just barely recall, he saw the cracked, jagged black stumps of her teeth. She pointed at him and it felt like an accusation.

Behind her, the shadows were twitching and flickering, drawing to themselves enough substance to form bodies of their own. And they were bodies that Bill recognized. The one directly to her right was a tall, broad-shouldered man of about forty, dark-skinned and flinty-eyed, dressed in an American soldier's uniform. His leg from the knee down was missing, though something that might have been a tendon dangled from the side of the kneecap. The missing piece of his leg didn't seem to impede his ability to stand perfectly at attention. A bib of blood flowed from a gaping wound in his neck down the front of his uniform. When Bill looked into the face of the man, he saw the same signs of decay around the eyes and mouth that the girl showed.

He recognized the man, of course. It was his combat platoon leader, Lt. Harry "Notso" White. Lt. Notso had been a goddamned hero, by Bill's estimation. He'd pulled Eddie Rivers out of a hailstorm of gunfire, and dragged Marko Riggs off the battlefield when both of the latter's legs were blown off from machine-gun fire. He'd even gone back to get Desmond Whittier when a Vietcong's machete had severed the young private's shooting hand right from his arm and he panicked. Bill would have died for the man—almost did—and found something earnestly painful in seeing his old lieutenant on the front lawn. The last time he'd seen Notso, the man was screaming for the lower half of his leg, and no one was pulling *him* to safety. No one had time. The man with the knife standing above him had slit his throat before they could even raise their guns. Bill did anyway, blowing the back of the murdering bastard's head off.

To the girl's left was most of Roger Kline. Bill had always thought Roger was kind of a prick, but he was part of Bill's platoon and so he was a brother. He hadn't lasted long in the war; he was too much mouth and not so much on the reflexes. It showed in the ragged piece of meat mostly hovering on the grass. His right arm from the elbow down was missing. His whole right leg and his left foot were gone. His chest was a ragged mess of churned-up skin and shredded uniform and he had burns all along the left side of his face. He attempted to wave at Bill with his remaining hand, and when he smiled, blood spilled out of his mouth and over his chin.

Bill hovered in the doorway with his gun. It wasn't that he didn't think he could bring himself to shoot his fellow soldiers if he had to, but he couldn't imagine why they might be putting him in that position. Why were they there? If the request he'd made in his letter had indeed, for some reason, been somehow twisted into this, then he could understand the hitchhiker, but then why the others? Why—

Then he remembered Evie—sweet little Evie, a young twentysomething redhead with a schoolgirl crush on an older man. She had been employed in the eighties as a dispatcher, right out of college. A good girl, always waiting at the station with a coffee for him in the mornings and a wish for him to be well every time he went out on a call. She was a pretty little thing too—innocently, almost cluelessly sexy—but Bill had always been a hard man to get close to and she was too young besides. He kept her at a distance, but it never stopped her from watching him, sometimes starry-eyed and sometimes thoughtful. She always used to say that he looked sad—haunted, she said, by ghosts of the past, and once he'd made the offhand remark that the war had done it to him. That year at the department Christmas party, they'd both had their share of punch and gotten drunk, and she'd confided in him that she'd spent her one opportunity to use the Door to wish that the ghosts of war that haunted them would be laid to rest. He'd been touched, but also a little unnerved by her confession. It was such a serious gesture for such a young heart, and he hadn't known what to say. He'd thanked her by keeping an eye on her that evening and seeing that she'd gotten home safely and without any of the other officers sniffing around her, looking for an easy time. Bill knew a number of them thought that was because he was staking a claim and that he'd seen her home so he could sleep with her himself. In truth, she'd made it perfectly clear that it could happen just that way, and a part of him very much wanted it to.

It had been the memory of the hitchhiker, actually, that had caused him to end things at her front door, gently and without any damage to her ego or her reputation. She'd been a little shyer around him after that, but the looks she gave him underscored her appreciation.

All those years later, it was a memory he'd filed away with the few warm and proud ones, that serious, selfless thing Evie had done for him in asking the Door to take his war horrors away.

But now Evie's request had been rescinded too.

It was then that he suspected something had happened with the Door that had never occurred in the collective memory of the town.

Their letters, it seemed, were being overturned.

He closed the front door and locked it, sinking to the ground with his back against the wood. He listened to the strangled sounds that were meant to be voices trying to form words. They went on for a long time—almost until the sun came through the windows, before falling silent. It was only then that Bill curled up on the floor and finally fell asleep.

* * * *

A few nights after the opening of the Door, Deets and his friend Chuck sat at a booth in the Once More Tavern. Though it was generally thought of as kind of a dive, the tavern was comfortable enough and honestly, the only local watering hole; there were worse ways in which to spend a Saturday night. The place had always been a combination of dark woods, paints, and pints, with fake leather seats and lantern lighting and well-stocked bar shelves. Once there had been a miasma of smoke almost as thick as the spilled beer scents and interior gloom, but even in that last refuge of minor vices, smoking inside had been banned.

The boys had been there for hours already, and had already built little phalanxes of empty beer bottles on the table between them. The wooden dance floor in the center of the tavern had already begun to collect a shoulder-to-shoulder crowd that was eager for the live music to begin. Conversation between Deets and Chuck had mostly petered out due to the sound check of the bar band and the comfortable buzz surrounding each of them. It occurred to Deets among the non-thoughts in his head that this was the first time since he'd tucked his letter under the Door in the woods that he wasn't feeling anything at all about it—not apprehension or guilt or fear or anything. He felt the way he had before the accident and it was nice. It was so nice, in fact, that at first he didn't notice the furtive figure moving across the dance floor without seeming to touch anyone. It was that feat, though, of physical avoidance that caught his musing attention, especially considering the way the boy was limping.

The boy's head was bowed, but his shaggy brown hair looked wet in places, glistening under the slowly alternating lights of the dance floor. He clutched one arm closely to his chest, as if deformity or injury made it necessary to protect the limb. He was short, small in stature all around and hunched over besides, and Deets wondered in amusement if the kid was underage, sneaking in and trying to blend in with the crowd so he could drink.

The boy wasn't holding anything, though, in either the injured or the functioning hands. He looked like he was simply trying to navigate the crowd to reach the seating flanking the dance floor.

The crowd parted for a moment, giving Deets a better glimpse of the boy, and he frowned. The sight pierced the comfortable bubble of intoxication in which he'd been hovering. The boy's jeans had dark stains all over them and he was missing one of his shoes. That was bad, but not so bad as the odd backward angle at which that latter leg was bent, as if his knee was facing the wrong direction, or that he was dragging some shoeless bird leg behind him instead of a human one. Deets noticed that the kid left a sock-smeared trail of blood as he glided and limped, glided and limped across the floor. He turned his back to Deets, who then saw the boy's spine visibly poking through the back of his T-shirt, a snake kinked at some very wrong angles. No wonder he was hunched over; with his spine in that kind of shape, it would have been a miracle if he could have straightened up at all.

"Hey, man," Deets muttered. "Look at that kid there. Someone should help him."

"What kid?"

"That one right there," Deets pointed. "Can't miss him." The other people on the dance floor seemed oblivious to him, though. No one cast any uncomfortable or sympathetic sidelong glances at him or the bloody mess he was making on the floor. No one moved away from him. No one even seemed to notice he was there.

Something was wrong. He felt it full-on, but had trouble defining its outlines in his mind. That kid wasn't supposed to be there.

"Wha kid?" Chuck slurred. "Don' see no kid."

"He's—" Deets stopped. His mouth hung open with the next word on his lips—*hurt*—because the kid was more than hurt. He was facing Deets now and stood as upright as that broken spine allowed. The face, streaked along the cheek with blood, was pallid and angry. There was hate in the filmy eyes. Yeah, that kid was more than hurt. He was dead.

Deets was sure about that, sure in his soul, because Deets had been the one who'd killed him.

He scrambled back in the booth seat, knocking over an empty bottle and sending it arcing around the table.

"Whoa, whoa," Chuck said. "Whassa matter?"

"The kid," Deets muttered.

"Deets, man, there's no kid—"

Deets was already on his feet, his eyes on the dead boy only ten feet away. The boy watched him go with those dead eyes, but made no move to follow. Chuck called to him from the booth, but the sound was eaten up by the first notes of the bar band's opening song and by the drunk-fuzz in Deets's head.

He had to get out of there.

When he hit the cooler air outside, he felt a little better, a little clearer. He began to walk toward the parking lot until he realized that Chuck had driven them there. Lurching a little on unsteady feet, he quickly shifted gears and started walking in the direction of home. It was a moonless night and a little chillier than it ought to have been in late August, and Deets shivered as he stumbled along the sidewalk. It would be about an hour walk in his state, probably. That wasn't so bad.

As long as that dead kid wasn't following him, that was.

Deets slumped against the front wall of a bank, his eyes searching the night for signs that he was being followed. He didn't think so, but then he wasn't sure what he was supposed to be looking for. A blood trail on the sidewalk, maybe. The limp gliding sound of a single shoe and a mangled foot on the sidewalk.

He listened. He heard nothing.

He dug into his pocket for his cell phone. *Fuck this paranoid shit*, he thought. He'd just call Chuck to come pick him up.

His pockets were empty. He'd probably left his cell phone on the table next to his beer.

Shit. Shit shit shit. Now what?

He'd have to walk. With any luck, Chuck would drive by on his way home, see Deets, and pick him up.

Pushing himself off the wall, Deets began the long walk back to his house.

After a while, the town center fell away and he was on a rural road with no streetlamps and no sidewalks. It was just him now and the pavement barely two lanes wide, the vast stretches of farms to either side, and the occasional barn or silo. However, he knew the road and it was relatively close to home. About a mile up, he would turn right onto Beakman and then make a left onto Quaterdale and he'd be in his own neighborhood. No sweat. The only rough part would be this mile stretch of road…or was it two miles?

It didn't matter. He could make it. No one was following him. The air was starting to clear the drunk-haze from his brain. He'd seen something, sure, but he was drunk and the lights had been low in the tavern and he thought it very likely that he could chalk it up to stress or guilt in the morning. He just had to get home and sleep it off. He could do that.

The glare of headlights behind him sent him veering off-road. He certainly didn't want to get hit. That would be irony, he thought, and snorted to himself—he walking down the road, and there comes Chuck or some other asshole, drunk off his ass and swerving in his big boat of a car, clipping Deets, bending his leg backward or kinking his spine in some very wrong ways…

He shivered again and walked faster, looking back at the approaching car behind him.

Except that there was no car. There was no light. He stopped short, glancing around. There was no place to turn off or park on that road. The headlights had been practically on top of him—close enough so that even if the car had stopped and killed its lights, he still should have been able to make out the outlines. His eyes had mostly adjusted; he would have seen something…if there had been something to see.

"What the—?" Deets turned again and, head down to the chill wind that had begun to pick up, he broke into a hurried walk bordering on a jog. He was firmly on the belief that people shouldn't have to run unless being chased by cops or psychos with chain saws or some other A-level emergency of that sort. Nonetheless, he didn't want to be on that road anymore, or out in that not-so-empty night.

Then he heard the thump. It was a sound he knew but couldn't place, the kind that jarred the bones. It was, in fact, a sound of impact with bones, of their cracking and breaking.

He was afraid to look up, but did anyway. Around him, there was only an unbroken darkness.

"Hello?" His voice was a croak. He cleared his throat. "Uh…is somebody…?" He let the question hang unfinished. He didn't really want someone to be out there, and the thought that someone might answer him seemed worse just then than not knowing. He took a few tentative steps forward and a huddled shape came into view maybe twenty, twenty-five feet ahead of him.

The shape was shivering…no, it was convulsing. Some nerve had been hit or severed or disconnected from some other part, and the whole quivering, twitching shape was in shock, working through its own death throes. It didn't look like a person—*people don't bend like that*—but rather like a shrunken mannequin or like a marionette tossed carelessly into a heap. Beneath it, a blackish pool was spreading outward toward him. Either it or the shape—Deets wasn't sure which—made a humming noise too, which could be felt as much as heard as his feet brought him closer. He was walking toward the shape without really thinking about it and he could feel its vibrations in his sneakers, going up through his legs.

Stop! his semi-lucid brain screamed at him. *Don't go near it, for God's sake! Stop walking, you stupid shit.*

His feet didn't listen, though. Unsteady as he was, he was closing the distance between himself and that huddled shape.

It was the dead kid. He knew that before he got close enough to see the injured arm and bloody jeans, the shoe that had landed halfway across the road. On some level, he'd known it when he heard the thump and saw the silhouette. He didn't understand why; his request seemed to have gone well enough, and he didn't think that there had been any time limit imposed on it. He thought he'd gotten what he asked for.

Yeah, and maybe his gramps had too. Maybe that was exactly what his mother was afraid of. Maybe sometimes it was just as bad to get what you asked the Door for as it was not to.

"I'm sorry," he whispered to the dead kid. His voice was hoarse. "I'm so sorry."

The kid's glazed eyes didn't blink. They didn't look at Deets. The pained expression on the face suggested the brain inside that deflated head was too preoccupied to care what Deets had to say. In fact, he wasn't sure the kid had even heard him until he heard a grinding sound and saw that the legs were trying to unfold themselves. This was followed by a cracking inside that heap of flesh that made Deets's skin crawl. The splintered bones moved under the skin of the boy's forearms as he planted a hand in the sticky pool around him and tried to hoist his upper half up.

Deets backed away. The boy was trying to get up.

The grinding and cracking sounds continued, bones shifting and sliding and breaking in new places to accommodate the boy's rough, jerky movements.

This time Deets's brain screamed at him to run, to get moving somewhere, anywhere, so long as it was away from the thing that was literally unfolding itself before him. His feet wouldn't listen, though. It was as if they were caught fast in the blood that was engulfing the pavement beneath them.

He stared, slack-jawed and silent, and the boy attained a reasonable facsimile of a standing person, or at the least, like clothes hanging from a clothesline. Deets tried to tell the boy again that he was sorry, but his mouth wouldn't work any better than his feet. He felt warmth along the inner thigh of his left leg and when he looked down, he saw a dark stain climbing his pants leg. He couldn't be sure, though, if he'd pissed himself, or if the blood from around his shoes was reaching up for him.

Deets looked up again and saw the boy raise a hand to him as if telling him to wait. Then the boy snapped that hand into a fist and Deets felt a sharp throb of pain in his leg so intense that he stumbled and fell over. He looked down to see his shinbone protruding out of the skin just below his knee. The pain was immense, a solid thing devouring his lower leg. It made the world go white for a bit and his stomach lurched. He tried to drag himself away, to break the boundary of the blood pool into which he'd landed, but the lightning in his leg was too much.

He looked up at the boy, pleading. He felt very sober then and very scared. "Don't do this, please. Please! I'm sorry. I'm sor—"

The boy made another fist and an explosion of pain folded his forearm backward so that his fingernails grazed the crook of his elbow. The world did slip away from him then, but only for a second, and he found himself lying on the pavement, his cheek in the blood that might have been his now. His head was too heavy to lift. His arm and leg were on fire with pain. Spots marred his vision, but he could just make out the boy hovering above him now, actually floating off the ground. The boy made a gesture like he was folding something and fireworks of agony exploded up and down his back.

Then the spots in his vision grew bigger and bigger until they swallowed everything in his field of sight, and Carl "Deets" Dietrich's secret swallowed everything else.

Chapter 7

Files on the Zarephath Door in hand, Kathy Ryan left her stark apartment and the sexy Irishman in her bed at about nine in the morning that Sunday. An old friend, a retired sheriff living in Zarephath, Pennsylvania, had put in a call about an hour before regarding the Door. He hadn't given her much in the way of details, but he sounded worried. She'd started packing the minute she hung up. In her estimation, that Door was an inter-dimensional time bomb waiting to blow, and although the townspeople treaded lightly around it and everything related to it, that didn't mean that something, or damn near anything, could go wrong with it at any time. Bill, like the other people in the town, was not given to knee-jerk reactions about the Door, so his call was of particular interest to her.

She put the files on the passenger seat of her car and pulled out of the driveway. She glanced in the rearview mirror, taking in the scar that ran down through her left eyebrow and across her cheek to her jawbone. She hated that scar. Reece Teagan, colleague and live-in lover, had often told her the scar did nothing to mar her beauty, but to Kathy, it was a glaring white reminder of everything that never quite healed right inside—all her jagged memories and pockmarked thoughts.

She shook her blond hair out so that it covered some of the scar, put the car in drive, and began the hour and a half's drive to Zarephath. As she drove, she remembered a conversation she'd had with Bill about the Door and what was behind it. It was hard to say whether the townspeople thought there were sentient beings behind the Door or some type of force, or something else entirely. Bill called the things "them behind the Door."

"What are they?" she'd asked him. "I mean, what do *you* think they are?"

Bill had glanced at the Door with an expression that bespoke a weight of decades. "Alien gods, maybe. Best I could ever come up with. Why? What do you think?"

"Well, they do grant wishes, right? In mythology and folklore, a lot of powerful beings did that, in exchange for gifts. Djinni, faeries, and yeah, even the old elemental gods and goddesses...Could be something like that. Or more likely, an alternate dimension's equivalent. Your aliens, so to speak."

"I dunno," Bill said. He put a hand gently, almost paternally, on the Door. "A smart man I once knew said them behind the Door were sorrows. Secrets and sins. Fears and nightmares. Malicious lies and cruel truths. He called them 'Brocken spectres of our secret selves and all the little darknesses of which we wish to unburden our souls.' He said there are many words for them, but no true names. And he was convinced that they trade with us to build their number, to grow stronger." Bill sighed. "Maybe they're all those things—what you said and what he said."

"Sure. Both, or something in-between. It's as good a theory as any," Kathy said. She thought from the look in the older man's eyes that he believed that smart friend of his, that maybe he had personal reason to believe it. He had once used the Door, after all, though he'd never told her why and she knew better than to ask. She didn't ask him what he was thinking just then, either. She knew that look and it meant that if he'd wanted her to know, he would have told her.

"Maybe the worst parts of us are banished there, collected and bound in whatever place lies beyond this Door. There would be, hell, decades, maybe centuries of hate and pain."

"Maybe, but whatever they are, they don't seem to have either the ability or inclination to come back on you...so long as that Door stays closed, I imagine."

His mouth twisted in a small, bitter smile. "I was always told to never, never open the Door. Folks before even my time had that rule as their first and foremost. I'm guessing they knew it wouldn't be too wise to underestimate the resourcefulness—or the resolve—of them behind the Door...especially if they really are both trapped and angry about it. But yeah," he continued, turning back to her. "So long as the Door remains closed, then theoretically, this particular Pandora's box of fear and loathing should be of no imminent danger to anyone. At least, anyone it hasn't already hurt in granting a request."

Kathy thought suddenly of her brother, locked away in a high-security cell at Connecticut-Newlyn Hospital, formerly Newlyn Hospital for the Criminally Insane. Theoretically, monsters locked away behind doors shouldn't be able to hurt anyone. In reality, though, Kathy knew that wasn't always the case.

It was the Door itself that fascinated her. Kathy had dealt with portals before, but they were usually far more ephemeral and insubstantial. They were seldom like the Door, a long-standing, solid object both known and accepted as a quirky reality by the people around it. The portals Kathy had experienced in the past were usually open both ways, which is what made them so dangerous. They allowed passage of things not meant in this dimension. The Door in Zarephath was closed and still managed to affect the people nearby.

It was really more akin to an altar or temple, in that pleas or prayers were offered at a site believed to be connected to some powerful force capable of granting them. It made her wonder who had built it, and whether it had been built on this side or the other, and to what end. Had it been meant as an altar to or portal for alien gods? If so, why had it been closed? What could be on the other side that even the Door's builders were afraid of?

She wasn't sure what was happening in Zarephath, but she hoped that whatever was behind that Door was still locked away.

* * * *

On Sundays, Grant didn't open the garage until one p.m. This gave the guys who worked for him the freedom to blow off steam Saturday nights without blowing off work on Sunday mornings. It gave Grant a bit of a break, and it allowed Flora to sleep in until it was time to do the accounts. Grant had often thought of just closing the garage on Sundays, but he liked to work. It gave him a sense of purpose and accomplishment, working with his hands. It made him feel useful. Still, he was getting up there in years now and his aching muscles and creaking bones had gotten him to think about taking things slower.

He and his wife, Flora, had decided to put off the weekly paperwork for a bit and catch an early Sunday breakfast. They expected Bill to wander in some time around noon, and Edna after her nail and hair appointment. For the time being, though, they had the place to themselves, which was good, because Grant had something important to tell his wife.

"Cicely told me that the Bartkowskis are having a terrible time of it. Anne's in the hospital. Her cancer's back, and with a vengeance, by the sound of it," Flora was telling him in a hushed voice. "Remember, Joe wished it away at the Door. And Alice—you remember her from the church?

Well, she's pregnant. She's fifty-seven, Grant!" Flora glanced around, then lowered her voice again to continue. "She's convinced it's the baby she asked the Door to take away when she was fifteen. She's having a hell of a time of it, though. Sharp pains, like something's gnawing at her from the inside out, she said. I'm telling you, Grant, there's something going on. Something to do with that cursed bunch of planks out there in the woods. Never trusted it. People are panicking all over town."

Grant cleared his throat. "Honey, about that...."

"And Rita Nunez, remember her? Folks are saying she started bleeding in the middle of Barney's Market, like she had her period, only really heavy, you know? Just blood streaming down her legs. Then it started coming out of her eyes, her nose, her ears...." She waved her hand as if to brush away the mental image and looked out the window, perturbed. The parking lot beyond was nearly empty. "Poor girl. Can't even begin to imagine what the Door undid on her to cause *that*."

"Flora—"

"Grant, I'm worried. What if the Door is leaking or something? What if whatever space is behind the Door is full now, like a closet where you keep stuffing all your junk until one day, you open the Door and it all comes spilling out?"

"Flora, listen to me, please. I have to tell you something."

She turned to him, a little startled. "Oh, sure. Sorry. What's on your mind?"

"It's about the Door."

Grant could tell from the way his wife paled that she knew the gravity of his secret, if not the content. He hated to see her upset, but she had a right to know.

He cleared his throat again. "Do you remember that wooden chest I brought home in '89, the one that was all locked up?"

She thought about it and then nodded slowly. "The one that biker gave you in exchange for fixing his Harley? The one you were going to hold until he picked up the money and you traded. It was like collateral."

"That's the one." He gave her a nod and a tiny smile. "Remember how I asked you never to try to open it?"

"Yeah...?"

"That's because I didn't want you mixed up with whatever was inside it. It wasn't payment for fixing a bike. I owed *him* money. Gambling. My last big loss."

Grant had been only just barely dodging that loose boundary between gambler and addict. It had never gotten so serious that he'd put up the house as collateral or anything, but it caused problems financially on a regular enough basis that Flora had nipped it in the bud early on. She'd given him an ultimatum: her or the gambling. Wisely, he'd chosen her. By his estimation, it was one of the only wise decisions he'd ever really made in his life. But the chest…that had been just shortly after he'd made the promise to her. It had been the unfortunate result of a final game that would have stripped him of his house, his car, and consequentially, his wife. The biker, Avis Morgan, had cut him a deal he couldn't pass up: *"Take the chest. Hide it for a week, week and a half 'til I pass through town again. Then I'll pick it up."* Grant couldn't believe that was all he had to do to pay off his debt, but Avis assured him it was. So he'd done it. He'd done it because he was scared of losing everything and besides, what could possibly be so bad and yet small enough to fit into that little chest? It was no bigger than a bread box and made of flimsy wood. He doubted it was anything that anyone but Avis, who was more than a little crazy in his own right, would have put any great value on.

"What was in the box, Grant?" Flora asked after his explanation.

"Something bad. Very bad."

"What was in the box, Grant?" Flora repeated, her voice no louder but noticeably thinner.

"He never came to get it. I know I told you he did, but he didn't. That was the thing, see. He wanted to be rid of it, and I guess he figured my being scared of him would keep me from ever opening it, but I …I had to know. After a while, the curiosity gave me no peace. I had to know."

"Grant—"

"It was a shiny black stone shaped just like a deer's heart, with these veins of blue running through it, and it was sort of…sort of see-through, like it wasn't totally there in the box. I didn't touch it. I don't know if I can explain why, but just looking at it filled me with such revulsion." He shuddered. "Even so, I couldn't really understand why Avis would care enough about some stone, especially that one, to keep it all locked up like that…until I found the secret compartment. It was under the box. Only accessible from the inside."

Flora said nothing. She watched him with that same pale, anxious look.

His voice dropped almost to a whisper, even though they were practically alone in the diner. "There was a little paper, rolled up like a tiny scroll. It was an apology, Flo. An apology for ever having wished for an object from the place behind the Door. I don't know if it's true that the stone was from…there, beyond. If it is, I don't know how Avis came to get ahold of it, or if he was the one who wrote the note. All I know is, when I saw that, I tried to get rid of it. I threw it away. I tossed it in the woods. I even tossed it in the lake. I was afraid to destroy it, but I sure as hell didn't want it. It scared me. It felt...dangerous. Alive. Volatile. And every morning after, there it was, locked up in its little chest, sitting on my workbench in the garage. But I knew it was just a matter of time before it hurt me. I could sense that it wanted to. I know it sounds crazy, but I could *feel* intent radiating from that box. Actual evil intent. I don't know why it didn't kill me. But you remember, that was the summer with all those fires, those strange accidents, that series of suicides out in the woods...."

"Oh my God," Flora murmured.

"So, I gave it away. I figured, that was how Avis had gotten rid of it, so maybe that was the only method that worked."

"Who did you give it to?" Flora had gone from looking pale and worried to horrified.

"Well, I figured if the thing was cursed, I didn't want to give it to anyone I liked. Nobody innocent and good, ya know? I couldn't saddle them with that burden. I didn't want to hurt anybody, but then...then I...I gave it to Mark Westerfield."

Her eyes had gone shiny with tears. She looked hurt and angry now, those subtle changes in expression that he'd come to read after almost forty years of marriage. He knew her pretty well, or at least, had always thought he did. He thought he knew the signs of her having an affair with Mark Westerfield. It turned out he was wrong, but he hadn't known that and probably wouldn't have believed that anyway back when he gave Mark the chest.

"He died of a heart attack," Flora said as if to fix that truth in place. That was what the coroner had determined, that Mark's heart had given out, possibly due to some great shock. Grant thought he knew what the shock was, or at least where it originated.

"Yes...outside the Door. He did. And they never found the box. It didn't come back to me. I figure he used the Door to wish it right back where it had come from. Maybe hell's on the other side of that Door and that stone was a little piece of it. I don't know. Maybe I should have been the one to wish it away, and then it would have killed me instead."

"It was a heart attack," Flora whispered, as if unable to let the idea go. "How—how could you—"

"I'm so sorry. Flora. I'm sorry I did it and I'm sorry I never told you everything."

"I never—"

"I know you didn't."

"So why?" She looked crestfallen and he flushed with shame. He couldn't look at her.

"I thought you did at the time. I was an idiot."

"That thing you gave him killed him."

Grant looked her steadily in the eye, though the rest of him felt shaky. "Probably. I was so afraid of losing you...I didn't think. I just felt. But Flora, there's more."

The waitress came by to top off their coffees and they fell silent. When she was out of earshot, Grant said, "It's back."

Flora gaped at him a moment, then said, "The chest?"

"Found it on my workbench in the garage this morning."

"Oh, Grant," she said, putting her hand over his. "What are we going to do?"

He appreciated the gesture and the inclusion of herself in the planning of a solution. He'd expected a lot more anger and distance from her. "I...I honestly don't know. It's back and it shouldn't be, and I don't think we can wish it away again with all this weird stuff going on around town. I don't know how to get rid of it without...without...." *Getting myself or someone else killed*, was what he was going to say, but couldn't bring himself to do it.

She patted his hand. "We'll figure something out. Look at me—we will, okay? It's going to be okay. That chest—it's in your garage right now?"

"Yeah," he said.

"Okay. Okay, good. Let's give it some thought and this evening we can discuss our options. Let's not jump to any hasty reactions." She was mad about Mark; he could tell. She had every right to be. He'd sentenced an innocent man to death, one way or another. However, she was still there with him, still in the thick of it with him, and that meant the world to him.

"All right," he said. "Flora, thank you. I mean it. I love you."

"I love you too, hon," she said, and tried to give him an encouraging smile. "We'll figure this out together."

Caught up as they were in their conversation, they never saw Ed, confronted by his own secret, out in the parking lot.

* * * *

Ed Richter had wanted a cup of coffee. He considered himself quite a connoisseur of the coffee bean, his taste buds in tune with all the subtleties of flavor, and aside from importing the expensive stuff, the best coffee in Zarephath was served at Alexia Diner.

Unlike Grant, the mechanic down the street from his store, Ed did close up shop on Sundays. The handymen and do-it-yourselfers in Zarephath knew to get what they needed on Saturdays and get their work done on Ed's day off. It had been working out nicely that way for the last few years.

Ed liked going to the diner on Sunday mornings because he liked watching the families. They came in after church services mostly, young parents with their broods of children. He didn't have a family of his own, knowing that even as a young man that particular path in life would be a disaster. He wouldn't have admitted to being lonely, exactly, but he did find some comfort in the presence of other people sometimes.

And of course, there were the boys. He especially liked watching the families with the little boys.

He had managed to cross the better part of the lot, his thoughts on coffee and people-watching, when a force hit him from the side, knocking him to the pavement. He felt the jarring thud in his bones and wondered if any of them were broken. He looked around for what could have hit him, and at first saw nothing.

He heard someone mutter "pervert." Startled, he scanned the parking lot for the speaker, but found he was the only person outside. Puzzled, he pulled himself painfully to his feet and made his way across the rest of the parking lot.

He supposed it could have been vertigo—he was getting up there in years—but it had never been a problem before. Besides, he had never heard of cases of vertigo producing auditory hallucinations. It could have been some new budding guilt, maybe brought on by all the time he'd been spending with Toby. The guy was weak-willed and soft, burdened like Lon Chaney's tragic character Larry Talbot with a beast inside himself that he couldn't accept and couldn't control. Maybe some of that was finally starting to rub off on Ed in his old age. He doubted it, though.

There was one other possibility, one he wouldn't have thought of if not for all the talk around town that week. He didn't want to give it any credence, but he guessed he'd have to consider it and plan accordingly.

Ed hadn't exactly been honest when Toby asked him if he'd ever used the Door. He had once, but not for the kind of altruistic purpose that Toby had. Ed had been a young man with the kind of secret that, in a small town like Zarephath in 1963, could have gotten him tortured and killed on a good day. Ed had used the Door to ensure his safety. It had seemed like simple self-preservation at the time. He'd written a letter asking that he never got caught or prosecuted by the law for any crimes he had committed or would commit against children. He'd also asked that he be protected from vigilante violence or mistreatment by angry or suspicious townspeople. He was painstakingly careful in how he worded it all. He knew requests could backfire and his, if not properly laid out, could blow up in his face in horrific ways. He took his time with it and delivered it only once he was satisfied he'd minimized risk to nearly nothing. And in the fifty-four years since, all he'd asked for had been given to him. He was a careful and secretive man by nature, but his letter had assured him a veil of secrecy that had protected him even at his most careless.

Until now.

The waitress, a nice girl named Tara, led him to a booth by the window. He said hello to Grant and Flora as he passed, but didn't linger too long; they were clearly in the midst of discussing something private, and he didn't want to interrupt. Once he was seated at his own table and had ordered his coffee, he gazed out the window again. His wrist and hip ached where he'd landed on the pavement, and the side where he'd been hit was surely going to bruise. But who—or what—had hit him? So far as he could tell, he'd been completely alone in the parking lot.

It might be worth preparing himself for the worst-case scenario. If it turned out something had gone wrong with the Door, if people's letter requests were being upended somehow....

He felt a wave of sickening heat despite the diner's air-conditioning. He was genuinely afraid for the first time in fifty-four years. His gaze swept the diner, but no one else was paying him any attention at all. Good. For now, he was—

Then he saw the napkin. He was sure it hadn't been there when he'd sat down, and no one had come close enough to the table to slip it to him, even when his attention had been turned to the window. He would have felt or heard someone go by. There it was, though: an unfolded napkin with a message hastily scrawled in pen.

We know what you did.
We're going to put you down like the sick dog you are.

The world wavered in front of him. He picked up the napkin with shaking hands and scanned the diner again. No one was watching him or glaring from behind a menu, taking in his reaction. He knew he must have looked pale and sweaty, but no one noticed. He looked down at the napkin again, then crumpled it into a ball and stuffed it in his pocket.

He slid out of the booth and toward the door as fast as his protesting body could take him.

By the time the waitress returned with his coffee, Ed was gone.

Chapter 8

Kathy met Bill Grainger at the entrance to the forest in Zarephath, on the edge of town. He was pacing by his truck when she pulled up, a serious look on his face. He waved as she parked. She cut the engine and got out of the car, then gave him a hug. Bill was never terribly comfortable with expressions of affection like hugs, but Kathy could tell it pleased him deep down.

"Good to see you, Bill."

"You too, hon. How've you been? How's that Irish guy?"

"Reece. He's good. We both are, thanks. So…tell me about the Door."

Bill exhaled loudly. "Right to business, huh?"

She winked at him.

"Okay," he said, gesturing for her to follow him. "This way. The Door's about an hour's hike in. I'll tell you on the way."

As they hiked through a mostly pathless forest, Bill filled her in on the rumors about town—Anne Bartkowski and the cancer that her husband Joe had wished away, Alice Cromberg and her baby some forty-two years overdue and the complications she was experiencing, and poor Rita Nunez, who started hemorrhaging in the middle of Barney's Market. He couldn't confirm firsthand that last event was related to the Door, since Rita had died en route to the hospital, but folks talk, and they claimed her last words before passing out from blood loss were, "No…no, it was supposed to be okay! It was supposed to be taken away!"

"So," Kathy said, "you're saying the requests people made using the Door are… what? Being undone? Reversed?"

"Sure looks that way," Bill said. "I'm sure there are other examples I don't know about yet that could confirm it. People are, as you might imagine, kind of reluctant to talk about using the Door. But I'd guess far more than

I know about are going through some similar things, or worse. Thing is, I don't know why. Nearest I can think is the Door somehow opened. All we put away came spilling back."

They made the remainder of the hike in relative silence, reaching the Door at one-thirty in the afternoon. It was, to her relief, shut. Even so, she eyed it warily. Kathy had seen it a number of times before, but it never failed to incite a mild anxiety in her. It was clearly a thing from another space and time, incongruous with the forest around it. As she approached it, she felt that familiar hum in her chest. She touched the wood and drew her hand back quickly. It was like petting a thing ready to strike. It hadn't exactly moved under her fingers, but she could feel a kind of tension there.

"Well," she said, turning back to Bill, "it's closed now. Is it possible that someone opened and closed it again? Or it closed itself?"

"Possibly. Either way, I think the damage was done, wouldn't you say?"

"I would. I'll take some energy readings and whatnot, though just the physical effects of standing near it seem to support your theory. It feels different here. The energy is different. And honestly, I'm more concerned with identifying and containing whatever may have come through. For that, I think we're going to need to talk to those people you mentioned. I think—"

Her words were cut off by a low buzzing so much like a saw that Kathy jumped away from the Door, convinced that something from the far side was trying to cut its way through. The wood groaned outward but didn't break. Evidently, even from the other side, that Door was indestructible.

Kathy and Bill listened to the buzzing, their gazes fixed on the Door, until the sounds subsided. Kathy became aware of a metallic smell that coated her throat and nose. She coughed, making a face.

"That's new," she said.

Bill grimaced, took her arm, and pulled her back toward the oaks. "We should go."

Kathy nodded. "But Bill, we're going to have to get the people together—a town meeting. As soon as possible—maybe Wednesday? We've got to tell them what's going on."

* * * *

Toby had tried to reach Ed all day. He had an unshakable feeling that something bad had happened to the old man, living all alone in that house on the edge of town. Ed hadn't opened the hardware store on Monday, which was very unlike him, and he wasn't answering the phone. Monday night, Toby made the decision to drive to Ed's house and find him.

When Toby was little, his uncle Seth had died. He'd spent a lot of summer vacations alone with his uncle, and some parts of the vacation were good. Uncle Seth had taken him fishing and hiking, had bought him ice cream and a new bike. Some parts, like watching those movies and practicing those wrestling moves that his uncle said were special, secret things that only the two of them shared, were awkward and uncomfortable and Toby tried not to think too much about them. He'd had mixed feelings about Uncle Seth, but in the end, he'd felt bad when the man died. Uncle Seth lived alone too, like Ed, and had dropped dead from a heart attack at sixty-three. No one had found him or even thought to look for him for about two weeks, since most of the family, especially those with children, had by then eschewed his company. What police found was gruesome; that was how Toby's mother had described it. And Toby couldn't help but wonder what Uncle Seth would have looked like by then, rotting away for two weeks in the summer heat of his hunting cabin, alone with country vermin. It had felt to Toby like a horrible indignity to be so disconnected from the concern of other human beings that indifferent nature took more of Seth than his relatives cared to bury.

Sure, Ed was a predator and perhaps by some people's standards, more deserving of gruesome things happening to him, but then so was Toby. And Toby needed to believe that both deserved better than to be left to rot alone.

He arrived at Ed's around eight-thirty that evening, and as if to show impatience with summer's last dregs, the sky was already growing dark. The house itself, little more than a trailer home without wheels, had a single light on inside, the one in the den where they drank beer, and outside hung a naked bulb trying its damnedest above the front door. Ed's beaten-up old Buick was in the driveway. He appeared to be home. Toby parked and got out of the car.

"Ed?" he called out. The den window was open and he thought he saw the curtain stir, but he received no answer. "Ed, you in there? You okay?"

He made his way to the front door. Moths and other winged insects swarmed around the weak light above the door, but remained absolutely silent. Toby frowned. He found their soundlessness unsettling. The distinct absence of buzzing or tiny flapping of frenetic wings encouraged the same surreal unease in him that his dream had produced. Toby shooed the bugs away and knocked loudly. The sound was muffled, distorted in Toby's ears. "Ed," he said into the door, "it's me. It's Toby. You in there?"

"Toby?" a weak voice floated out the den window. It was Ed. "Hold on."

He heard Ed shuffling to the door and fumbling with the lock, and a second later, the door opened. Ed stood there in an undershirt and sweatpants. The smell of whiskey wafted out the screen door. Ed's hair was slick with sweat and his eyes, red-veined, hung in dark sockets. He had a bruise on his cheek and another on his forearm, and something that looked like a bite mark on his opposite shoulder.

"You look like shit," Toby said, opening the screen door. "Are you sick or something?"

Ed moved to let him in. "No," he muttered. "What are you doing here?"

"I was worried. You're not answering your phone, you didn't open up the shop today, and you live out here alone."

Ed scoffed. "I wish. I haven't been alone all day."

Toby glanced around the little hallway, peering where he could into other rooms. No one appeared to be anywhere in the house with them. He gave Ed a puzzled look.

"What I mean is," Ed said, gesturing for Toby to follow him to the den, "I've had visitors. I guess they're gone now. Well, for the time being. Maybe because you're here."

"Who?" Toby asked. "Bill?" In the den, Ed sank back into his usual spot on the couch while Toby took the armchair across from him. Ed offered him the whiskey bottle, which Toby declined, before answering.

"Nah, not Bill. I don't know who they are. Can't see 'em."

Toby frowned. "What do you mean?"

"I mean," Ed said, "that whatever they are, I can't see them. But they're mean sonsabitches, I'll tell you that."

Again, Toby gave a cautious glance around. There were no signs anyone but Ed had been there in weeks. "It's just you and me here, Ed."

"Yeah, now."

"But before…?"

Ed gave him an impatient sigh. "I ain't senile and I ain't drunk, Toby."

"Didn't say you were."

"So don't patronize me. You used the Door."

Toby bristled a little. Where was this conversation going? "Yeah, so what?"

"So I'd be mighty surprised if you were to tell me nothing odd's been going on in *your* life right about now."

Toby's face grew hot. "Some bad dreams, yeah. A few mental setbacks. Certainly not the long-term results I'd hoped for. But what does this—"

"You listen and listen good," Ed broke in. "Folks been coming into the store, grumbling about that Door out in the woods. Folks do that, you know, 'cause they know I ain't got nobody to tell. They say things—things like how whatever they asked for any time from days to decades ago are going haywire. And even when folks don't say nothing, you can see it in their eyes. Something's gone bad out there. And I think we don't even know the half of it yet. That Door's giving back more than just returned letters, you get me?"

This time, when Ed handed him the whiskey bottle, Toby took it. "I hadn't heard the talk. Been trying to avoid people as much as I can until I got a handle on why these feelings came back. Thought maybe I'd written the letter wrong or something. Like maybe I hadn't specified how long I wanted the feelings to go away. Thought it was just me. But you say it's happening to everyone?"

"Everyone who used the Door, so far as I can figure. Which is a hell of a lot more people than one might think. I didn't put much stock in it until yesterday, to be honest, but then one of them things attacked me."

"One of what things?" Toby was trying to understand, but Ed wasn't making a whole lot of sense.

"I told you, I don't know what they are. I'd have to be able to see them to describe them, wouldn't I?"

"Yeah, sure. But you keep bringing up the Door. I don't get how this stuff happening to you is related if you've never used the Door."

Ed sighed again and gestured for the bottle. Toby handed it to him and he took a long swig from it. Ed shook his head. "I lied."

Toby raised an eyebrow but said nothing.

"I asked it once to make sure I never got found out and never got caught. That what I might have done or might someday do, you know, with the boys…that it would never come back to haunt me. I was just a boy myself, really, when I asked."

"And you're saying, what? That your letter essentially got returned to sender?"

Ed made a face, evidently finding Toby's response distasteful. "In a way, I guess. I keep hearing things. People muttering things, calling me names and such, leaving little threatening notes all over the house, but when I look, no one's there. And these bruises," he gestured at his face and body. "It's like getting sucker punched, only I can't see nobody punching me. Sure as hell feel it, but there ain't nobody around. Mighta thought it was a stroke or something. Dementia, something like that. But it ain't. I know that. Something's wrong with the Door."

"Okay. Okay, then. So what do we do about it?"

"I don't see that there's much we can do. Ain't like we can call the police and file a complaint." He laughed, but it was a brittle, bitter little rattle in his throat.

"Ed, you can't keep going on getting the shit beat out of you."

"Don't have much of a choice, do I?"

"Maybe you could leave for a while, get away from that Door and whatever influence it has. Pack up and run." It was what Toby had done after Dingmans Ferry. He'd packed up and left and hoped nothing would follow him out to Zarephath. The law hadn't, certainly, but his own guilt had always been a step or so behind him.

"Wouldn't do no good. People have tried to outrun the reach of the Door after foolishly sending some second letter or after them getting not quite what they wanted. Ain't no one ever been successful, though. I suspect running away ain't going to matter much."

"So what, then? Let invisible monsters beat you to a pulp?"

Ed cast a forlorn look out the window. The night had collected along the tree line at the edge of the woods, and Toby figured that to Ed, it must have seemed like a gathering of those invisible enemies, amassing for a moonless attack. It wasn't too hard for Toby himself to imagine shapes in the shapeless, and an animosity in the inanimate.

"Do you want me to stay tonight?"

"Why?"

"In case they come back."

Ed turned to him, too intoxicated and too exhausted to hide his gratitude. "Yeah, if you're not busy. I'd appreciate it."

"No problem," Toby said.

The two watched outside the window, standing guard over the advance of the night.

* * * *

People in town were talking.

There had been an announcement in the Monday paper, a flier at the market, a folded note in Kari's mailbox from the sheriff's office. There was to be a town meeting that Wednesday, and all were strongly encouraged to attend. Evidently, the mayor and members of law enforcement wanted to discuss a problem with the Door.

Kari felt sick to her stomach. She thought she knew exactly what problem they wanted to discuss. She and Cicely were discussing it over coffee on Cicely's front porch. Kari had been watching the wind chimes, taking in the way the wind stirred them, but then carried away their music, out of earshot. She thought of telling Cicely that they might be broken, but decided it wasn't that important.

The older woman seemed disinclined to leave the house, though. From the way she kept glancing back through the screened upper portion of the door, she seemed uncomfortable with being inside as well. She looked exhausted.

Cicely had been telling Kari about Rita Nunez and Alice Cromberg, neither of whom Kari had ever met, though she'd heard the names from Cicely before. Alice, a friend of Cicely's from church, had freely admitted to her church lady friends that she was pregnant, despite the fact that she was seven years strong into menopause. The woman was as far along as she'd been at fifteen when she'd delivered a panicked letter to the Door, asking for her to have never been pregnant at all. Alice was a talker, comfortable in the center of attention even when those around her weren't, and didn't mind telling people that she hadn't wanted to kill the baby, but only make it disappear, and she had worded her letter as such. Then she woke up three mornings later simply *not* pregnant, and had cried in relief and not asked too many questions. There was no doubt in her mind that her unpregnancy, as well as her current situation, were due to some magic from that Door. And she wasn't the only one.

Kari was more worried about Cicely, and inquired about her health.

The old woman paused, seeming unsure how to answer. Then she said, "Bad dreams, I guess. I hope that's all they are." She smiled sadly. "Actually, I suppose it's more than that. It's…" Her voice trailed off and she smiled shyly. "I've never really talked about this before. See, I was married once. I may have mentioned that."

"In passing," Kari said, nodding.

"His name was Reggie. Aw, sugar, when I met him, it was love at first sight. He was handsome, strong, funny….We used to have these long talks out on this porch here, just sitting and rocking and looking up at the stars." Cicely's smile faded. "Men change sometimes, though. They disappoint you—some men do, at least. Reggie…well, he could be cruel too. Had himself other women from time to time, and never took any guff from me about it. He'd get so angry over such little things, mostly when he drank. He'd pinch and hit and kick…once, he burned my stomach." Cicely had a sad, faraway look on her face as she rubbed her stomach just above the navel. Kari said nothing, waiting for her to continue. It was difficult to hear, but it was the most Cicely had ever revealed about her life.

"I married him when I was nineteen," she told Kari. "We were married forty-nine years. And then one day, I'd had enough."

"You left him?" Kari asked.

She chuckled dryly. "He left me, in a manner of speaking. I used the Door. I wished him away." She sipped her coffee.

Kari stared at her a moment, unbelieving. It seemed so bold a thing for Cicely to do, and yet at the same time, it struck Kari as exactly the solution Cicely would come up with. "You...and it worked?"

"Oh yes," Cicely said. "Three days after I asked, he went off to work and never made it there. Police found his car out on the road by the woods, where we parked that time I showed you the Door, remember?"

Kari nodded.

"Out there, they said. They found his car, his wallet with his license and credit cards. They even found his shoes. Didn't find him, though. No trace. No blood or bone or hair or anything."

"Wow."

"They searched the woods for days after. I remember them bringing in the dogs. And I remember the sheriff at the time, Bill Grainger—he was kind. He often came out to the house when Reggie got too loud and the neighbors called the police. He knew what kind of man Reggie was. And he told me, sugar—he said, "Maybe some things are a blessing, Miss Cicely. Maybe some lost dogs don't really need to be found, eh?"

Her eyes filled with tears. "And I agreed. I was so...so relieved. And Bill called off the search that day." She shook her head. "They weren't ever gonna find him anyway. The Door had worked its magic. Gave me just what I asked for. And God forgive me, but I couldn't help hoping that them behind the Door had taken him to their side of things, because I didn't just want Reggie out of my life, I wanted him out of this world."

Kari squeezed the woman's knee and Cicely smiled gratefully. "Aw, sugar, I'm sorry to be unloading on you. It just feels good to talk, you know?"

"Any time, Cicely. You can talk about anything, any time."

"Aww, you're a good woman, sugar. I appreciate that."

A terrible thought occurred to Kari then, and she gasped. "Wait, so... with all that's been happening with the Door, things undone and whatnot... what does that mean for you?"

Cicely glanced back at the screen door. "Heard him once through the bedroom door and seen him twice. Out on the streets of town, I've seen him. Every time, he's someplace closer to the house. Frankly, I don't know what I'll do when he gets here. And I know he's coming."

"Oh, Cicely...."

Cicely patted Kari's knee that time. "It's okay, sugar. The Lord will look out for me, one way or another. I just worry about other folks. So many have used that damn Door and now...."

It took all of Kari's will to stifle the guilt and confess to Cicely that she'd opened the Door. That had to be the cause of all these people's problems. They were suffering bizarre aftereffects that appeared to be related to their use of the Door and that—well, that was more than likely *her* fault. If she'd just chosen to move forward into a state of ignorant bliss, none of this would be happening right now.

She was so lost in that particular thought that she missed Cicely's question.

"Mm, I'm sorry. What did you ask?"

"I asked if *you* were doing okay. Feeling any effects with all that's going on?"

Kari nodded. It was an honest answer. "Been thinking of Jessica more than ever," she replied. "Sometimes, I think I even see her."

That was an understatement. Since she'd opened the Door, Kari had been seeing a lot of upsetting things.

That past year, once the grief had settled in as a part of Kari's soul, the suicide note came back to haunt her. Who was the man referenced in the note, and what had he done? She thought she could guess at the latter. Once she'd found a bloody pair of panties beneath her daughter's mattress, and at the time she had assumed they were stained from menstruation and Jessica had been too embarrassed to tell her. Now Kari thought differently, and the rage became another part of her. One of the most frustrating things was not knowing who had hurt her little girl, or how long it had been going on. It withered a part of Kari's soul that she hadn't been able to stop it because she'd never known it was happening. She felt helpless. She couldn't undo anything that had been done and worse, she didn't even have a name that she could hang the blame on.

She should have given the police the suicide note. She knew that. Maybe they could have found him and thrown him in jail. She hadn't been thinking, though, of anything other than hiding that note and by doing so, making it somehow less true, a little bit less awful to have found her little girl lying dead on her pink bedspread. As time passed afterward, she was afraid it would somehow make her look suspicious that she had hidden that note. After all she had lost, she couldn't bear to be thought of as neglectful or complicit in her daughter's death. She hadn't just done it to protect her daughter; she had done it to protect herself, to assuage the guilt of not knowing, of not having ever seen the signs her daughter was being hurt. Jessica had felt so helpless and ashamed that death seemed like the only answer, and Kari always felt that was as much her own fault as the man mentioned in the note.

There was a part of her that had always hoped she would be the one to discover who that man was and make him pay without any police intervention, but she was no detective. She had been an average working mom from Dingmans Ferry with the perfectly average dreams and aspirations of a suburbanite. She wanted a new dishwasher and to fix the roof over the garage. She wanted her daughter to get good grades and her husband to like the dinners she cooked.

Now she was responsible for unleashing what at best looked like a curse on an entire town full of people.

She still had the note. She didn't keep it with Jessica's other things, but in a little locked box inside another box way in the back of her closet.

The night she opened the Door, she'd found the note unfolded on her pillow when she'd gotten home. She'd just held it, rereading it until she was crying so hard she couldn't see the words anymore.

I can't stand what that man does to me.

She'd burned it that night, but found it intact and uncharred on her night table the next morning. So she'd locked it back in its box inside another box and hidden it even farther away, down in the basement. After that, it wasn't the note she kept seeing, but glimpses of Jessica herself.

She'd always believed she'd give anything to see her daughter's face again, but...not like that. She saw Jessica, heard her, but the girl she loved was now an angry thing with bluish skin and vomit down the front of her clothes and hemorrhaging in her eyes. Kari couldn't bear to look at her, or to listen to the gurgling sounds the girl made in an attempt to blame Kari for not protecting her. Could she have? Her child's death was not the result of a tragic accident or lingering terminal illness, but a suicide, deliberate and violent and terrible. However, like any mother oblivious to the secret life of twelve-year-olds, she had never imagined her daughter could find anything regarding the facets of middle-class suburban life so egregious as to no longer be bearable.

That man had been unbearable. She should have used the Door to ask that the man pay for what he'd done, but again, she hadn't thought it through. She'd only thought of her own pain.

"Cicely," she said, her voice weary from the thoughts behind it, "do you think what's going on with the Door can be stopped? Like, do you think someone knows how to fix it?"

Cicely sipped her coffee, her rocking chair creaking thoughtfully. "I hope so, sugar. I certainly hope so."

Chapter 9

It took Bill pulling a few strings to get the town together on such short notice—calls to the current sheriff of Monroe County, a great bear of a man named Timothy Cole, as well as Mayor Forsythe, the folks at the *Zarephath Ledger*, and Amanda Pulaski at the Historical Society, since the only space big enough to hold a town meeting was in the basement of the History and Heritage Center. Bill pulled it off, though; Kathy was impressed. By Wednesday evening at seven, those notable heads of town and county were gathered at long folding tables equipped with microphones. The sea of folding chairs set up in neat rows across the rest of the basement were filled; other townsfolk stood behind the chairs near the door.

After the mayor and current sheriff had their official say, Bill took the mic. "Thank you, Mayor Forsythe, Sheriff Cole. And ladies and gentlemen, thank you for coming out tonight. We appreciate your participation tonight. From what I understand, this is the first meeting in almost seventy years regarding the, uh…the Door in the Zarephath woods."

There was an agitated murmur from the crowd that Bill silenced by holding up his hand.

"You may be aware of some unusual events happening in town. Before we get too far into the discussion of the nature of these events, I think it's important to stress that not every misfortune is or should be necessarily associated with the Door. That could lead to potentially dangerous misunderstandings. Hear what I'm saying, folks: Please do not jump to conclusions about your or other people's misfortunes or difficulties being related to the Door.

"That said, as I'm sure at least some of you have noticed, the Door or some force connected to it seems to be reversing or otherwise undoing requests made of it, reaching back for the last few decades."

The uproar of frightened murmurs took longer to quiet that time. Questions sprung from the crowd:

"Oh God—why?"

"How do you know?"

"What happened? Are we in danger?"

"How can we stop it?"

"Please, please," Bill said into the microphone. "Please, settle down. That's what we're here tonight to discuss."

The crowd settled back into their seats, but their expressions and body language spoke of deep fear. Kathy couldn't help but wonder how many of them had been tempted or had succumbed to the temptation of using that alien version of a wishing well in their midst.

Bill continued. "This is still a working theory, but seems to be supported by the limited firsthand evidence reported by townspeople. We've brought in an expert in matters relating to this sort of thing, and she will speak to us about the situation and answer any questions you have to the best of her ability. Please welcome Kathy Ryan."

There was a smattering of uneasy applause as Kathy stood and took the mic from Bill. "Uh, hello. My name is Kathy Ryan. For over a decade, I have been a consultant to law enforcement agencies across the country regarding crimes with distinct occult, preternatural or supernatural elements and aspects. I am well aware of your Door, and have spent some significant time and resources amassing what information I could about it." She paused. The crowd before her was silent. She felt their eyes on her, on her scar. She saw some of them balk at her tone, which was so practiced a mix of authority, confidence, and inarguable reassurance that it pervaded all her speech now. She waited a few seconds to see if they would argue her credentials or ask questions, but no one spoke. She supposed any town so used to the unusual in their everyday life would feel no need to question a woman claiming to be an expert in the unusual. That was good—one hurdle jumped.

She continued. "We suspect that sometime in the last week or two, the Door opened. We don't know on which end. It is closed now, but we suspect that something came through nevertheless, and we believe whatever it was is responsible for the reversions. We would like to identify and contain this force if possible, and minimize further risk to you, the people of

Zarephath, particularly users of the Door and those marginally involved with it by association or involvement in the letters others have written."

As she spoke, she noticed a lot of poking and prodding between the people, whispering and grumbling. Her understanding was that the cardinal rule for living in Zarephath was to never, ever, under any circumstances open that Door. She understood their panic, but mob panic was always a dangerous thing. If she could have seen a way to gather information on a smaller, quieter scale, she would have. However, she believed time was of the essence and where her files were lacking, only the townspeople could fill in the blanks. So she kept talking.

"I understand that many of you are frightened at the prospect of an unraveling of requests and what it will mean in terms of the well-being of yourself or others. That is why it is going to be of vital importance that you lend us your assistance—anonymously, if desired. Yes, I'm saying that in order to help you, I need you to help me. Understand that I am not here to judge you and frankly, I don't care *why* you used the Door. But if you want to save yourselves, your families, and friends, I just need to know *that* you did, and what you have been experiencing as a result this past week. Sights, sounds, smells, and of course, any physical contact. I need to be able to identify what, specifically, is attacking you so that I know how to fight it."

After that, the crowd did erupt in noise, and it took the mayor and Sheriff Cole to herd them into some semblance of order to ask their questions.

"Are you really going to take this information anonymously? What if folks don't want anyone to know they used the Door?" The question was posed by a harried-looking middle-aged woman with a messy bun of mousy brown hair. She wore a T-shirt that read *Aliens took me...and brought me back*.

"Absolutely. We'll be setting up interviews by phone and written request, to meet at a time and place that is both convenient to you and discreet. The interviewing team will consist only of myself, retired sheriff Bill Grainger, and Sheriff Cole. No one else will be aware of your participation if you wish to remain anonymous."

A male with a baseball cap and gray T-shirt stood up and asked, "How did the Door open? I thought it was locked." There was a chorus of agreement on that point. It had likely never occurred to a number of people to even try to open the Door under the assumption that it had some kind of cosmic lock.

Kathy replied, "We don't know at this time how or why the Door opened, although given what we know about the Door, we don't think it's likely it was opened from the far side." Outrage rippled through the crowd, so she added, "This does not mean we're accusing anyone here or blaming anyone for opening the Door. Please do not take it upon yourselves to try to assign blame to your fellow neighbors. That Door you have out there is not from this dimension. I'm sure you know that. As such, we can't be one-hundred percent sure at this time how to predict its behavior. We can offer theories based on patterns we have seen from years of field research and observation."

"So you've seen other Doors? Doors like that one out in the woods?" an old man in a wheelchair hollered from the far side of the room.

"Other portals, yes. Not like yours, though; not exactly. In many cases, the portals could only be opened or activated from one side. The Door in Zarephath seems to possess many characteristics of a portal like that. Other portals can be opened from either side, given someone has a key and knows how to use it."

"Can you keep the Door from opening again?" a young girl in the front row asked. She looked about nine and absolutely terrified.

Kathy softened for a moment. "I hope to. I'll certainly do my best, sweetie."

"We have time for one more question," Bill cut in. "Then we'll give you information on setting up appointments to speak with us privately."

A man in the back of the room raised his hand. Despite his boyish handsomeness, his eyes looked haggard, as if sleep had eluded him those last several days. "Can this force you mentioned, this whatever it is that escaped from behind the Door—can it kill us?"

The room grew silent, awaiting her answer. She paused—not long enough for them to pick up on it and panic, but long enough to think through how to answer that.

"That," she said, "is what I'm hoping to determine from you fine people. I suspect there is a physical-interaction component, to be honest with you. But I promise I'll do everything I can to keep it from hurting anyone."

"I hope you can," the man said softly.

* * * *

Bill awoke in the darkness, one foot in the real world and one foot still in his dream. He turned to his digital alarm clock. It read 4:00. He'd been having a dream, though the details were fuzzy. He thought it might have been about the night with the hitchhiker, but he could only remember streaks of blood mixing with rain. It was already fading, though, and he mashed the remnant sleep from his eyes with the heel of his hand. With a groan, he got up and trudged to the bathroom and stood over the toilet, waiting for the stream of urine to begin flowing. He'd found that the older he got, the longer it took to get his dick going, regardless of what he needed it to do. He'd also discovered the need to make these nightly bathroom visits more frequently, which wreaked havoc on his sleep.

When he was done, he splashed some cold water on his face and headed back to bed. Still groggy in his head, he almost didn't notice the shape moving on the bed. He got within a few feet of it before his brain registered what his half-closing eyes were seeing.

Something was moving beneath the covers in the dark.

Immediately he was awake, trying to gauge the distance between the thing on the bed and the gun in his night-table drawer without taking his eyes off the shape for too long. It looked to be about the size of a large dog, but the contours weren't right for an animal. It appeared to be struggling to free itself from the blankets he'd thrown back a few minutes before, and whatever it was, it was making wet smacking sounds beneath them. Bill inched toward the night table.

The thing must have heard the creaking of his feet on the floorboards, because the sounds stopped suddenly, like it was waiting and listening. After a few moments, the smacking, slapping sounds resumed, and Bill crept closer to the night-table drawer. Beneath the blanket, it looked like a number of snakes writhing in different directions. Blood soaked the portion of the undersheet exposed by the moving blanket; Bill could see a wet shadow dripping down the side of the bed. He quietly eased open the night table and pulled out his .38. In one fluid move, he threw back the blanket and drew the gun on the shape on the bed.

He almost dropped the gun. The thing lying where Bill had been moments before looked like the hitchhiker from the waist up, though it was worse off than when Bill had seen it on the lawn. The plastered blond hair looked leached of color and mangy spots on her head suggested it had been pulled out or fallen out in random clumps. The eyes had flattened in their sockets and were a dull gray color now, and part of her bottom lip was missing. Her breasts were lopsided, one sliding nearly into her armpit and the other flattened against her chest. Her nipples were purplish-gray. There was nothing remotely human below her waist, which was itself a tattered and bloody mess of flesh where thin, knotted cords of blackish muscle grasped at the soaked sheets. And her stomach…

What he had mistaken for snakes were long tentacles waving and snapping at the air. They reached out to him from a hollowed-out cavern in her gut, slick with blood and some substance the sickly yellow color of phlegm. The hitchhiker's arms reached out for him too, as if pleading with him to embrace her.

When the thing sat up, he emptied the gun into its face. It shrieked once, then folded in on itself. It was like watching a rag get pulled through a pinhole, and then it disappeared with a tiny plop. Bill stared at the bloody spot on the bed for several seconds, his brain still trying to process how the monstrosity that was there seconds ago was now gone. He took a deep breath and with a shaking hand, put the gun back in the drawer.

Then he heard the shriek outside.

He rushed to the bedroom window and peered out. Looking up at him from the surrounding darkness below was the thing that had been on his bed, except that instead of the hitchhiker's face, there was a cavernous emptiness. It looked to him like a hole poked in a piece of paper, but the void behind it was endless, deeper than the body, deeper than the world. It was dizzying to look down into it, with those matted clumps of hair dangling into the abyss like cilia and those tentacles whipping up a frenzy all around it.

Another shriek emanated from that black hole, a thin, unnatural sound overlapped onto the air rather than moving through it. Bill was about to grab his gun again when the thing ran off on its stomach tentacles, disappearing into the night.

Bill watched the space where it had been for some moments after, scanning the darkness in an ultimately futile attempt at discerning where the thing had gone. The world outside was silent; even the crickets, tree frogs, and cicadas had packed it in for the night.

He looked at the mess on the bed, stripped off the sheets and blankets, and left them in a heap on the floor. Then he went downstairs and grabbed a kitchen chair, hauling it awkwardly up the stairs to the bedroom, where he set it down facing the window. He took his .38 out of the night table, sat in the chair, and with the gun in his lap, he waited for the dawn.

Chapter 10

Setting up interviews to question the townspeople about their experiences with the Door and the more recent results of having used it proved tricky. Most people were not as forthcoming about their use of the Door as Alice Cromberg, who, shortly after giving her statement in the makeshift interrogation room of the Heritage Center's basement, had to be rushed to the hospital. She had been experiencing some cramping during the interview, but as she'd gotten up to leave, she'd been wracked with a spasm of pain that nearly dropped her to the floor. Kathy, worried that she might be miscarrying, had called an ambulance.

She'd gone to the hospital earlier that day to talk to Joe and Anne Bartkowski about the aggressive return of Anne's cancer—the poor woman looked ravaged from the inside out—and had even managed to pry from Bill that an old dispatcher with a crush on him had wished away his Vietnam-related PTSD. Their stories more or less conformed to the town gossip she'd already heard. What they proved in terms of illuminating and useful information about the Door was frustratingly little. None of the people she'd talked to so far had visited the Door or the woods or even given much thought to either since their initial letter. In all those cases, the Door had delivered with little to no negative side effects everything the letter writers wanted, pretty much the way they wanted. All that suggested was that good wishes had finally gone bad, and Kathy knew the sampling was far too limited to make the determination that it only applied to such a narrow set of circumstances.

She was particularly interested in some of the upcoming interviews over the course of the week that had not made the town circuit of gossip. Ed Richter, the owner of the local hardware store, had informed them that a number of townsfolk had laid their confidences on his counter regarding their interaction with the Door, and that if it could save people's lives, he could part with a few names and basics that Kathy, Sheriff Cole, and Bill Grainger could use as leads. Ed had made only one request, and it was that they come out to his house to talk with him, as he was not well at the moment. In truth, he'd sounded terrible on the phone even to Kathy, and those who knew him said he sounded like death warmed over.

Her next few appointments were with a Toby Vernon, a Kari Martin, a Cicely Robinson, and a Mr. and Mrs. Grant and Flora Kilmeister. The couple she would have to speak to last; Sheriff Cole had informed them recently of the tragic vehicular homicide of their employee, a young guy named Carl Dietrich, and they were pretty shaken up about it. Apparently, it had been a hit and run; someone had mowed the boy down in the street. The others had requested various clandestine meetings out of the town's watchful line of sight, and the trio of interviewers had agreed.

Kathy had reiterated to each of the townspeople she had spoken to that contents of the interviews would remain anonymous. What she couldn't promise them was immunity from prosecution, should one of them implicate him- or herself or someone else in a crime. Sheriff Cole had stepped in on that point, uncharacteristically sensitive and soft-spoken, and had assured worried townspeople that prosecution was not their aim. Saving the lives of the people of Zarephath was priority number one, and anything else could be reasonably and discreetly sorted out later. Kathy wasn't sure if the man was lying to them or not, but it put people's minds at ease and got them talking, and for that, Kathy was glad.

An elderly woman by the name of Edna Tremont had been first on their list. They met her at three p.m. at a local scenic spot, Carner Park, at a picnic table under an elder tree. She always went to the park during warm months and sat at "her" table, watching the children play and feeding the birds. There wasn't much else for her, she explained, as she was something of the "town crazy," as she put it. The thing was, the longer Kathy spoke to her, the surer she was that Edna had one of the sharpest minds in town. Her stories about the Door were a veritable gold mine of information into its working, despite the fact that she had never used it herself.

First, she told them about some of the observed odd effects of reversed wishes whose letter writers were no longer among the living. It made for some very unsettling conversation. Some things seemed to her like big, important things, and she started with those. She tossed her bread crumbs and smiled at games of tag while she told Kathy, Cole, and Bill about a man she'd known in the forties by the name of Jeff Dietrich. Jeff was born with one leg shorter than the other and limped his whole walking life as a result. Edna told them that he saw it not only as a physical limitation, but a social and emotional one as well, and one that made him inferior to his older brother Greg. He also had a temper shorter than his leg, and had shot his brother in the head for teasing him about it, then poured gasoline on him and set him on fire. In a fit of guilt, Jeff had written a letter wishing to trade places with his brother, then hobbled out to the Door alone to deliver it. Three days later, his charred remains had been found curled up in front of the Door with a bullet wound in the blackened skull. He'd waited his three days outside the Door to make sure that his request was honored, and it was, but not with the second lease on life Jeff wanted for his brother. Greg, now burdened with the guilt of murder on his soul, had hanged himself from the very same big elder tree in Carner Park under which Edna and Kathy and the others were sitting. That was in '48. Edna told them last Tuesday's visit to her picnic table had led to the discovery of a pile of bones beneath a noose that was hanging from one of the branches of a tree and that she'd noticed one leg bone was significantly longer than the other.

Some things were littler, but somehow more horrifying in that there was no explanation forthcoming. These, Edna said, were things like doors in different places than they'd been days ago, a metal bar running through a cherry tree, a rusted-out car parked on a side street with a single grocery bag of dried and rotted fruit in it, and the park's outdoor basketball court carpeted with the corpses of dead goldfish. From an abandoned house down the street from her own home, Edna could hear arguing and crying, but no one was inside. She also claimed that from the empty lot where the old theater in Zarephath had once stood, she could hear singing, but only when she stepped where the audience seats used to be. There were graves with different tombstones on them. There were people with different faces. She'd found a severed skeletal arm in a birdbath on Pine Street and on the double lot on Elm, a shed-sized pyramid of stone in which there was an old sneaker, a flashlight, and a bloody pillowcase.

Edna assumed these small, strange reversions were due to letters written by the now-deceased. She could only begin to imagine the secret dreams and desires, envies and fears that had left these orphaned things to haunt places where they had once mattered so much to someone.

She also had stories to tell of living neighbors and friends, though these were no less tragic or terrible. Edna had recalled a man who had lost a leg in Korea asking for his leg back. She'd gone to check in on him with a chicken dinner, as she often did on Sundays, because he was a bachelor without a wife to properly cook for him. She had found him in his old wheelchair, looking miserable. The leg that had been returned to him had developed a fast-spreading kind of gangrene or sepsis or something, she couldn't remember which, and had begun rotting right off his body. She'd called an ambulance for him and the last she'd heard, they were going to have to amputate. Edna also told them about a woman who had been burned in a fire in '84 wishing for her beauty back. She continued modeling for almost twenty years after that. The police—Sheriff Cole confirmed it—had found her in the woods on Tuesday. The animals had gotten to her and gnawed off more than half of her face.

By the time the interviewers were finished with Edna, they were exhausted. So much tragedy and horror had visited the town of Zarephath, and Kathy could see how people would try to fix it using the Door. It was human nature that in times of fear or sorrow, people leaned toward wanting to believe in something over nothing, to take whatever god was available to them: even faceless, nameless gods behind a freestanding door in the woods. It was sad, in a way, but not surprising that their trust in those gods was so often misplaced.

It was almost six thirty in the evening when they left Edna Tremont at her picnic table and headed back to Bill's truck. Their other interview that evening was with Ed Richter, owner of the local hardware store. They were scheduled to meet him at his home on the edge of town. Kathy remembered passing the house on her way to meet Bill in the woods. It was the only one that far out, and Kathy suspected Ed liked it that way.

As they drove out to the place, Kathy asked, "So this guy Ed… what's he like?"

She noted that Bill and Cole exchanged a subtle glance before Bill said, "He's been a townie his whole life, far as I know. No family, few friends, though he knows everyone. Seems okay—quiet. Mostly keeps to himself."

"Sounds like a serial killer. That all you've got for me?"

"Not much else to tell, really," Cole added. "Kind of an odd guy. Bill and I never got complaints about him, though. He's never been arrested. Guy's never even gotten a parking ticket."

Kathy thought there was more to their opinions of Ed Richter, that they were leaving out something they suspected, though perhaps couldn't prove. She'd known a lot of cops in her line of work, and had come to understand all the little tells that clued her in on how they thought. She was especially observant of the ways they hid all kinds of things they might not be inclined to tell her. She decided not to press the issue for now, and leaned against the backseat window.

Outside, the sun was sinking fast behind the tree line, almost too fast for this time of year. Ever since Connecticut, weird weather and light cycles made her suspicious and a little anxious; it wouldn't have surprised her if the Door could somehow effect time as well as space.

They arrived at Ed's house a little after seven pm. As the three got out of the car, Kathy sensed something wrong. The air felt off, subtly crackling with an energy that grazed the skin and raised the tiny hairs all over her body. The house itself seemed unwelcomingly quiet. The car in the driveway slumped against the pavement on four flat tires. The light bulb above the door was broken and the windows were dark. There was a smear of something rusty-brown along the siding of the house just below the front windowsill.

"None of that's a good sign," Bill muttered, gesturing at the house. Cole clicked the safety off his gun.

The three approached the front door. Bill knocked heavily. When no sounds came from inside, Bill called out, "Ed? Ed, it's us. You in there?"

"Looks like we got blood," Cole said, examining the smear by the window. "Can't see much inside."

Bill nodded, and he and Kathy moved out of the way so Cole and his gun could enter first. Cole tried the front door and found it unlocked. He eased the door open, gun raised, and the three went inside.

* * * *

Across town, Kari was bleeding heavily. Jessica had come just as the sun had begun to sink behind the trees.

The first time Kari had seen her since her death, the girl had looked much like she did when Kari had found her. That night, her skin had been cold and clammy, bluish around the lips and fingertips, and she hadn't been breathing. There was vomit on her chin and all over the front of her nightgown. Kari had found that despite her whimpering panic, a current of measured control coursed through her that allowed her to think, to turn Jessica on her side and then call 911 on her cell. It had been too late, though. Jessica had stopped breathing an hour or so before Kari found her, having chosen to take the pills right after Kari had tucked her in and kissed her good night. Kari hadn't seen her again until she herself came up to bed and went in to check on her daughter.

Now, when Jessica visited, she looked like she was falling apart. In so many of Kari's worst dreams, Jessica, her only baby, was rotting alone in the cold ground, the little life that Kari had a hand in creating snuffed out, and its delicate little shell putrefying, devoured by worms. Those dreams would leave her gasping for air, clawing the dark toward wakefulness. Even now, the thought gave her panic attacks. She couldn't bear to think of her beautiful little girl like that. And every time Kari felt a chill and a hum in her chest—the usual indications of Jessica's return—the decaying waif that came to confront her embodied every horror Kari had ever feared.

Also, please let her rest in peace knowing, wherever she is, that she is very much loved by her mother and father, Kari had written in her note. It hadn't occurred to her when she'd opened the Door that this specific part of the note would be undone too. It had been stupid of her not to remember—stupid, stupid, stupid. Now her daughter was a restless, rotting thing deprived of the simple comfort and security of undoubtable parents' love.

If that thing was her daughter, that was. Whether it was or whether it was some kind of manifestation of her daughter that the Door was using to punish her didn't much seem to matter; the feelings were the same. The result was the same. The implication was the same: that her daughter had once again been wronged by her own mother.

Jessica didn't physically hurt Kari at first. In the last day or so, that had changed. At first, it was just little scratches to the face or small, ineffectual fists on her back. Kari had been surprised that Jessica could actually touch her. She'd harbored the thought in the back of her mind that despite the emotional and mental pain the girl was capable of causing, Jessica was still just a phantom or thought form brought into being by her guilt, Jessica's unrest, or the Door's malevolent whims. It had never really been a concern that Jessica could or would hurt her.

Dusk was descending on Zarephath, and when Jessica lunged at her from the shadows, Kari cried out in surprise as much as pain. Jessica had been a blur and a hum and a banshee cry of anger as she flashed by, and her punch rocked Kari back a little. The blood gushed from her left nostril in a hot stream, pattering onto the hardwood floor of the hallway where she stood, shocked.

Kari screamed a few seconds later, a leak in the dam holding back her pain and frustration. The sound hung in her daughter's wake. Where had Jessica gone? Was she coming back?

A sharp crack to the back of Kari's head answered her question. Kari saw white fireworks in front of her eyes for a second before she could wheel around and face her attacker.

No one stood behind her.

"Jessica?" she cried out. "Jessica! Why are you—"

Kari caught a flash of angry eyes before a sharp blow to her gut forced the rest of her sentence out as a huff of air. She doubled over, clutching her stomach. She managed to stumble toward the den before what felt like a kick to the ribs toppled her over onto her side. She groaned, trying to roll over onto her knees and get up. A flurry of brown hair and another blow to her face split the skin along her cheek, and another knocked her down again.

She looked up, glancing around the room in terror. She saw no sign of Jessica anywhere. The blood on her face was growing sticky and the back of her head felt wet, her hair matted. She pulled herself to her knees once more and began to crawl toward the kitchen. Her purse was in there and her cell sat inside her purse. She had to call that lady from the town meeting, the one who could make them behind the Door stop.

Little feet blocked her way, bare and crusted with dirt and hovering just an inch or so off the floor. Kari looked up. Jessica glared down at her, skinny arms folded beneath the beginnings of breasts. She wore the dress that Kari had buried her in, though it was shredded now along the hem, crusted with vomit along the front. One sleeve was torn at the shoulder and hung almost to her elbow.

"Jessica," she breathed. "Stop this. Please!"

Jessica said nothing. Kari knew that stubborn look well, that expression of preteen defiance that had promised only to get stronger and more unmanageable as Jessica grew older.

"Please, baby. Let's talk. Talk to me. Tell me what happened so I can try to make it right." Her words had sounded weak in her own ears, but it still hurt to hear such derisive laughter from her daughter. *Make things right?* that laughter said. *When have you EVER made anything right?*

The girl above her sank to the floor and crouched down. She moved in toward her mother so that her face was close, very close to Kari's. Every fiber in Kari's being screamed at her to flinch, to move away, to escape the miasma of rot that Jessica's skin and hair gave off, a cloying smell that crept down Kari's throat. The part of her brain that could focus through her own fog of pain was tensely coiled, expecting a bite or some other savage attack to the face.

It was hard not to look into those eyes. They had always been so beautiful, so blue, and now they were misted with the desiccation of unblinking death, a film that prevented Kari from truly seeing into her daughter, and likewise, from Jessica truly seeing out.

Her face was so close. Her teeth....

The girl twitched and flickered.

"Jessie, baby—"

The girl wavered out of focus for a second, two, and then was gone.

Kari crumpled to the floor and bawled, her tears and blood mixing, drawing the dust on the floor to adhere to her skin. She lay there a long time, letting those fluids of life and feeling drain away. When she finally sat up, she felt dried out and a little dizzy. She managed to pull herself to her feet, groaning from all the places that hurt, and shuffle over to her purse on the counter. She fumbled with the phone, but eventually found the number she had entered for Kathy Ryan. She pushed the little green *call* circle on the screen and listened to it ring.

When the voice mail picked up, Kari said, "Ms. Ryan...It's Kari. They can hurt us. They can kill us if they want to. And it's my fault. I don't know how to fix it. I opened the Door. I closed it again, but I guess I wasn't fast enough. Please, please stop them. They're going to kill us. Please check on Cicely."

Then she hung up. The world was dissolving into little pinpoints of white. She managed to drop the phone back into her purse before she fainted, dropping heavily to the floor.

Chapter 11

The hallway of Ed Richter's house was absolutely silent, so much so that Kathy's internal alarm bells went off. It wasn't just the absence of the sounds of human life—breathing or snoring, rustling of clothing, shuffling of footsteps—but the utter lack of sound throughout the residence. No clocks ticked softly into the room, and no TV or radio shilled indispensable products or mindless entertainment. There was no groan of old water pipes or creak of settling foundations, no buzz of latent electricity or trickling of water. There was no music of crickets and tree frogs from the open window. Although a house missing any one of those sounds was nothing unusual, a house missing *all* of those sounds certainly was, particularly given the proximity of Ed's house to the edge of the woods where only an hour's hike in stood the Door. It was as if sound was somehow dampened, if not swallowed entirely inside the house; even their own footsteps and whispered words seemed hollow and devoid of substance.

Cole checked and cleared each room as they made their way from the front hall to the den. Then Cole cleared the other rooms before returning to say, "He's not here. Doesn't look like anyone is."

"Maybe he stepped out," Bill said, but he didn't sound like he believed the idea any more than Kathy or Cole did.

Kathy looked around the den. Clearly, this was where Ed spent most of his time. There was a TV remote and a small forest of beer bottles on the side table by the couch and another handful on the coffee table. A large TV stood on an old wooden stand. A small oscillating fan in the den spun along soundlessly, generating its modest breeze. The window in this room was open; it was the one under which they'd seen a smear of blood. Kathy examined the windowsill, expecting to find more, but she didn't. Instead, she found streaks of something bluish, almost the consistency of grape jelly.

"Did you see any blood in any of the other rooms? Signs of struggle?" she asked, turning to Cole.

The big man shook his head. "Nothing like that. Some indication that he burned a bunch of Post-it notes in an ashtray in the bedroom, but otherwise…." He shrugged.

"Guy's old," Cole said. "Maybe he forgot we were coming and went out."

"Car's in the driveway," Bill said. "Maybe someone picked him up?"

"Maybe," Kathy mumbled. "Or something dragged him out."

Cole cocked an eyebrow at her.

Kathy pointed to the bluish substance on the windowsill. "There's that—don't touch it. If it's from something that came from behind the Door, it could be poisonous."

Cole drew his fingers back, wiping them on his uniform anyway.

"So…what's the likelihood he's still alive, then? What are we looking at here, a missing person or a dead one?" Bill threw up his hands.

"Hard to say. I think we should proceed with this as a missing persons situation. Does Ed have any friends? We should start there, then maybe try the woods in the daylight. We still don't have conclusive proof of these things being able to kill anyone."

Bill shot her a look. "Kathy, you know they can. People are hurt, sick, dying. The Door is doing that."

Kathy squeezed his shoulder. "I know that. I know. I believe the townspeople are in real danger. I do. But we won't know exactly what kind of danger until we get more information. We need to find Ed and at this point, gather up anyone else we haven't talked to yet, or we might not have anyone left to talk to."

Bill nodded. "We could try Toby's place."

"Who?"

"Toby Vernon. He's…well, he comes out here to see Ed sometimes. I guess you could say they're friends. If Ed's still alive and not here or at the store, there's a chance he's with Toby."

"Okay, good," Kathy said. "Let's start there, then. I have his address in my notes. Let's pay Toby Vernon a visit."

She pulled out her cell phone and noticed a missed call from an hour before and a voice-mail message. She frowned. She'd never heard the phone ring.

"I have a missed call," she said, checking the list. "Looks like it's from Kari Martin." She put the phone on *speaker* and played the message.

"Ms. Ryan...It's Kari. They can hurt us. They can kill us if they want to. And it's my fault. I don't know how to fix it. I opened the Door. I closed it again, but I guess I wasn't fast enough. Please, please stop them. They're going to kill us. Please check on Cicely."

The three stared at each other.

"This puts a wrinkle in things," Bill said.

"We'll have to split up. Sheriff Cole, would you mind picking up Kari and this Cicely she mentions?"

"Sure thing," Cole said. "Just drop me back off at my patrol car."

"Thanks. Bill and I will check out Toby's place. We'll meet back at the Heritage Center basement at ten-thirty."

"Sounds like a plan to me," Bill said, digging his keys out of his pocket. "Let's go."

* * * *

Bill dropped Sheriff Cole off at his patrol car in the parking lot of the Heritage Center and waited while the big man got out his keys. They couldn't afford to lose anyone else and Bill wanted to make sure Cole got off safely. The sheriff honked as he drove off, and Bill pulled back onto the road.

"Things are falling apart," Bill said softly. "This whole town...it's falling apart."

Kathy, who had spent the better part of her life uncomfortable around men's pain, looked out the window. "All towns fall apart. And people rebuild them. It's going to be okay. Not every place is Thrall."

"Where?"

Kathy turned and smiled at him. "Never mind. My point is, we'll fix this, okay? We'll find a way."

"It was going to happen sooner or later. I always knew it. We weren't ever meant to have things like the Door in our world. It ain't something human beings should ever have had to live with. Too much temptation and too much of stuff far beyond most folks' comprehension. It ain't right."

"No, it isn't," Kathy agreed. "But it isn't as uncommon as you might think. You know how I know there's a place for us to go after death? Huh? You know why I know there's an afterlife?"

Bill shot her a sidelong glance. "Tell me you've seen heaven."

"Oh, hell no, not that I know of. If I knew there was a heaven, I'd have found a way to get out of here years ago. But I have seen other worlds, or at least doorways to them. Some of them are absolutely terrifying. Some spin on axes of utter indifference and some are fueled by malice and hate. But some of them are beautiful and safe, Bill. And what is heaven, really, but a beautiful, safe plane of existence different than ours? Heaven and hell are, theoretically, beyond most folks' comprehension, and yet humans have lived thousands of years alongside those concepts, living and dying, fighting and sacrificing for them." She patted his shoulder. "Your townspeople here, they're strong. They're not perfect, but I think for the most part, they strive to be good. They try to be better than they were yesterday, better than those who came before them. And they've lived a long time alongside that Door. Whatever is going on, they'll weather it. We'll weather it."

Bill offered a small, grateful grin. "Thanks, Kathy."

"No problem," she said.

Bill looked like he was about to say something else when his expression fell and suddenly, the car swerved. He rolled to a stop on the side of the road.

"What happened? What's the matter?" Kathy asked.

"Sorry. Sorry. Thought I—you okay?"

"Yeah."

"Thought I saw something," Bill finished. "In the road."

Kathy paused. "Something from the Door?"

"Yup." Bill pulled back onto the road, checking his rearview every so often.

"Want to talk about it?" Kathy watched his expression. He seemed genuinely unnerved by whatever it had been.

"Not...not yet. I'll tell you. Just not now."

"Okay," Kathy said.

He surprised her when, after a few moments of silence, he said, "It was a girl. Met her after the war, after my wife left me. I was drinking a lot then and she gave me drugs. We had sex. I think I might have hurt her."

Kathy waited for him to continue.

"I didn't kill her. I don't think I killed her. She ran away. But I hurt her. And I don't remember damn near anything about it. I asked the Door for her to be okay." He paused. "I've never told anyone that before."

"It's okay," Kathy said. "Everyone has secrets. Yours isn't going anywhere."

"I just wanted her to be okay. And if everyone's requests are being turned around on them...."

"You tried to do right by her."

"I can't remember hurting her. I wish I could take it back."

"I know, Bill."

"They call it PTSD now. That and the drugs...and I can't remember—"

"Bill, it's okay." She got him to make eye contact with her. "You've got nothing to explain to me. Really."

That grateful look returned, but there was no smile.

"Has she hurt you?" Kathy asked.

"Physically? No. Not yet."

"Okay, good," she said. "Let's keep it that way."

They drove on in silence for a few minutes before Bill slammed on the brakes, his arm shooting out in that parental gesture of keeping momentum from hurting the passenger. His wide-eyed gaze was fixed on a figure out in the street.

"Can...can you see her?"

Kathy squinted. The figure standing in the farthest reach of the headlights vibrated so quickly that it blurred. This movement was punctuated by the occasional pause in which the figure became motionless, and in those seconds, Kathy could indeed see it clearly.

"It's a rotting girl," Kathy said. "At least the upper half of her is. Blond once, looks like. Not sure what that mess below her waist is. Tentacles, maybe. Is that her?"

"Yeah. You can see her, then." It was part question and part statement of relief.

"Yes, I can see her."

"What should I do?" Bill asked. "If she can come at me and you can see her, maybe that means she can come at you too."

"Hit her," Kathy replied coolly.

"What?"

"With your car," she explained. "Hit her. Now."

Bill turned to Kathy. She could see he wasn't quite taking her words in.

"She's not the girl you knew," Kathy told him. "That girl, I'm assuming, had legs. This thing doesn't. Kill it."

Bill turned his attention back to the road and slammed on the gas. When his car made jarring impact with the thing in the road, it popped like a balloon, tiny girl-shards fluttering everywhere. Then it pulled itself back together and skittered off into the night.

"You saw that too, right?" Bill whispered.

"I did," she whispered back.

Bill started back down the road again, and the two drove the rest of the way to Toby Vernon's house in silence.

* * * *

Sheriff Timothy Cole had always been a man for whom the cold, factual, logical reality of his job and the ephemeral and intangible nature of the supernatural had never really conflicted. He'd been raised by God-fearing and churchgoing parents who had instilled in him the sense of the spiritual, and despite the mundane horrors of his job, that spirituality had never quite left him. He didn't talk about it much with the officers under his supervision because it wasn't any of their business and because he learned early on in his career that rationality went a long way toward earning and keeping respect. Nevertheless, it was difficult to be sheriff of Monroe County, under which Zarephath was part of his jurisdiction, and not encounter from time to time the weird and unexplained.

He hadn't been thrilled at first about the idea of an occult expert joining them as a consultant, called in by his predecessor, no less. There were plenty of people who claimed to be experts in such things who were little more than dangerous dabblers unable to understand the power behind Zarephath's Door. Kathy Ryan, however, appeared to be an exception. He had investigated her background as thoroughly as he was able, which was exceedingly more than most, given both his spiritual and law enforcement connections. Hers was a secretive profession, with many of the cases to her credit locked down tight in various records departments. Getting information on them usually required an inside person or a high security clearance. Still, Cole had managed to find out enough to be satisfied that Zarephath was in some competent and capable hands. He respected her because other people who had earned his respect the hard way respected her. They weren't always at liberty to give details about cases she had worked on with them, but they unanimously agreed she knew her stuff.

Cole wouldn't have let just anyone go messing around in Zarephath. If it had to be someone other than him or Bill, he supposed Kathy was a pretty good candidate.

During the time that he had spent with her and Bill, he had grown to feel confident in their ability to beat whatever was stalking the residents of Zarephath. He was, by nature, a man secure in his own abilities and not easily frightened. He had to be. He was the law, the guy with the gun, the one that ran toward trouble instead of away from it. But chasing invisible monsters was not the same as chasing perps who had knocked over a liquor store. His gun wouldn't matter too much and running toward the source of trouble could very well get him killed.

He assumed the fact that Kari Martin had called Kathy and not 911 meant that Ms. Martin was not in need of an ambulance or of police assistance. It was not an assumption he felt comfortable relying on, but he did hope that at least he would find her alive. He also hoped to find her alone; if whatever had prompted her to call and confess to opening and closing the Door was still with her, he wasn't sure what the most effective course of action would be.

Sheriff Cole had never used the Door. He occasionally thought that put him somewhat at odds with a number of the townspeople of Zarephath, who seemed to think of it as almost an insider's rite of passage. He supposed they thought he might not be inclined to believe their stories about the Door or that he was missing some experience necessary to truly understanding the situations arising from its use. So far, that had never proven to be the case, and he'd hoped to solidify their tentative faith in his ability to help by joining the task force involving Bill and Kathy.

Now, though, he wasn't so sure their faith was rightly placed. He didn't like this mantle of self-doubt settling on him. It didn't suit him.

When he pulled up in front of the house, he was relieved to see the porch light come on. He parked and as he stepped on the sidewalk, the front door opened. A light-haired brunette in her thirties stood there, pretty enough to look at, but beaten up pretty badly. She had a deep gash on her cheek that she was trying to hold together with a bandage strip, and her bare arms had sporadic bruises from shoulder to wrist. One arm clutched her side.

"Ms. Martin?" Cole asked as he came up the walk.

She nodded slowly. "Kari."

"Are you all right? Is anyone in the house with you?"

"No…no, I'm alone."

"Do you need medical assistance? Would you like me to call an ambulance?"

"Did Kathy Ryan send you?" the woman asked. "I called her…."

"Yes, she did. She asked me to pick you up and bring you to her, if you're able."

"Oh yes, please. I need to talk to her. It's really important."

"Are you sure you wouldn't like me to take you to the hospital first?" Cole noticed another gash on the back of her head, the dried blood clumping her hair.

"No, please—just take me to Ms. Ryan. I need to talk to her."

"Come this way, ma'am." Cole gestured toward the police car.

The crash from inside the house made them both jump.

"Ma'am? Ma'am, I'm going to ask you again. Is anyone inside the house?"

Kari looked confused. "No…I was here alone. I've been alone for at least an hour and a half. No one should be in there."

Cole drew his gun. "I'm going to have to ask you to stay here, okay? I'm just going to go inside and look around."

"Please don't," Kari said. "I just want to get out of here. I don't know what's inside—"

"That's why I need to check it out. I'll only be gone a few minutes, okay? You can wait by the car."

Kari looked hesitant as she stood on the porch, hugging herself and shivering. She seemed to concede then, descending the steps and passing him on the way to his car. He followed and let her into the backseat.

"Please be careful," she said through the window.

"I will," Cole told her. "I'll be right back. Please stay put, okay?"

"Okay," she agreed.

With Kari secured, he turned his attention back toward the house.

The front door stood open and beyond it, he could see the front hallway. He moved cautiously forward, his gun trained on the doorway. Another crash made him flinch and he glanced back at Kari, who was watching him nervously from the car. He turned back to the house and kept going.

The front hall extended toward the back of the house and ended in what appeared to be a kitchen. To the left was a doorway and a staircase leading to the second floor. To the right was another doorway. He stood on the threshold and listened. Banging sounds, more faint now, were coming from upstairs.

With a final glance back at Kari, Cole entered the house.

It was easy enough to ascertain that no one else was in either of the rooms off the main front hallway. With an eye on the stairs, he checked the kitchen, as well as the den and a bathroom at the back of the house, as well. Then he made his way back to the stairs.

Above him, the banging sounds continued. He could also feel a slight, unpleasant hum in his chest, ears, and stomach that was not quite painful, but certainly uncomfortable. With his gun pointed at the darkness of the second-floor landing, he slowly climbed the stairs.

The sound was coming from the bathroom. The door was shut, but there was faint light coming from under the door—a night-light, perhaps. Cole checked the two bedrooms on that floor, one of which Kari was evidently using for an office. Both of those were empty and Cole was glad for that. He could be reasonably sure, then, that whatever he was dealing with was confined to that one upstairs bathroom.

He crept toward the door. His training suggested he identify himself and tell whoever was in there to come out, but his gut told him that this wasn't the kind of situation covered by any of his training. He hovered outside the door for a few seconds, wiped the nervous sweat from his brow, and then threw open the door.

The faint light he thought he'd seen was gone, so he felt for the light and flipped it on, worrying in those seconds that whatever was in there would bite him or spear him or spit acid or—

Light flooded the bathroom. There was nothing there. Confused, Cole searched the shower and even looked in the cabinets. The window, he noticed, was open, but when he looked out, he could see nothing but a little patch of backyard lit by moonlight.

As much as he was bewildered, he had to admit to himself that he was relieved. He had no game plan for fighting off whatever had come from behind the Door. He let out a low whistle and flipped off the light.

Then he heard Kari Martin scream.

He took the stairs two at a time as he flung his bulk down to the first floor. He tore out of the house, but skidded to a stop on the porch when he saw the thing on the hood of his patrol car.

There was little distinction between the head and body of the thing; its shape appeared to be a fluid thing, like liquid in zero gravity. Its bones, if that was what they were, swam under the skin, shaping and reshaping appendages it used to smack the windshield. Occasionally, a glowing, yellowish eye like that of a shark would swim up out of the surface of the hairless, brackish, mottled skin, sink back beneath the surface, and reappear someplace else. One fairly constant feature was the abundance of mouths. They worked open and closed but made no sound. Occasionally, one would yawn and Cole could see other mouths inside, an endless fun-house mirror reflection of mouths inside of mouths inside of mouths, endless teeth and long, sharp adder tongues flicking wildly inside.

"Oh my God," Cole whispered, and began to fire at it.

It stopped pounding on the patrol car's windshield and an eye emerged to look at him. He stopped shooting, dumbfounded by the alien curiosity of the eye. A number of tentacles formed around it, waving in his direction. Cole thought they might have been sensing or assessing him somehow, even more so than the eye itself, and it made the hairs on his arms and the back of his neck stand up.

He fired again, aiming for that one big eye, but the bullets just sank into the amorphous flesh. The eye dove back beneath the skin and a mouth emerged to replace it, opening on an endless gullet of spiraling teeth. That odd hum he'd felt in his chest inside the house assaulted him, not exactly louder but more intense; it felt as if all his internal organs were vibrating and it made him nauseous.

Cole glanced at Kari. She was desperately trying to work the handle of the door and get out of the car, but it was designed not to open from the inside. Cole turned his attention back to the thing on the hood of the car. Keeping his gun pointed at that endless mouth was due more to training than practicality, but it was something between him and that beast, and that was enough to get his legs moving.

He edged toward the car. He'd have to let Kari out himself.

The thing went back to pounding the windshield. Cole heard a glassy *crack* but kept moving. The metal of the hood groaned under its weight, and he made a mental note that weight meant substance—the thing had to be a solid, physical thing, at least to some extent. If it had a partially solid body, then it might very well have a weak spot, a way to kill it.

He had closed half the distance between the house and the car when the thing turned its attention to him again, a number of eyes surfacing to watch him. He froze.

It formed tentacles on its underside and used them to climb to the roof of the car. The eyes stared down at him, daring him to get closer. The gun shook and it took all the strength in his hands to steady it again. The centermost eye disappeared and a mouth stretched wide, but this time, Cole was prepared for the bone-jarring hum. He fired into the mouth until his gun clicked through empty chambers. The humming sound broke off, a sensation like one's ears popping during an altitude change, and he realized he had closed his eyes. When he opened them, the thing was folding in on itself. Its roar seemed to be coming from the gaping hole where its mouth had been, and reminded Cole of the rush of air in a wind tunnel. That hole was sucking the rest of the creature into it, bending it and—it looked to Cole—the world around it, into odd shapes before swallowing the last of the creature. A second later, the distorted space above the roof of his car righted itself, and all trace of the creature was gone.

Cole laughed in disbelief. Had he killed it? Sent it back to where it came from? It didn't matter; the thing was gone and Cole wasn't about to wait for it to come back. He jogged around to the driver's side and let himself into the car. Immediately, he was flooded with thanks from the backseat.

"Oh my God! Oh my God, did you see that? Thank you! Thank you so much! Oh my God, that was in my house! Thank you!"

"Just doing my job, ma'am," Cole said with a smile, but he was pleased with himself too. He may never have used the Door, but he'd fended off something that had come from behind it, and had discovered some useful information about it to boot. "Now, in your voice-mail message to Kathy Ryan, you mentioned someone named Cicely?"

"Cicely Robinson!" Kari exclaimed. "Please, we have to go see if she's okay! I—I'm afraid she may be in more danger than I was."

Cole started the patrol car. "Then let's go get Cicely Robinson."

Chapter 12

When Kathy and Bill pulled up in front of Toby Vernon's house, they found the man sitting on the front steps of his house. He was alone, which didn't bode well for Ed, in Kathy's opinion. He rose when he saw them and limped toward the car. Kathy recognized him from the town meeting. His young, handsome face looked pale and terrified, and a large rip across his chest had split his T-shirt in two.

"Ed," he said. "They took Ed."

"Toby?" Kathy asked.

The man nodded.

"Who took Ed?" she asked.

He looked dazed, and it took Bill clapping a hand on his shoulder to snap him back to the here and now.

"I don't know what they were," Toby said. "At first, they looked like children. Little boys and little girls. But they weren't children."

Kathy and Bill ushered him toward Bill's truck. "They have Ed. I tried to stop them. We tried to run. And I thought we were safe…but then they took Ed."

"Okay, tell us everything that happened," Bill said. "Start at the beginning."

Toby looked at them, a new texture of fear overlaid onto his features. "I—I—"

"We're not judging you," Kathy said, trying to curb her impatience. If he clammed up because he was afraid of his secrets being revealed, they might never find Ed. "Right now, we're only interested in what happened tonight."

Toby considered that for a moment, then nodded. The three got into the truck and Bill headed for the Heritage Center.

"Just go slowly," Kathy said. "Start at the beginning and talk us through it."

"Okay," Toby said. "Okay. Well, it started when I went to check in on him tonight."

* * * *

Toby had gotten to Ed's around seven in the evening. Toby had been making it a nightly thing, sometimes staying the night, since the town meeting. Ed had been having a hard time of things lately, since the Door had gone bad. Toby hesitated, then explained it simply as, "He was being harassed. He couldn't see who was doing it, but it had escalated to violence in the last few days. Ed's an old man. He can't be getting the shit kicked out of him on a regular basis, you know?"

Kathy and Bill nodded noncommittally from the front seat and waited for Toby to continue.

When no one answered his knocks on the front door, Toby had let himself into Ed's house and found the old man half-drunk on his couch.

"You okay?" he asked.

Ed nodded miserably. "They were back tonight."

Toby looked around the room. "Are they still here?"

"No. I think they cracked a rib." He groaned as he shifted on the couch.

"We have to get you out of here," Toby said. He'd brought an empty gym bag and began looking around the room for things to pack. "Ed, this isn't safe. Look, come stay with me. I have the room. We can fight them off together."

"Maybe I deserve it, Toe."

Toby stopped stuffing the folded blanket he was holding into the gym bag and looked at Ed incredulously. "What?"

"I've been thinking about it. Maybe this is how it ends for me. I sat here counting last night and I've hurt twenty-three people since I was sixteen. Twenty-three people and never felt a single consequence, not once. It ain't natural to keep karma from coming around and making things right."

"You're drunk," Toby said uncomfortably and finished packing the blanket. "I'm going to grab your clothes and stuff from your room."

"You oughtta go," Ed said sadly. Even from the other room, Toby could sense the mixed feelings in the suggestion. "You ain't any safer here than I am."

At this point, Toby blushed deeply. Kathy saw it in the rearview mirror, where she'd been steadily watching him as he talked. After a few seconds of silence, Kathy gently urged him to go on, reminding him that they weren't there to judge and certainly not there to compound his problem. He and his secret were safe with them.

Toby looked out the car window. It had begun to drizzle and the moonlight through the droplets on the window created tiny, strange shapes on his face.

He had not answered Ed then because it wasn't really an arguable point. Toby had had his own issues, as he fully intended to tell the trio of interviewers the following day. He was nervous about that and those nerves probably didn't contribute any to his mood as he swept around Ed's house, scooping up toothbrush and hairbrush, shirts and pants, socks and underwear for the old man. When he came back into the den with the gym bag packed, Ed was peering nervously out the window.

"What is it?" Toby asked.

Ed held up a finger and the two waited in expectant silence for several seconds before Ed whispered, "The woods are glowing."

Toby joined him at the window, searching the tree line anxiously. There was indeed a faint glow coming from between the trees, a soft bluish-green that morphed to yellow and back again. He also saw movement, though it was hard to discern what, exactly, was moving.

"You see that?" he whispered. "There—something's moving."

"What is it?" Ed whispered back.

Toby squinted. Against the glow, tiny, human-shaped silhouettes were marching into view. "Looks like...people."

That it was people coming for them from the glow in the woods terrified them more than some hulking, slithering, flapping thing from behind the Door. They had both, in their way, been expecting angry mobs their whole lives. Angry mobs were the boogeymen of their adult dreams, and had been built in their minds into torturous, berserk hordes far more capable of atrocities than the unseen, unknown stuff of closets and the undersides of beds.

"We've got to go," Toby said. "Now, Ed!" He grabbed the old man by the arm and dragged him out of the house and toward the car.

The angry mob was still a ways off, but Toby could see now that they were children. If he had to guess their ages, he'd have said they ranged from eight- or nine-year-old boys to twelve- and thirteen-year-old girls.

"That's pretty specific," Bill cut in, and again, Toby flushed a deep red.

"Yeah," he said. "It is."

Toby went back to his story without further explanation.

He and Ed got into Toby's car and Toby started the engine. When his headlights came on, they flooded the driveway ahead of the car. A line of children stood blocking the way. A little boy balanced on one leg. He was missing an eye. The girl next to him stood a little taller and on two legs, but she was missing most of her lower jaw. A clump of her hair was torn out. She did not scare him so much as the girl to her left, a brunette with vomit covering her chin and the front of her nightgown. Her blue eyes glowed, then flashed to yellow. She unhinged her jaw and opened her mouth and more vomit, stringy and gray, spilled out. In its wake, Toby could see spiraling rows of teeth.

"Fuck," he muttered. Next to him, Ed began to laugh, and the sound was like the cracking of bones in Toby's ears.

Toby threw the car into *drive* and slammed on the gas, aiming for the children. The ones closest to his bumper burst into little flesh confetti as the car hit them, then reassembled into the same monstrosities. Toby glanced at them in the side mirror, then peeled off into the street and didn't look back.

The drive back to Toby's was relatively uneventful. Ed was lost in his own maudlin thoughts, and Toby was busy with the road ahead of him and the hope that nothing was following behind. When he finally parked in his own driveway, he exhaled a long sigh of relief.

"Come on," he said to Ed, grabbing the gym bag out of the backseat and handing it to the older man. "Let's get inside."

"They'll find us," Ed muttered. He took the gym bag with shaking hands and got out of the car. Before Toby could do the same, there was a blur and Ed was gone. The echo of children's laughter still hung in the air.

Without thinking, Toby got out of the car and searched the property. It only dawned on him as he turned his attention to the skies that whatever had swooped out of nowhere and snatched Ed and his gym bag could do the same to him. He kept looking, though.

That's when he saw the little girls. There were three of them: a blonde, a redhead, and a brunette. He thought they looked vaguely familiar, though that would have meant they'd be grown women by now. They stood on his front lawn, little hands on slim hips, pale skin flaking off their bodies and the stains of leaking fluids on their clothes. They were barefoot and their feet made odd crackling sounds in the grass as they began to advance on him.

He wanted to move, but couldn't. It was like a dream he'd had a while back, where he'd wanted to run, to escape the clawing attention of these little girls, and his legs had been immoveable, only this time he was awake and terrified of what they'd do to him when they descended on him.

The redhead reached him first and tried to tear off his T-shirt. She managed a good slash with one of her fingernails before her fingers fell off into the grass at his feet. The blonde, who had come up behind him, grabbed a handful of his hair and yanked his head back so that the brunette could bite at his throat. The redhead, meanwhile, tried to fiddle with the zipper of his pants, but without fingers, she was unsuccessful. The brunette helped, deftly licking his neck while unzipping his pants. They grabbed at him through his underwear and he tried to scream, "No!" but then the brunette's tongue was in his mouth and he couldn't breathe.

Toby lashed out at them, glad to find his arms and hands still worked. He clawed at the brunette. Her face disintegrated into ruddy, wet sand between his fingers and he felt a wave of horrified nausea splash through him. He spit out her tongue onto the grass. Then he swung at the redhead, his fist cutting a sandy swath through her rib cage. Her upper half thumped onto her lower half before toppling over into the grass and coming apart in rough, grainy clumps. He shoved the brunette, blind as she was without a face, and she too came apart upon impact with the lawn. He managed to get ahold of the blonde and whittle her down with his fists. He didn't remember much more about fighting them off; pure adrenaline kept him pounding them down into clumps and then breaking the clumps into grit that, moments later, sank into the grass.

He still heard them laughing, though. Little-girl laughing, the kind of laughing that accompanied the telling of delicious secrets, still too innocent to be the derisive laughter of women, but heading there.

Toby went and sat on the front steps of his house. He almost wanted them to come at him again, to carry him off like they had Ed. Maybe the old man was right, but there was only so much even the damned could take, and Toby had reached his limit. If he was an animal, so be it; he was ready to die like one.

That was when Kathy and Bill had showed up.

* * * *

The truck was silent for several minutes after Toby stopped talking. He had never clearly spelled out what he'd asked the Door for, but it was pretty obvious that it had to do with his interest in little girls. Kathy thought that for Toby's sake, it was good that Cole, who had four little daughters of his own, was not around to hear the story. Bill's gaze remained fixed on the road. Kathy surmised that her friend was working through his initial revulsion and instinct to hit the man in his backseat. She herself, while harboring no love for those who hurt children, felt that their current situation did not allow anyone to judge another's sins or secrets. If for no other reason in heaven or earth, they had to remain united in order to fight off what had come from behind the Door. She thought both Toby and Bill understood that on some level, but she let them process, each in his own way, anyway.

When several minutes had passed, Kathy said, "We're meeting others at the Heritage Center. We can figure out where to look for Ed from there."

"Will Sheriff Cole be there?" Toby asked. It was hard to read from his tone if he was frightened or not by that prospect.

"If all went well gathering some of the other townspeople, then yes," she said.

Toby went back to looking out the window. "Is he picking up Grant?"

"Grant Kilmeister?" Bill asked without taking his eyes off the road.

"That's the guy."

"Why would he?" Bill glanced at him in the rearview.

Toby shrugged. "Ed told me the other day that Grant said he had something he had to get rid of. Something to do with the Door."

"What kind of something?" Kathy turned in her seat to face him.

"I don't know," Toby answered. "Ed was kind of drunk, but he said it was something that came from there. From behind the Door. And it was deadly."

Bill's truck screeched to a halt. "This might have been useful information to have."

Toby blinked. "I thought you would have known already."

"Do you know where this Grant Kilmeister lives?" Kathy asked Bill.

"It's on the way to the Heritage Center. Looks like we're making one more stop."

* * * *

Sheriff Cole had radioed back to the sheriff's office and informed his deputies to advise the townspeople of Zarephath to meet at the Heritage Center for their own safety. He told them to go door-to-door if that's what it took, starting with the list of names on his desk of people who were known to have used the Door. Sheriff Cole thought it was in the best interests of the townspeople to stick together, as many as possible, in one place. The forces from behind the Door were no longer just dangerous to those who had made requests of them; now anyone who encountered them could be at risk. Kari was impressed with how authoritative he sounded. Sheriff Cole was clearly not a man to argue with.

When he was finished, she had tried to call Cicely on her cell, but got no answer. They were on Dingmans Turnpike, heading toward Cicely's house, and Kari was anxious. She watched out the window, wishing the patrol car to move faster. Cicely hadn't told her too much about her ex-husband, but she'd said enough to worry Kari. If Reggie was back the same way Jessica was, then Cicely was in a lot of danger. The rage of a twelve-year-old girl was one thing, but the rage of a grown man?

Kari shuddered. "You're the police. Can't you go faster?"

"Ma'am, I'm going as fast as—"

"There! There she is!" Kari cried. They happened to be passing the Alexia Diner and there Cicely was, in their usual booth by the front window. The patrol car had almost sailed right by her.

"Where?" Sheriff Cole said, turning the car in the direction she was pointing.

"The diner. Hurry!"

Sheriff Cole pulled into the parking lot of the diner. As soon as he parked, he was out of the car. He moved fast for a big man, and was opening her door a moment later. Kari sprung from the car and raced to the diner steps, the pain in her side a knife between her ribs. She pulled open the door, Sheriff Cole right behind her. Her gaze went right to the usual booth where she and Cicely usually sat.

Cicely wasn't there.

"No," Kari muttered. "No, no, no."

"Can I help you? How many?" a waitress asked, looking to seat them.

Kari turned suddenly to her. "I'm looking for someone who was just in here. Cicely Robinson—she's a regular. An older woman, African-American. Pink sweater. She was sitting right there." Kari pointed to the booth.

The waitress shrugged. "I'm sorry, I haven't seen her."

"Are you sure? She was sitting there. We—I—saw her through the window."

"I'm sorry," the waitress repeated. "No one here like you described."

"She was right there, like, two minutes ago!" Kari shouted, drawing the attention of the few other patrons.

The waitress, a skinny little waif of a thing, looked flustered. "I—I'm sorry. I don't think anyone's been sitting at that booth all night."

"No, that's impossible. I…I just saw her."

She felt Sheriff Cole's arm on her shoulder. "Ms. Martin—"

"Officer," the waitress said, "I swear, I haven't seen the lady she's looking for. Do you need me to get my manager?"

Kari broke out of the sheriff's grasp and ran to the ladies' room.

"Cicely!" she called out. "Cicely, are you in here?" No one answered. The room was small: two sinks and three stalls. She glanced in the mirror above one of the sinks and groaned inwardly at her beaten-up face. She looked unstable, to say the least. No wonder the waitress had looked at her like that.

As Kari turned to the stalls, her head began to ache. She was probably overdoing it, considering her injuries, but she needed to find Cicely. If Reggie hurt her, it would be all Kari's fault and she couldn't, just *couldn't*, be responsible for another death.

The doors of two of the stalls were open, and as she passed each, Kari could see that no one was inside. She approached the third stall and knocked on the door. "Cicely? Are you in here?"

She thought she heard a wet, sloshing sound. In her mind, she pictured some horrid-looking fish, an unfortunate intestinal escapee, a by-product of a questionable serving of diner food, splashing about in the toilet bowl. A hysterical laugh almost broke loose from her.

"Cicely?" She pushed on the stall door, but it didn't budge. Was someone in there? She tried to peek through the thin crack between the stall door and wall, but could see no one. She bent down, looking for feet beneath the door, and a wave of dizziness caught her and threw her off-balance. She slumped against the back wall, trying to blink that low hum out of her head.

She pulled herself back up, using the wall for support, and the dizziness subsided. The hum faded. She slowly bent again, looking for signs of someone in the stall. Again, that hum forced its way into her head and chest, threatening to drop her in a dead faint. She straightened up, backing away from the stall.

"Cicely," she muttered weakly.

"Cicely," a deep, gurgling voice from that far stall repeated. "Ci-ci. Ci-ci."

"Shit," Kari whispered.

"Ci-i-i…Ci-i-i…" The voice gargled the word in the thick fluid of its throat, and Kari had to fight to keep the world in focus.

She ducked out of the ladies' room and hurried back to where Sheriff Cole was talking with the confused waitress. He spotted her and opened his mouth to speak, ostensibly to ask if she was okay. Her nose was bleeding again; she could feel it trickling over her upper lip. She wiped it on her forearm.

"We have to go," she said, heading for the door.

Behind her, she heard the sheriff apologize to the waitress and then he was behind her, guiding her by the arm through the parking lot and back into the patrol car.

"We have to get to Cicely's. Something's wrong. Something's very wrong."

Sheriff Cole huffed, exasperated. "What was that back there, huh? What was that all about? You know, I've arrested people for less of a disturbance than that."

"I'm sorry. I'm sorry. Please, just get to Cicely's house."

Sheriff Cole started up the car, put it in reverse, then pulled out of the parking lot. "What did you see in there?" he asked after a minute.

Kari chewed her fingernail a moment, on the verge of tears. The hum had gone away, but her head felt like it was caught in the fist of something big and angry. "I don't know. I can't—I don't know."

The drive seemed inordinately long to her. The roadside scenery, mostly trees, was lost to the shapeless gloom of lampless roads. It was a little surreal, actually, how featureless Dingmans Turnpike was just then, and then Maple Street and then Oak Street, both of which should have had the faint orange glow of streetlamps and porch lights, but didn't. Beyond the curbs and slivers of sidewalks, the night had engulfed everything. Partial outlines of homes, parked cars, and signs were a blur, though she didn't think Sheriff Cole was driving so very fast. It made her feel isolated, near and yet not close enough to landmarks of familiarity and civilization. It was as if they were driving down phantom streets disconnected from reality and the rest of Zarephath. She sucked in a breath, convinced that they were getting farther and farther away from Cicely's house. They would end up lost on narrow ribbons of road that cut a path through nightmare lands of total shadow. When they finally ran out of gas, the unseen, unformed things with teeth would swarm out of the void around them and….

She shivered. Were they still so far from Cicely's house? Her instincts told her they should have been just about there, but it was hard to tell. She was about to turn away from the window and ask the sheriff when Cicely popped into view; the headlights caught her in their glare and then let her fall away, back into the dark.

"Wait! Stop the car!"

"Oh, come on—"

"It's her!"

"Are you sure?"

"Please, back up. I just saw her."

Grumbling, Sheriff Cole put the car in reverse and slowly backed the car up, searching the sidewalk for what Kari had seen. Even at that creeping pace, it was hard to make out anything recognizable. The moon had abandoned that stretch of road, and faint silhouettes served as the only suggestion that anything at all existed beyond the bounds of the car.

Suddenly, Cicely Robinson came into view again. She was standing on the side of the road in the near–pitch-dark. She looked disoriented, unsure which way to go, and so was shuffling a few feet in one direction before pausing, turning, and shuffling back the way she'd come.

"Cicely!" Kari cried through the window. She pounded on it to get the woman's attention. "Cicely!"

Sheriff Cole put the car in *park* and got out. Cicely only then seemed to notice them. She looked flustered as the sheriff approached her, explained something Kari couldn't quite catch, and then opened Kari's door. Kari slid over to let Cicely in.

"Oh my God! Cicely, are you okay? Why were you wandering around out here in the dark?"

"Reggie," Cicely murmured. "He was at the house."

"Jesus," Kari said as Sheriff Cole got back in the car.

"You ladies okay?" he asked, pulling away from the curb. "Mrs. Robinson? You all right?"

"Ms.," Cicely corrected him, still dazed. "I'm all right. I had to get out of the house."

"What happened?" Kari gently touched her friend's arm.

Cicely shivered under Kari's touch. "Well, I was in my kitchen, making a cup of tea—decaf, mind you, to relax me so I could go to sleep. I haven't been sleeping well, as you know." She smoothed the wrinkles on her pants nervously. "I thought I heard a noise upstairs. Well, maybe *heard* isn't right. I thought there was something wrong with the electricity. There was kind of an electrical hum coming from upstairs, do you know what I mean? The kind that makes those little hairs stand up and gives you a slight headache?"

"I know what you mean," Kari said.

"I figured maybe I left something on," Cicely continued. "The TV in the bedroom, most likely. It makes this sort of hum when it's in sleep mode. So I didn't think much about going upstairs to turn it off. But it wasn't the TV."

She hugged herself and shivered again. "I should have known it wasn't the TV."

Kari felt a pang of guilt in anticipation. Cicely was a good woman, a smart woman. She didn't deserve whatever she was remembering behind those eyes.

"I climbed the stairs," Cicely went on, "and saw a light on under my bedroom door, a sort of flickering bluish-green light. The hum was stronger on the second floor, but it…I know this sounds weird, but it distorted other sounds. Like my footsteps on the stairs or my own voice—it was like the hum ate into them, dampened them or something.

"I tiptoed over to the door and listened from the other side. I was afraid in the same way I used to be afraid of *him*. I was scared to open my own bedroom door. There were strange noises, though, coming from inside the bedroom. The hum didn't just dampen those noises, but seemed to stretch and snap them. They sounded almost like words, if random syllables were missing….It's hard to explain. There's a flow to normal sound in this world, and this just wasn't normal sound. It was broken. A jumble of pieces of sound in the wrong order." Cicely looked frustrated. "I don't know how to make you both understand, but those broken, unnatural sounds got inside me. They pulled at me, and I found myself opening the bedroom door even though my brain and my hands didn't want to. My eyes didn't want to see whatever was on the other side. My legs wanted to run, and I couldn't do anything but move through the door toward the sound. And that's when I saw Reggie."

Tears spilled down her cheeks. "That bastard was lying on the bed—*my* bed. Just lying there like he owned the bedroom and everything in it. He wasn't watching TV. That was off. The screen was black. But he was watching the wall above it." Her eyes grew big and she sank as far back as she could into the patrol-car seats. "It was like there was a big, rectangular screen on the wall—not just on it, but through it. It was a window in the world, looking out on a place the good Lord above had no part in creating. When I looked, I could see a sky with no stars, and a raging ocean, and a tall tower…then there was a static glitch—that's what it looked like—and then the scene was replaced by faces, melting and stretching and filling the space, except I don't think they were faces. I think they were masks. And they were screaming."

"Cicely—" Kari began. The old woman was rambling, lost behind the trauma of what she had just experienced, and she wasn't making a whole lot of sense.

Cicely held up her hand. "Look, I know how it sounds. But it happened just like I'm telling you. I know what I saw."

"Okay." Kari nodded. "What happened next?"

"Well, when I could finally turn away from those terrible shrieking faces and back to Reggie, he was staring at me. Lord, he was frightening. His hands were covering his eyes and blood was streaming from beneath his palms, but there were eyes on the backs of his hands, and those were the eyes that were watching me. And his mouth moved, but only those broken sounds came out.

"I screamed, sugar. Just like those shrieking masks inside the wall, I screamed and the sound was broken too. In the next second, Reggie was standing in front of me, face streaked with blood, and he had no eyes. It was like the lids had fused closed or…or like scar tissue had grown over where his eyes used to be. And then that spot split open—the skin just split—and it became a second mouth. He talked to me with both mouths. Both mouths moved and those broken-sound words came out, but I could understand. He said the most awful things. Told me seven years' worth of unspeakable things he was going to do to me. His hands were gripping my shoulders so tight…." She slid the shoulder of her pink sweater down and lifted the short sleeve of her blouse. Finger-shaped bruises mottled her skin. Her tears dripped onto the wounds and she sniffed, then pulled her sweater back up.

"I brought my knee up into his man parts. I'm not proud of that, sugar, but sometimes a woman's got to get fierce. So I kneed him and my knee sank into something cold and sort of like jelly. I panicked for a second, but it was evidently enough to make him let go of me and I ran, down the stairs and out of the house and into…this." She waved at the dark outside the car window. "I kept running until my chest hurt and then I walked and walked…and I don't think I got more than a house or two away from my own. How—how is that even possible?"

"I don't know, hon," Kari murmured. "I don't know." She didn't think it was wise to mention, given Cicely's state of mind, that she also would have sworn she'd seen the old woman in the diner, at their usual booth, and that something in the ladies' room had recognized Cicely's name. That would have been around the same time that Cicely was lost in the dark.

An uneasy silence settled on the patrol car as each thought about what Cicely had said. Cicely finally broke it by asking, "Where are we going?"

"Heritage Center, ma'am. We're meeting the occult expert, Kathy Ryan, and Bill Grainger and some of the other townspeople to discuss our next move."

"And what is our next move, Sheriff?"

Sheriff Cole cleared his throat. "I suppose that'll be up to Ms. Ryan."

Cicely said something then that neither Cole nor Kari could quite make out.

"Beg your pardon, ma'am?"

Cicely looked confused for a moment, perhaps not realizing she had spoken out loud. Then she said, "I…it was something Reggie said, before I ran. *Na-mor-graph-un. Va-ur-med-sef.* I don't know what it means."

"We'll tell Ms. Ryan. Maybe she'll know. Maybe it can help," Kari said. She wasn't so sure, though, that anyone or anything was really going to help them survive what was happening.

In the quiet gloom of the patrol car, Kari thought the others felt the same.

Chapter 13

When Kathy, Bill, and Toby arrived at the Kilmeister residence, they immediately saw that the garage door was open and the interior was illuminated by a faint bluish-green glow. The garage was a detached kind at the end of a long driveway, wide enough for two cars but used instead as some kind of workshop. Kathy could see rows of carpentry tools hanging neatly on pegs along the walls. Paint cans, tucked into the front corners, stood half-covered by drop cloths. An obviously new table saw stood in the center, flanked to the left by a rough-plank sawhorse and a folding chair tucked under a board serving as some kind of counter, and to the right by a rough workbench with a wooden box on it. More drop cloths were heaped in untidy piles toward the back of the garage.

The faint glow from within was the only light on the property, or in fact, anywhere in the neighborhood, which did not escape Kathy's notice. The Kilmeisters' house blended into the night, a vague silhouette against the sky, as did the other houses on the street. As they got out of the car, Kathy found it hard to shake the idea that the shadows were too thick, too heavy around the houses, and most certainly, not empty.

"So, the garage, then?" Bill started for the glow and Toby grabbed his arm. Seeing Bill's expression, he quickly let go.

"Look, I don't know if that's a good idea," Toby said. "I've seen that kind of light before—out in the woods. Before the children came."

Bill and Kathy exchanged glances. Then Bill said, "I'd guess that's all the more reason to go check it out."

"Why?" Toby regarded Bill as if the latter had suggested using one of those garage tools to dig an errant eyelash out of one's eye.

Bill gave him an impatient look. "If that glow means something from behind the Door is in that garage, be it an object we might be able to use or a critter we might be able to kill, then we best get on that before either does any harm to the Kilmeisters."

Toby didn't seem to have an answer. Bill turned and began walking again, with Kathy close at his side. Toby followed reluctantly behind.

The garage was surprisingly deep, more like the size of a large boathouse than a garage, and Kathy wondered briefly if the Kilmeisters had remodeled it to make it bigger. It was a pale gray, concrete in most places, organized with assorted odds and ends in jars and on shelves and pegs, though decaying into chaos toward the center of the space. As they got closer, Kathy could see that the glow was coming from the box on the workbench. It occasionally flickered, casting erratic shapes of light and shadow all over the garage. The box itself was a flimsy-looking thing, bowing along one of the sides, with a cheap lock on the front. It—or more likely, whatever was inside it—was giving off the same kind of nearly soundless hum that the Door did, and as she got near it, she felt the dull beginnings of a headache.

"Oh shit," Toby suddenly exclaimed. Bill walked over to where Toby was standing by the drop cloths at the back of the garage, looked down, and sighed.

"Jesus," Bill said. "Kathy, you better come over here."

With a reluctant glance back at the box, Kathy joined the men at the back of the garage. It was obvious, once she cleared the sawhorse and table saw, that the drop cloths were draped over two bodies, a male and a female, facedown. What Kathy had mistaken for paint stains on the canvas cloths was actually dried blood, seeping up from underneath in irregular patches. The body closest to them, the male, appeared to have tried to claw his way out from under the cloth covering him from the neck down. The head was half-turned on its cheek, and Kathy could see one eye, wide and glazed in death, rolled back in its head. The mouth hung open in a crooked scream, the bottom jaw shifted too far to the left for any natural position, even in death. Most of the teeth were missing, and given the sticky pool of blood under the right eye, Kathy assumed there was some severe damage there too. Her gaze glided along the shape of the body and although the drop cloth was thick and bunched in some places, it struck her that the outlines indicated bones that were not just broken, but shoved into impossible contortions.

The woman behind him had fared no better, apparently. Her clotted hair covered her downturned face entirely. The contours of her body under her makeshift death shroud ended somewhere beneath the waist. There, the cloth was completely deflated and soaked through.

"Mr. and Mrs. Kilmeister, I assume?" Kathy said.

Bill nodded, whistling low. "I've known Grant and Flora for decades. Sent me a card when my grandson made the police force. She used to make me chicken and rice soup. Good people. Something sure made a mess of them."

"Something that might still be here," Toby pointed out, and Bill glared at him.

"Bill, can you turn them over? Just so we can assess the damage?"

He nodded, grabbing a pair of rubber work gloves off the crude counter and sliding them on. He took a deep breath and threw back Grant Kilmeister's drop cloth.

The three of them collectively shrank away from the bodies. Something certainly had made a mess of them. Although shirtless, Grant still wore jeans and a single sock, but those were a mess; his bottom half had been folded backward so the backs of his knees cupped his shoulder blades. One foot had been crushed to a pulpy mess that dangled just below his ear. The sock was still hanging onto the other, but from the shape and the stains, there was not likely to be much of a foot in there. As she took in the extent of Grant's injuries, Kathy saw that pretty much all of the straight lines of his body were bent in one way or another, the jagged bones that had once kept them rigid now rising up out of the flesh like the tips of icebergs. Bill, crouching near the body, looked up at Kathy, then took Grant by the shoulder and rolled him over.

His jaw was definitely broken, tearing clear through the lips and cheek on that side. What few teeth were left in his head were visible through the rip in his cheek. The rest of the skin on the right half of his face was stringy, almost plastic-looking, as if held close to extreme heat. Where his eye should have been was a putty-like glob of skin, tinged with swirls of blood. A jungle of broken ribs distorted and bruised the front of his torso. His entire body was frostbite-rigid, a captured moment of death, though Kathy couldn't begin to imagine what had caused so much damage leading up to it.

"You okay?" Bill asked her.

"I'm fine. Let's get a look at her."

Bill pulled back Flora's drop cloth.

"Fuck," Toby whispered. "What did that to her?"

Flora too was topless, but her torso faced upward, making the nasty, bruised twist of her neck so much more horrific as it disappeared beneath the hair on the back of head. Both of her arms below the elbows had begun to change, as had the lower half of her body. A mottled, leathery hide had begun to overtake her soft, fair skin, arrested in its climb upward likely by her death. The hide still quivered, though, frustrated and dying alien flesh bound to dead meat. Within that alien hide, new body parts had begun to form.

Beneath Flora's navel, a mouth had begun to take shape in the leathery skin. It hung slack-jawed against where her pubic bone should have been. Most of the area below that was a coil of slimy, fibrous tubes that could have been entrails or tentacles. Kathy didn't want to get close enough to find out. She and the other two flinched when the end of one of those coils snapped at the air above it, a lazy snake woken from the cozy dark beneath the drop cloth.

Bill turned Flora over and recoiled in disgust. Her face was missing entirely. The split down the middle of that blank plane of leathery skin emitted a huff of air that smelled like rancid meat. Something like a long tongue poked through and then came to rest on what used to be Flora's chin.

Bill stood, peeling off the gloves and tossing them on the floor next to the bodies. "Now what?"

Kathy turned back to the box on the workbench. She had no doubt that the thing inside it was the cause of the Kilmeisters' death, and the worst thing for the town would be to run the risk of that box getting lost or ending up in the wrong hands. Still, if it was capable of such visceral and brutal violence and worse, how would they transport it and where would they keep it?

"We have to take that box," she said flatly.

The men turned to the humming, glowing thing. It was vibrating slightly. If Kathy hadn't known better, she would have thought it was giggling with glee.

"Did that thing do...that...to them?" Bill asked.

"I think so," she replied. "We can't let it do that to anyone else."

"So...is it safe to move it? I mean, what triggers it?"

It took all her stubborn Ryan will for her to answer, "Let's see," and walk over to it. In her experience, there usually was some catalytic event that set off such objects. It was an educated guess that just picking it up would not be enough to unleash what was inside. It was still a guess, though.

"Go outside, both of you," she said.

"Kathy, wait a minute—"

"Do it," she said, and was relieved that her tone had convincingly left no room for argument. Toby followed Bill outside to the driveway, where they watched her with anxious expressions.

She picked up the box.

She thought she heard the guys outside exhale a collective sigh of relief.

It thrummed with life in her hands and was alternately cool and warm to the touch. It aroused a revulsion in her that she could almost taste, and she resisted the urge to hurl the box against a wall and smash it. The thing inside knocked against the lid as if trying to get out. That was good; that meant the lid was locked, and also suggested that the wood, flimsy as it looked, was perhaps the one thing protecting her from what was inside. Maybe the Kilmeisters had opened the box. Maybe that was what had killed them. Another guess....

Very gently, she turned the box over. She noticed an inscription on the bottom written in the same set of runic symbols carved around the stone frame of the Door in the woods. She'd spent a significant amount of time trying to translate the runes around the Door after her first visit, and thought she might be able to make out what the inscription said if she could compare it with her notes.

A rattling sound drew her attention away from the box, and she looked up to see the garage around her had come alive. The tools hanging on the walls, picking up on the humming of the box, were rattling on their pegs, threatening to fly loose. There were shears and axes, screwdrivers and hammers, jars of nails of various lengths, extra saw blades...a lot of very sharp things, trembling with murderous excitement.

And Kathy and that damned box were standing right in the center of them.

"Well, shit," she muttered under her breath.

"Kathy!" Bill called.

"Ms. Ryan, I think you might have another problem on your hands."

"Thanks, Holmes, Watson. I'm on it," she said evenly. She took a tentative step forward and the nail gun fired a warning shot past the tip of her nose. She froze. To her right, the table-saw blade began to shake.

The garage door rumbled and slid forward an inch.

Slowly, very slowly, Kathy lowered herself into a crouch.

"Bill," she said, "I need you to take the box."

Bill started forward warily, his eyes on the tools.

"No, don't come in here. I'm going to slide it out to you."

"What about you?"

"What about me?" she asked.

"Stop fucking around," Bill said through his teeth, "and get the fuck out of there."

"I will. But take the box first...you know. In case."

"Kathy, don't do this...."

"If this box doesn't make it back to the Door, then what happened to the Kilmeisters could happen to a lot more people. In fact, I can guarantee it will." Seeing his expression, she added, "Please, Bill. Do this for me."

His expression softened. "Okay," he said softly. "Give it here."

Kathy slid the box along the floor. It skittered a few feet and tipped over. She held her breath for a second, but it remained closed. Still, it was too far for Bill to reach.

"Dammit," she spit. "Hold on." She crept forward and had just closed a hand around the box when a sharp bolt of pain in her hip made her cry out. A hammer clanged to the floor beside her. Quickly, she grabbed the box and shoved it the rest of the way. Bill leaned in, snagged the box, and pulled it over the threshold just as a rain of nails fell to the cement where the box had been.

Kathy had a moment to feel relief before her right shoulder erupted in fireworks of pain that radiated down her back and arm. She reached around and felt the handle of a screwdriver; a good portion of its tip was buried in her shoulder. She wanted to pull it out, but thought the better of it. Instead, she army-crawled forward. Above her, the garage door rumbled again, falling like a guillotine halfway between the ceiling and the ground.

"Fuck!' she shouted, and a blaze of pain across the back of her calf made her whimper. She turned and saw the hedge clippers had sheared a bloody gash across the back of her leg. She leaned over to look at it when a thump in the wall tore her attention away. A small hatchet blade bounced off a metal leg of a shelf inches from where her head had been.

She got on her knees and crawled faster.

There was a clatter outside and then a metal garbage-can lid skittered to a stop beside her. She looked up to see Toby waving at her.

"A shield!" he called.

She gave him a small smile of genuine gratitude, grabbed the garbage-can lid, and held it in front of her like a shield, scuttling backward toward the opening. A crowbar glanced off the edge of the lid and clattered to the floor, followed by a number of nails and screws, some of which stuck in the metal. She moved faster, awkwardly dragging herself on one hand and her non-injured leg.

When the saw the blade fly off the wall, she screamed and ducked behind the lid. She counted several seconds, waiting for the pain or the warmth of blood, but when she felt neither, she opened her eyes. Some of the blade's teeth had chewed through the metal of the lid, but the latter had done its job admirably as a shield, stopping the blade from burying itself into her face.

She allowed herself a little victory crow and a pair of pliers hit the lid, denting it. She launched herself backward on her good leg. The garage door took a few more inches of open space away. She scooted backward, telling herself with each rough grasp of that cement floor that she wasn't going to make it, that she was too far away, that the door would close on her and break her spine, that—

Her hand slid roughly over the threshold of the garage, and the door came down onto her lid, denting it. She let go. Strong hands grabbed her beneath her arms and yanked just as the force of the garage door sent the lid flying into the center of the chaos, and the door came crashing down.

She sat on the driveway, breathing heavily and bleeding onto the asphalt.

"Toby, get the duct tape in the back of the truck. Go now!" she heard Bill's voice say behind her. She couldn't stop staring at the closed door. Beyond it, she could hear the tools in an uproar, flinging themselves against the walls and each other. Their thumping and clanging made her feel cold all over beneath her skin.

She felt Bill gently move her hair out of the way, then yank the screwdriver out of her shoulder. She muffled a cry of pain against the crook of her opposite elbow, and a moment later, heard the ripping sounds of duct tape as Bill patched her up.

"Should hold for now," he said over her shoulder. "Not as deep as I thought, but still…."

She turned to him. "*Thanks* doesn't seem like a big enough word, Bill. You saved my life."

"We should get you to a hospital," he said, and although it was too dark to tell, Kathy thought he might have been blushing. Taping up the wound on her leg, he added, "But of course, you won't go."

"Not now," she said. "We need to get to the Heritage Center. We need to get that box somewhere safe. Where is it?"

A bolt of panic seized her that was worse than the pain in her shoulder and leg combined. She didn't see it—couldn't see anything, particularly the glow of the box—but then Toby, who had been hovering near Bill in the dark, said, "It's in the truck, Ms. Ryan. No worries."

"Call me Kathy," she told him. "And thanks again. I never would have made it out without that garbage-can lid."

Though she couldn't see him too well, she got the impression Toby was even more uncomfortable with gratitude than Bill. "Glad I could help. Do something right for once."

Bill and Toby helped her to her feet and guided her to the truck. She thought she could walk okay on her leg, but she moved more quickly with their help. The interior glowed a soft blue and Kathy saw the box on the passenger seat. She picked it up with one hand and could feel it vibrating again, this time in anger. Who knew what it could do to the truck? Force it off a cliff? Make it explode? As the guys got her and themselves into the truck, she looked around the interior, hoping for a bigger box, preferably made of lead or iron, something with the right properties to contain the one in her lap.

There was a toolbox by Toby's feet, large enough, Kathy thought, for the wooden box to fit inside.

"Toby, hand me that toolbox, will you? Bill, what is that? Aluminum?"

Bill shrugged as he pulled away from the curb. "I think so."

Toby handed her the toolbox, and with an apology to Bill, she dumped his tools on the floor and then put the wooden box inside, closing the lid and fastening the clasp.

"Is aluminum some type of special protective metal or something?" Toby asked.

"Not really," Kathy said. "It's too new an alloy to have any historical occult significance, but it's been effectively used in place of mercury, which is poisonous, but believed to be significant when it comes to transdimensional transportation. Newer occult philosophies attribute some protective power to both mercury and aluminum, but I'm an old-school kind of girl." She smiled at Toby. "I guess we'll see if they're right, huh?"

Toby looked as worried as he did confused. "You're the expert."

Chapter 14

Deep in the woods of Zarephath, the Door hummed.

What was left of Ed Richter in this world was tugged at by winds that kept sending the oak trees above into a nervous rustle and made the ropes that hung from them, the ones that had strung up Ed for a while, creak like old bodies.

There wasn't much of Ed for the winds to play with, just some scraps of flesh and a few bones that had been pulled out of his right leg. The animals, few that there were in the vicinity of the Door, might drag them off soon enough, but not while the Door emitted that hum that was almost words.

There was a little blood too. Not much, not anymore, but a smattering on the fallen leaves which, this close to the Door, were in a perpetual state of late autumn.

What was left of Ed on the other side of the Door screamed until his face changed into something that was nothing like a face and the soft parts of him were devoured by hungry, impatient gods.

* * * *

When Kathy, Bill, and Toby arrived at the Heritage Center, they were glad to see Sheriff Cole's patrol car among others already parked. They were even happier to see the man himself in the basement, sitting on folding chairs with two women who he introduced to Kathy as Kari Martin and Cicely Robinson. The rest of the room was more sparsely filled than Kathy would have liked—maybe thirty-five of the sixty or seventy that had shown up for the town meeting. Odds were that far more people had used the Door, and thus were in danger of backlash, than the small group gathered and milling about the basement. What Kathy supposed the number meant was that a small town had grown somewhat smaller, and quickly.

She recognized a few faces from the town meeting, including the lady with the alien shirt (now in a checkered pink and blue blouse), a few middle-aged men, and the little girl and her mother. It pained Kathy to see the little girl there and know that she still couldn't follow through yet on her promise to protect the town. What bothered her even more was the idea that, given their presence, either the girl or her mother had used the Door, or both. All three prospects were equally horrible to Kathy.

She set the toolbox at her feet and sat in one of the folding chairs behind the women. Toby sat behind her and Bill sat behind Sheriff Cole. Kathy's presence drew the others in the room closer. Townspeople took seats in the surrounding folding chairs or hovered nearby in the aisle.

"Hello, ladies," Kathy said to the two women. "It's nice to meet you. I'm glad Sheriff Cole was able to get you here safely." To the others, she added, "Everyone, I'm happy you all made it here. I choose to find it encouraging that there are some of you, rather than discouraging that there aren't more of you."

Her statement was greeted with cool stares and unsure grumbling. They were waiting on her for answers. Many looked exhausted. Some looked physically hurt.

Cicely shivered, pulling her sweater tighter around her. Kari looked miserable. She also looked just about as badly beaten up as Kathy felt. Her face was an assortment of bruises and she clutched the side of her ribs as if trying to massage a persistent pain.

"I got your message," Kathy continued, looking at Kari. The other woman began a jumble of half-started sentences, mostly apologies and explanations, and Kathy held up her hand.

"Look, it's okay, Kari. May I call you Kari?"

The other woman nodded. Kathy continued. "I figure you had your reasons, and I'd even go so far as to guess they were good ones, or seemed good at the time."

"What does she mean?" Cicely asked, looking at Kari. "Your reasons for what?"

Kari's eyes, red already from crying, spilled new tears. "I opened the Door." There was a surprised gasp from those assembled nearby. Cicely in particular looked especially wounded.

"Sugar," she said, and there was the slightest ice-sharp edge to her voice, "I told you that rule number one was that you never, ever open the Door for any reason. Ever."

"I was forgetting her," Kari said softly. "My own daughter. I was forgetting all my memories of her because of how I worded the letter and I just wanted to get it back. I begged with them behind the Door, really pleaded for my letter back. I asked them to cancel it. I tried to bargain, offered a trade, anything. I even tried to dig under the Door, but I couldn't reach and I thought, if I just opened it for a minute—"

"So this is her fucking fault all this is happening? 'Cuz she opened the fucking Door?" one of the middle-aged men said. He was a big guy with an unruly gray beard and an ample stomach over which was stretched a T-shirt and flannel. The T-shirt read *SEX MACHINE*.

"Sex machine, you got a name?" Kathy turned to the man.

"Ted," he said.

"Ted. Easy does it. This is no one's fault, okay? All of you have to understand something right now. If you blame or judge anyone in this room for their involvement with the Door, for whatever they asked to be undone or taken away or given to them, then we won't need to worry about the Door killing everyone. You'll do the job yourselves."

Again, the chilly silence, but Kathy could tell from their expressions that they knew she was right.

"No blame, no judging, do you understand? The day after all this is fixed, you can go back to your lives and hate each other as much as you like, but tonight, and until we resolve this problem, no one here has any higher moral ground than anyone else. You need to work with me. We need to work together. I don't care what bad you did. I want to see what good you can do."

Nods and murmurs of approval from the crowd satisfied her, so she turned back to Kari.

"I need to know how long the Door was open and what you saw. I need to know what came through."

"It...it was only open a few minutes. Maybe five or six minutes, tops, and probably not even that long. It took some effort, but I got it closed again. I swear, I never meant for any of this to happen." Her pleading gaze swept the assemblage. "I swear I never wanted anyone to get hurt."

"We know," Kathy said in her best attempt at sounding soothing. "Tell us what you saw."

"It was...another place. Another world, I think. Outside of our universe."

"What makes you say that?"

Kari's hands fidgeted in her lap. "Everything was different in that other place. The air felt different. It was so quiet, except for the hum. The ocean, that limitless ocean, was so quiet, even though it was raging. And there were no stars in that other sky, just an endless expanse of black…."

She thought a minute, then added, "Well, it was more like purple, but a shade so dark that it was just about black. There was nothing familiar about that sky. Nothing. Nothing at all."

"Did you see anything else?" Kathy asked.

"A tower," Kari said. "A dark gray tower with carvings on it. It had to be huge. I think it was the tower that created the humming that ate all the sound."

"Did you see anything living?" Bill broke in. "Any people?"

Kari chuckled, but the sound stuck in her throat. "No people. Nothing like people at all. If those things I saw are the gods behind the Door, then we've been laying our secrets and sorrows and fears on an altar built for monsters."

"Can you describe them?" Cole asked. The others in the room were dead quiet, hanging on Kari's words.

"Brownish. They didn't really have one consistent shape. I think their bones moved by themselves under their skin. And their eyes and mouths appeared and disappeared at will. They could reshape themselves as needed, to create parts like tentacles or…or wings."

She shook her head, the tears dripping off her chin. "I closed that damned Door before they flew out. I'm sure I did. Closed it right on one of them before it could push through. I swear not a one of those things crossed through that opening. So…how did they get here?" Her tear-streaked face held an expression so broken and confused that Kathy genuinely felt sorry for her.

"Well," Kathy said gently, "other dimensions are not beholden to the same rules of time and space that we are. Their physics and ours don't always work the same. They could have come from under the Door, after some seal had been broken in opening it. Or you could have seen their escape out of order, chronologically. It's hard to say for sure. But you've done really well here tonight. You've given us a lot of useful information."

"I have?"

"Yes, you have," Kathy said. "I'll add what you told me to my notes, do a little comparing, and hopefully we'll find a way to get everything back to normal, okay?"

She glanced at the little girl as she picked up the toolbox and rose. "There's a room in back here, an office, that we can speak to each of you privately in, if you have anything at all to contribute about the Door. Even if something seems little or unimportant to you, let us know anyway. It could be that little, seemingly unimportant detail that serves as the last piece of the puzzle. As for the rest of you, I would caution that at least for the next few hours, you remain here. Make yourselves comfortable. We'll put a pot of coffee on. Kick off your shoes. But please stay here. We're pretty sure that these things are more likely to attack when you're alone, or in small numbers. Bill, Sheriff Cole—a word, please?" She indicated the office and the two men rose to follow her.

Once inside the office, she set the toolbox down on the desk next to her file on the Door of Zarephath. Mrs. Pulaski of the Historical Society had been kind enough to lend both her office and her desk to the three of them as a command center. Kathy was going to need it now more than ever.

The men sat in chairs opposite the desk and Kathy sat behind it.

"Those things Kari Martin was describing—I saw one," Cole said. Kathy and Bill gaped at him, but his gaze was fixed on the toolbox. "When I went to pick her up. I heard noises in the house and went to check it out. She was in the back of the cruiser then. And when I came out, one of those things was on the hood."

"Did you kill it?" Kathy asked.

"Tried to," Cole replied. "I don't know if I killed it or hurt it or just pissed it off. The first few times I shot at it, nothing happened, but then I nailed it right in the mouth, and that got the thing all bothered. It sort of...well, it's tough to explain, but it sort of sucked itself up into itself. It disappeared."

"So they have weak spots, at least," Kathy said. "Good work, Sheriff Cole."

"Thanks," Cole answered, looking surprised. "I was just focusing on how to get it off my car and get Ms. Martin here safely. Now, I gotta ask—what's in the toolbox? Seeing as how you look a bit worse for wear, if you don't mind my saying so, I figure it's important enough. Me, I'm hoping it's some kind of interdimensional rocket launcher."

"Nothing as fun as that, I'm afraid," Kathy said. "We found it in the Kilmeisters' garage. All we know is that Grant Kilmeister was in possession of this thing, and that it comes from the other side of the Door. I'm not sure how it got here, and it looks like the only people who can tell us are dead or missing."

Cole looked floored. "The Kilmeisters?"

"Both dead," Bill said.

"And Ed Richter?"

"Toby Vernon says he was taken. By what or to where, we don't know."

Cole frowned. "This is turning out to be one hell of a shit show."

"No kidding," Bill agreed.

"And what's in this box," Kathy said, "could make things much worse. We need to keep it locked in this office until we figure out what to do with it. There's an inscription on the box inside this toolbox, and it would be useful to know what that inscription means."

She opened the file, stuffed with papers messily paper-clipped and stapled to each other or the folder itself. Flipping through the pages, she unclipped a packet with runic writing and handwritten notes on it, turned it around, and slid it across the desk to the men.

"What's this?" Bill asked, leafing through the packet.

"As much of the language carved in the stones around the Door as some colleagues and I have been able to decipher. As you can see, we have most of the inscription figured out, thanks to a faint second set of characters, almost like a shadow to the prominent ones." She handed them a close-up photo of the Door and pointed to the stonework surrounding it. "Your Door was never meant to be a wishing well. In fact, it came with a warning; the first few words are essentially *Enter not, nor give your soul to them behind this Door.* It's a rough translation, of course. The word *soul* is probably closer to the idea of *essence*, and *them* may be a more literal translation than a pronoun. Anyway, there's this missing piece here, and the words *key* and *lock* and what we think might be some sort of time frame.

"We aren't sure, of course, who inscribed the stone or why—clearly, it wasn't our god-monsters warning people away from feeding them. More likely, these inscribers built the Door or were Travelers who used it. That second set of inscriptions we discovered," she explained, pointing to a thinner, fainter set of runes around the Door's frame, "were actually Latin words, while the primary runes were in an alien tongue. It was like whoever inscribed them wanted to make sure that no one from either side made the mistake of opening the Door. And the aspects we can't translate are the parts where the Latin version is too faint or worn away completely.

"Now, my guess is, if those inscribers built or used the Door and even they couldn't remove it but only warn others about it, then we don't stand much of a chance of getting rid of it, either. Your town may be stuck with the structure itself. However, the inscription does mention a lock and key. My theory is that however this box got here, that process triggered the unlocking of the Door. Maybe it was a letter some unthinking, curious individual wrote asking for a little keepsake or knickknack from that other dimension. Maybe it was a remnant of those ancient Travelers, unearthed somewhere and then forgotten about in an attic until the Kilmeisters came to be in possession of it. But I think its materializing in this world may have acted as a sort of key. And maybe none of it would have mattered if Kari Martin had never actually opened the Door. But she did. My hope is that we can use this thing to relock the Door. I just need to work out how."

The men were quiet for several moments, thinking about what she had said. She thought she read a lot of mixed feelings into their expressions, and so kept quiet, letting them process. Confusion led to panic and she needed them to be clear and in control.

Finally, Cole broke the silence. "We need to ask that Toby Vernon fella everything he can remember Ed telling him about this box. Bill and I could talk to him while you work on whatever's written on the box in there." He gestured at the toolbox. "In the meantime, I'll call my deputies back in and have them guard this place. Guns...well, they don't do much other than scare the things off, far as I can tell, but at least that could buy us some time, keep those things at bay for a bit."

"And after we talk to Toby, I think we ought to round up these other folks and give them something to do. Keep their minds occupied," Bill said. "We don't need any nervous breakdowns. Asking them about the Kilmeisters might be helpful. Putting them to use in some plan I hope you're forming in that pretty little head would be better."

Kathy winked at him. "Great ideas. I'm genuinely glad you two are on this case with me. You've both been invaluable."

The men looked pleased, even if they did their best to mask it behind fidgeting and clearing their throats.

"Hey," Bill added, "I saw that guy Ted sitting with the Latin teacher from the local high school, Rob Sherman. I can give him the heads-up that you might need his expertise, if you want."

"I'd appreciate that," she said.

The men got up to leave. At the door, Cole turned and asked, "Is, uh... is that thing poisonous? I mean, is this a quarantine type of situation?"

Kathy said, "At the moment, no. If there was a biological threat, you'd have all been infected long ago. It's not dangerous like a disease, locked up like that. It's more like...a caged tiger. If we open it, though...."

"Got it," Cole said with a nod, and he and Bill let themselves out of the office.

Kathy sighed as she sank into the desk chair, her injuries howling and her body exhausted.

It was a valid concern that Cole had raised. What had been happening to Mrs. Kilmeister's body before she died suggested it was more than probable that something inside that box could change people into...something else. In most cases she had consulted on, contamination of that sort hadn't been an issue. Many of the dimensional beings she had dealt with were not capable of introducing alien pathogens except possibly when solid, and most chose not to be. Post-case scans of people and objects for trace remnants of other worlds returned negative results. Occasionally, she did find herself wondering if her very fiber, physically and mentally; her mind, heart, and lungs; her flaws and abilities; her thoughts and dreams, were impacted somehow by her exposure to elements from other dimensions. She was fully aware intellectually that every case she took on might be exposing her body, mind, and soul to a kind of supernatural radiation and that over time, it might very well change her. It was an occupational hazard, but generally not a serious consideration for the people in affected interdimensional hot spots. She didn't often let herself think of being caught decades from now in the grip of some alien cancer or mutation, but once in a while, it crept into her thoughts. It was one reason she had never had children—one of many, given her family's history, as well as her profession—and one reason that until Reece, she had never been much inclined to settle down. The doctors gave her a clean bill of health every year or so; sure, they told her to cut down on her drinking, but invariably, they were amazed that the amount of alcohol she admitted to consuming had done no discernible damage to her body. Both the drinking and the stunning lack of liver damage she believed to be by-products of her job, and so far, the only qualifiable or quantifiable effects. All those other worlds and other dimensions and the denizens within that she had pissed off were going to make damned sure she could never drink herself to death, at least until they could get a crack at her again. Lucky her.

She stared at the toolbox for several minutes before finally undoing the clasp and opening the lid. The blue glow was fainter, as if the thing inside the wooden box was sleeping. She reached in and very carefully, took the wooden box out and placed it on the desk. She frowned. There was a symbol carved on the lid that she couldn't believe she hadn't noticed back in the garage. It was crudely carved, an oversimplified pictogram, really, but it looked very much like the Door in the woods. Had that carving been there before? Or were the contents of the box so malleable as to be remaking themselves into what she needed them to be? Was that it? Did the Kilmeisters open the box expecting a monster, and so they found one?

Kathy shivered. It was the first artifact she had dealt with that genuinely scared her.

She turned the box over, copied the inscription along the bottom onto a piece of paper, and then put the box back inside the toolbox, closing the lid and fastening the clasps.

Then she got to work.

Chapter 15

As Bill Grainger and Sheriff Cole approached him, Toby felt a pang of unease that years of practice allowed him to hide well. He hated that cornered animal feeling, when all the muscles in his body were tense, ready to strike or run. He also hated how easily all the little manipulations and practiced survival mechanisms had come back to him since the opening of the Door. Police had always made him intrinsically nervous, but adding to his discomfort was Bill, an ex-sheriff himself, with a very dangerous bit of information about the predatory weakness in Toby's lifestyle, which he may or may not have shared with the local law.

Toby knew what happened to guys like him when there was any wiggle room whatsoever in dispensing justice. Toby would never make it to jail. What was left of his tortured and mangled remains would be dumped in a ditch on the side of a highway. It had happened to others he knew. Word got around on the forums. Rabid dogs were put down, not treated to a stay at a hospital or even a jail. One less rabid dog in a rural community was just fine by the folks who lived there.

Sheriff Cole was a very large man. Bill was a very strong-looking one, despite his age.

The men turned the folding chairs around and sat across from him.

"Can I help you gentlemen?" he asked evenly.

"As a matter of fact," Bill said, "you can."

"We'd like to ask you about Ed Richter and what he told you about that box you all found in Grant's garage," Sheriff Cole said.

"Don't know that I can offer much more than I have on the subject, but I'll try."

"Mr. Vernon," the sheriff began.

"Toby," he offered. If he could establish himself as a real human being, with a real name, he thought he might be harder to beat up in an alley somewhere later.

"Toby," Sheriff Cole said. "Please just tell us exactly what he told you, everything he said regarding Grant's box."

"Okay," Toby said, shifting forward in his seat. "Well, he mentioned a few nights before he—uh, Wednesday night, I guess. The night of the town meeting. I offered to stay on the couch again, but he said no, so I said I'd stay at least until he fell asleep. Safety in numbers, like Kathy Ryan said, you know? Ed hadn't been sleeping well, even with the booze. I think those things were at him day and night. When they weren't beating the shit out of him, then it was terrorism—leaving little threatening notes, spray-painting things on his walls, breaking windows, knifing his tires, leaving little signs and messages everywhere. He was exhausted from covering it all up."

"Covering what up? The paint?" the sheriff asked.

"Uh, yeah. The paint, the notes, everything. Ed was a private kind of guy and these...things...were dragging all his most personal stuff out into the light and throwing it in his face. Ed may not have been a saint—none of us are, really—but he was a good friend to me. He was an ear and a shoulder to a lot of people in this town. He didn't deserve to get beaten up like that, mentally or physically."

"I'll take your word for that," the sheriff said, "not being fully aware of what skeletons, exactly, were being dragged out of his closet."

Toby chose not to respond to the undertone in the sheriff's comment. "Anyway, he and I were watching the woods. He told me they usually came from the woods, and it turned out he was right. But that night, nothing came, and Ed and I hung out like we used to. It was...kind of nice, actually. I think for a little while, a couple of hours maybe, we both forgot about the Door.

"Then all of a sudden, he got this really serious look on his face. Dead sober, he said to me, 'You know Grant Kilmeister?' I told him I did; I knew Grant in passing. I'd brought my car to his shop a couple of times, saw him at the Alexia once in a while, that sort of thing. His wife was always friendly to me." Toby thought about the twisted, monstrous mess he'd seen in the Kilmeisters' garage and shuddered. "I asked why and Ed said, 'Told me at the diner this morning that he's got something from there,' and he nodded at the woods. So I said, 'What, the woods?' And he said, 'No, the Door. From there *behind* the Door, wherever that place is.' And I guess I looked like I thought that was bullshit because he shrugged and said, 'I thought the same thing—bullshit. Nobody's ever seen nothing from that side of the Door. But he swears he has it in a box and that he needs to get rid of it. Says it can kill people and he don't want to hold onto it no more.' So I asked him how Grant came to have it and he said he didn't know. I guess Flora came back from the ladies' room then and he got all quiet about it.

"I remember I asked him if he thought that this thing that Grant had was what was causing all this trouble with the Door. He said no, because Grant had had it for years, then…uh, didn't have it, then had it again. I don't know where it was when he didn't have it. Ed didn't know, either.

"And that was about it. Ed was talking about how all of us who'd asked the Door for something were screwed and got on this kick again that maybe we ought to be screwed, and I didn't want to go down that road with him again, so I changed the subject. Maybe twenty minutes later, he was asleep and I left."

"And tonight?" Sheriff Cole asked.

"Tonight," Toby answered, "the stuff in our letters came back to bite us in the ass."

"You told Bill and Kathy that Ed was taken away."

Toby eyed him evenly. "Yes."

"By what?"

"Children."

"Children?" Sheriff Cole cocked an eyebrow.

"They looked like children. At least, at first they did." Toby couldn't tell if the sheriff's expression was one of genuine confusion, or the disgust of a dawning realization. He fought every instinct in him to bolt out of that chair.

Bill said, "Tell him, Toby."

Toby looked away. It felt disloyal to his friend, but he said, "Ed had a problem. With little boys. I think it had been a while, since—well, Ed's an old man now. I don't guess the feelings ever go away, but I figure you eventually get too old to act on them, or even want to."

He still couldn't look at the men, but he could feel their eyes on him, and the waves of moral indignation rolling off them like heat. "He asked the Door once to protect him from the wrath of…well, everyone. Anyone who might find out, or even suspect. He asked to be free of ever getting caught. And he knew…these last few days he knew that what he'd asked for was wrong, that karma finds its path to you one way or another. Ed, he thought the whole lot of us, everyone who had ever asked anything of the Door, were all getting what we finally deserved."

"Do you believe that?"

"I don't know. There are as many kinds of sins as there are sinners. I don't think I'm in any position to judge what other people deserve."

"What about what you deserve?"

He turned back to the sheriff, whose accusation was as much in his eyes as his voice. Toby shifted uncomfortably and coughed. He supposed cornered animals couldn't hide their wounds forever. If it came down to it, he'd just bare his teeth. "Does it matter now? I mean, to your investigation— does it matter whether I deserve it, or for that matter, what form those things are going to take to come get me? Fact is, they're coming, and it doesn't look like there's a whole lot we can do to stop them."

"What did you ask the Door for, Toby?" the sheriff asked. His voice was uncharacteristically soft and somewhat disappointed.

Toby took a deep breath and looked the sheriff in the eye. "I asked that the feelings that made me want to hurt little girls be taken away, so that I never hurt anyone again."

The sheriff and Bill both must have seen something, some darkening or disconnect in Toby's gaze, because they both leaned back. Maybe they weren't expecting such a level of honesty, but Toby had to admit, it felt... good. It was a weight lifted, not to have to hide what he was or pretend to be part of the herd that he preyed on. The fear of repercussions had suddenly diminished to little more than a dull ache. When he thought about it, the terrible specters of perversion and the shame of giving into them, and worrying about what men like Bill and Sheriff Cole would do if they knew, had haunted him his whole life. Those things couldn't do any more damage than they had already done. At least dying like a dog in a ditch would stop the madness.

Bill leaned forward. "Look, Toby. As much as I don't like it, Kathy had a point about us keeping our anger in check. And out of respect to her, professionally and personally, it's something I aim to abide by. We need to put our collective heads together to fight this thing. Everyone has secrets. I just have one more question for you." He leaned in closer, uncomfortably close, and said, "That little girl over there...."

He tipped his chin toward a little blond girl of maybe nine or ten. Toby had seen her at the town meeting with her mother. The kid clutched her doll and fidgeted in the folding chair next to her mother. She looked bored and tired more than anything.

"I don't need to worry about her safety, do I?" Bill asked.

A number of things ran through Toby's head, but he thought better of all of them and bit his tongue. Instead, he said, "Of course not. She's safe from me."

Bill looked him in the eye and this time, his look was as hard and cold as anything in Toby's arsenal. "I don't want to have this conversation again. I don't even want to have to spend precious thinking time in this head space again. You get me? I don't have to worry about that girl. If I have to even think about what I'm seeing or hearing.... Don't make me kill you, Toby Vernon. We might need you."

Toby sublimated his shame and frustration and said, "On whatever's left of my life, I swear I won't hurt that girl."

Bill studied him a minute, nodded, got up, and walked away. Sheriff Cole sat for a minute. He didn't look like he was in any hurry to exit the interview, which made Toby somewhat wary. Then the sheriff said, "I have four little girls at home."

Toby answered, "I'm sure you love them very much."

"Of course I do. They're my whole world. I'd tear apart anyone who tried to hurt them."

"I imagine you would."

"It's taking every ounce of willpower not to hit you just on principle, you know."

"I know," Toby replied.

There was a pause, and then the sheriff asked, "Why did you ask the Door to stop you?"

Toby considered how to answer for a minute, trying to read the other man's face. He thought the sheriff was on the verge of snapping at him, Kathy's warning be damned, and that the slightest wrong answer, the tiniest waver in tone, might push him over the edge. It had been Toby's experience, though, that if someone was going to punch you, there was little you could really say or do to stop it. So Toby chose to answer honestly. "Because I hate that part of me, and I was scared that no matter what else I did, it would get worse. Because I can't undo what I've done, but I thought I could prevent myself from ever doing it again. And because I envy people like you, who have the kind of pure, decent, honest, normal relationships you have with your daughters."

The sheriff said nothing. That same unreadable expression held the features of his face fixed in place.

Toby said, "You asked me before if I thought I deserve what I get for using the Door. I guess I do, and then some. I'm usually too much of a coward to really think very long or hard about that. But I do believe wholeheartedly that a lot of little girls deserve better than to have to worry about a monster like me. I thought my letter would keep them safe. It's a sad, scary thing, though, to have to rely on something, anything other than yourself, to do the right thing. Now it's on me, where I guess it ought to be. I deserve that, but I hope I'm man enough to carry it."

"I hope you are too, Toby Vernon," Sheriff Cole said, and stood. He paused a moment and then said, "Good on ya for trying, though," and before Toby could answer, he walked away.

* * * *

Outside the Heritage Center, the moon slipped on diaphanous clouds as it moved across the sky. Neither it nor the surrounding stars were enough to pierce the gathering darkness that was swarming over Zarephath like spilled ink. The streets from the woods out by Ed Richter's house to the town center, though empty, were coated in pregnant shadow that devoured sound and left behind a faint hum.

Four of the officers from the Monroe County Sheriff's Department had found that between their two cruisers' high beams, they gained little visibility back, and it left them anxious.

In the first car, Deputy George Franks was watching that encroaching darkness with a wary eye. He'd been with the sheriff's department a long time, back when Bill Grainger had been sheriff, and he knew all about Zarephath's history of disturbances outside the norm. He'd seen some shit, he was fond of telling the younger officers—shit to tell the grandkids. And of course, there'd been some shit that no one ever had to know. That was the nature of police work in Zarephath. Sometimes upholding justice meant walking away, and sometimes it meant keeping one's mouth shut. Sometimes it meant burying the bodies, more often figuratively than literally, thank God.

God…He was a funny concept in Zarephath. It had never been lost on Franks that there was only one church in that town, a loose sort of nondenominational congregation as opposed to the socially encompassing Protestant, almost Puritan churches scattered heavily all over Monroe County. Outside of Zarephath, those folks were God-fearing folks, with their highway signs about Jesus and their country-music stations with catchy tunes about salvation. Such was not the case in Zarephath. Sure, there were devout families like the Robinsons and the Verbanas, the Edmundsons and the Smiths, but by and large, Franks thought the people in Zarephath didn't put too much stock in God anymore. Prayers never worked quite as fast as the Door, and God never seemed quite as present in their daily lives as the gods behind that pile of cursed planks in the woods.

Officer Kyle Edmundson—of the devout Zarephath Edmundsons—
was driving, and injected nervous chatter along the way. The boy's hands
were still shaking, though he was trying hard to hide that by gripping the
steering wheel. Edmundson had heard about the monsters overrunning
Zarephath from Sheriff Cole, but he admitted to not having fully believed
it all until tonight. They had been carrying out the sheriff's orders to
notify people in fear for their safety to meet at the Heritage Center. After
a public announcement at the Once More Tavern, they had come across
Edmundson's first monster in the parking lot. It was perched on top of the
dumpster, while beneath it was a pile of bones. They fired on the thing,
but their bullets had no effect until the creature opened one of its many
mouths. The bullet spiraled down its gullet, and the rest of it followed in
an astonishing feat of impossible physics.

The bones were small and Franks assumed they were animal until he
and Edmundson got close enough to see the skull. It wasn't quite the skull
of a child, not with those horns and bony protrusions, but Frank couldn't
shake the feeling that it had been a child once.

It had touched the thing they shot. That was the only answer Franks
could come up with.

They left the bones there and got back in the patrol car, Franks radioing
to Deputy Morgan and his rookie and well as Sheriff Cole about possible
mutation from physical contact with one of those creatures.

It was hard for Franks to tell if Edmundson was okay. He suspected
their encounter had shaken the boy's faith in the God of his parents, as
evidenced either by a beast that no good God in heaven would ever have
had a hand in making, or the deformed bones, which no good God would
have let happen to a child. He felt for the boy; it was a hell of a night to be
indoctrinated into the weirdness of Zarephath. In a way, though, Edmundson
was, in Franks's opinion, lucky.

The boy had never used the Door. The same could not be said of George
Franks. His marriage was over because of what the Door had flung back
in his face, and he was facing the real possibility he might never see his
daughter again. He didn't think it would lead to his being cut loose from the
force, but he was nearing retirement himself, and a career was a hell of a
thing, if it was the only thing, to have to keep one warm in his golden years.

In the other cruiser, Deputy Morgan and his rookie, McCoy, were
following closely behind Edmundson's vehicle. McCoy was pretty sure,
though he couldn't have said how, that with just enough space or a single
turn of the head or even a blink just a second longer than normal, that
the suffocating darkness outside would swallow up one car or the other

and the police force under Sheriff Timothy Cole would simply disappear. Another eerie story about Zarephath: the missing cops who just vanished one night, right out from under the watchful eye of another police cruiser. McCoy shivered.

"You believe Franks?" he asked, more to fill the silence inside the car. Morgan had been sullen, even more so than usual, and it had occurred to McCoy in a moment of semi-awe that the powerful, gruff man he'd been shadowing for weeks was actually scared. He didn't say so; Morgan was not a man to accuse of such things, but the idea made his mentor a little more human.

"Yeah," Morgan said. "And you better too."

McCoy tried to chuckle lightly, but the sound got lost in his throat. "Come on, though…monsters? Really?"

Morgan gave him a brief glance and then went back to watching the car ahead of them. "Remember that call we got last week? The wellness check on Agnes Warner?"

"Yeah, the old lady on Douglas Street, right?"

"That's her. Remember what we found?"

McCoy did—it had been hard to forget. His first dead body, the prone form of Agnes Warner had been there on her kitchen floor for days. It was a sad possibility with the elderly who lived alone, that they could pass away and have no one in their lives who would think to check on them. There was an odd aspect to the death that Morgan, at the time, had said McCoy would understand better with experience. The woman had been surrounded by the carcasses of chickens. Their rotting bodies had created a collective stink that had been too much for McCoy, and in fact, had to be cleared away before any significant investigation could be done regarding Agnes herself.

"I remember the chickens," McCoy said.

"And Ms. Edna? Remember her?"

"Of course. Can't forget it. I still see her stomach, all bloated with those bite marks, like that deformed thing inside her had chewed its way out…." McCoy cleared his throat. "What about them?"

"They're two casualties of the Door. You stick around this town long enough, you'll see dozens, maybe hundreds more cases like that. This town is and has always been fucked, and it's because of that Door."

"I kinda thought the Door was just a ghost story, you know? Something kids tell each other to scare themselves silly."

Morgan shook his head. "It ain't. Look, in other towns, you worry about gangs and meth heads and getting shot when you pull over some nutcase.

In Zarephath, you worry about anyone who's ever gotten too close to that Door. Trust me. If nothing else I say ever sticks in that big-haired head of yours, for Chrissakes, remember that. Now pay attention to the road."

"Yessir."

"Cole wants us on guard duty. Folks at the Heritage Center are scared."

"Morg, what exactly are we guarding them from?"

Morgan snorted. "Themselves."

"Huh?"

"You'll see soon enough, son."

* * * *

"Toby," Kari Martin said. Her face was streaked with tears. Toby turned in his seat to see Kari Martin, opener of the Door, and Cicely Robinson staring at him.

"Yes?"

"We couldn't help overhearing what you told Sheriff Cole and Bill Grainger," Cicely said. "We didn't mean to eavesdrop, but…." she gestured, indicating the fairly small basement.

Toby nodded.

"Is it true?" Kari blurted. "Do you really…you know?"

Toby tried very hard not to let his expression change. He thought he'd overheard that Kari was a mother who lost a daughter, and he didn't want to inadvertently add to her pain.

"Not in a long while," he replied. "I don't want to keep hurting them."

"How could you?" she whispered. "How fucking could you?"

Toby struggled to find words, but couldn't.

"You're sick," she hissed.

"I know," he answered.

"How old?"

"Excuse me?"

"How old were the girls?" Kari asked, loud enough to draw a few glances and raised eyebrows.

He settled back uncomfortably. "Eleven, twelve. Is this something you really need to know? Don't you think—"

"Don't," she said. "Don't even begin to suggest to me what I should think. I—I have to go." She got up and fled toward the ladies' room. Toby watched after her.

"Her daughter committed suicide," Cicely said. "She was twelve. It was what prompted Kari to move here in the first place."

"I'm sorry," Toby said, and genuinely meant it. "What was her daughter's name?"

"Jessica," Cicely said.

A wave of nausea washed through him. *Jessica.* That had been the girl's name, the one that made him want to stop. "Wh—where did she move from?"

"Dingmans Ferry, I believe."

It was sheer will that kept Toby together, his face stolid, his expression and body language betraying nothing. Inside, every part of him was soaked in guilt and self-hate. It was…oh God, it was his fault. That woman had lost her beautiful little girl and it was his fault. How could it not be? What else could have driven a twelve-year-old to such an extreme act? "I'm so sorry to hear that. I suppose she wishes I were dead."

"I…uh, I don't think she has that kind of hate in her heart."

"I would. Hell, in her shoes, I'd do what I could to make it happen."

"I don't think you would."

Toby wasn't quite sure how to take that. He said, "Would it surprise you, what I've done for little girls?"

"Tobias, I don't think—"

"If I had a daughter, you're damn right I'd do horrible things to a man who…to a man like me."

"Surely you don't mean that, Tobias," Cicely said.

"You seem to want to find some good in me," he said, not sure whether to be amused or suspicious.

"I need to," she replied.

"Why?"

"I'm not doing it for your sake," she said, her face and neck flushing. "I find it very difficult, if you must know, to muster up anything like human compassion for people…like you. But that goes against what the good Lord told us about judging others, and I need to believe in the good in *me*," she gestured to herself, "which means reconciling the almost instinctive loathing I have for those who do… uh, what you do to children with the notion of loving the sinner and not the sin."

He considered that for a moment before saying, "Okay, then. If it helps, I'm kind to animals and pay my taxes on time."

She stood. "I should check on Kari." She turned to go, the disgust evident in the look on her face, when he spoke her name. She turned, barely concealed impatience in her eyes.

"I appreciate what you're trying to do, Ms. Cicely. No, really, I mean that. Not many people would take the time to think of me as a human being at all. I know it probably doesn't mean much coming from me, but for what it's worth, I think that makes you a pretty darn good Christian woman."

The tiniest smile fluttered across her lips, and the look in her eyes softened. In the next moment, though, her primness took over and with a curt nod, she left the room.

Chapter 16

Kathy was having no luck with the inscription. A headache was beginning behind her eye just above her scar, and the small of her back complained loudly when she finally sat up straight in the office chair. She needed a break.

She figured the words were some kind of an incantation, partly because after poring through her notes, she believed even more strongly that the contents of the box were as malleable as they were mercurial, and much like the contents of various people's letters, the substance of that other world could very much be shaped by the thoughts and feelings of the one handling the object. She wanted the inscription to be an incantation that would send everything from that other world back where it came from, and so she thought that was exactly what it was trying to be.

Of course, it wasn't going to make things too easy. Most of the characters didn't match the known runes at all. There was a vague familiarity there and even some of the same lines and circles, but there was some obstacle there, some crucial piece of the puzzle her mind couldn't quite wrap around yet. She went to her purse and pulled out a flask, opened it, took a swig, then sealed and replaced it. She couldn't keep drinking until the barriers in her mind came down. That was how she usually worked, but she felt confident it would undermine these people's confidence in her. Still, she needed to step away for a second, so she quietly opened the office door.

Cole was by the steps leading up to the Heritage Center proper, speaking with two older men in sheriff's office uniforms. Bill was speaking to Ted and Rob, nodding and jotting things down on a pad of paper as they replied. Toby was sitting alone. Several seats away from him, the girl was curled up on the folding chair with a cheap blanket pulled up to her shoulders and her head on her mother's lap. She was clutching her doll. The mother was stroking her hair. Kari and Cicely were gone; Kathy assumed they were in the bathroom, but made a mental note to check on them if they didn't return soon.

Other townsfolk were milling about, discussing the situation in hushed, tense tones or strident, thin voices.

"I don't know why we can't just write a letter asking the Door to close and lock itself forever."

"Uh, because it's doing the *opposite* of what we ask it to do now. That would just open the Door."

"Okay, so write a letter asking the Door to unlock and open itself and set everything in it free on this world."

"Are you insane?"

"Am I? Maybe it would do the opposite."

"That's the stupidest—"

But it wasn't. It *wasn't.*

"Wait," Kathy broke into the conversation. It turned out to be between the woman formerly of the alien abduction shirt and a man in a baseball cap, both of whom looked startled to see her there. "Wait. He may have an idea there. Well, not exactly like how he said, but…yeah…yeah!"

And the barrier in her mind began to crumble.

She ran back to the office, slamming the door closed behind her in her excitement. Reversion. She *had* seen those characters before, except now, they were backwards and upside down. The inscription, written in the words of the Travelers, backward…it seemed to fit. She found comparisons, one by one, of each character. But were the words meant to be read backward? Were the sounds of those words meant to be pronounced backward? In many occult rituals, reversal of rites and incantations involved exactly that: words or actions done backward or in opposite directions.

She opened up some files on linguistics from a folder on her laptop.

That was when she heard the scream.

* * * *

Kari splashed more water on her face, patted it dry with paper towels from the dispenser next to the sink, and looked at her red-rimmed eyes in the mirror.

She'd had to get away from that man. Her sitting so close to someone who hurt girls like Jessica and trying to talk to him like he was just like any other human being overwhelmed her with rage and guilt and frustration. It had opened a wellspring of grief in her the likes of which she hadn't felt since the night of Jessica's death, and those emotions had surged up her throat until she couldn't breathe. She could barely see. She thought she might hyperventilate or pass out or throw up right there on Toby Vernon's shoes.

There in the ladies' room, though, after rinsing her face a few times with cold water and taking several deep breaths, the room was starting to right itself again. She didn't like the wild look in her eyes or the way her hands shook as she smoothed a flyaway strand of hair, but she was beginning to feel a little better.

She jumped when the door suddenly opened, but it was only Cicely.

"Just come to check on you, sugar," Cicely said. "You okay?"

Kari nodded and sniffled. "I just—I had to get out of there."

"I know," Cicely said, putting her arm around Kari and giving her a squeeze. "I know. It's going to be all right. We'll get through this." Side by side, the two stared at each other in the mirror. Cicely gave Kari a warm smile. "We'll get you through this."

"I just feel so…like I'm drowning, you know?"

Cicely's smile grew bigger. "I know, and that's natural—as natural as one can expect in this crazy situation." Her grip around Kari's shoulder grew tighter.

"Thanks, Cicely. I really appreciate—"

Cicely's smile had widened considerably. It now took up half of her face. Her lips, a pale clay color, were starting to crumble from the strain, and her teeth, discolored and filed to sharp little points, were impossibly large. Cracks began to form along the rest of her exposed skin, and from the myriad crevices waved tiny tendrils. Her grip tightened painfully, the long, rotting fingers digging into the skin of Kari's shoulder.

With its free hand, the Cicely-thing by her side reached up and pulled off its face as if it were just a mask. Beneath it was Jessica's face, which promptly vomited into the sink.

Kari screamed.

The bathroom door opened and Cicely came rushing in, looking worried. Kari spun around, her wild gaze searching the bathroom, but there was no sign of the thing that had been masquerading as Cicely.

"My God, sugar, are you okay?" Cicely touched her arm and she shivered. "Kari? Kari, what happened?"

"I don't know!" Kari began to cry again. "I don't know. You were here, then it wasn't you; it was some…*thing*…then it was Jessica, and then it was gone. I don't know what's happening to me!" She broke down. Cicely pulled her into a gentle hug. Kari let her, but the bathroom felt too small. She wanted to go back to where there were people.

"Can we go back?" she asked.

"Of course, sugar. Of course."

Cicely led her out of the bathroom. Kathy, Bill, and Sheriff Cole appeared at the far end of the hall and came running.

"Kari, are you okay? What happened?" Kathy asked, searching her face.

"She saw one of those things. In the bathroom."

"Is it in there now?" Bill asked.

Kari shook her head. "I don't know where it went."

"I'll go look," Kathy said to Bill and the sheriff.

"I'll come with you," Bill said, and they moved off toward the bathroom.

The sheriff and Cicely led Kari back to the main area of the basement. They sat on some folding chairs toward the back of the room. A few minutes later, Kathy and Bill returned to join them.

"Nothing in there now, or in the rooms nearby," Kathy said.

"How could they have gotten in?" Sheriff Cole asked. "I've got deputies at all the doors."

"Well," Kathy replied, "remember, these things are not always solid. They're not tied to the same laws of physics, nor do they necessarily exist in the time-space structures that we understand. Those deputies, they're mostly buying time. But that's all. Our best safety precaution is sticking together. Going forward, we should remind these people to move in groups wherever possible. Pairs, if nothing else."

"Okay," the sheriff said, standing. "I'll spread the word to everyone."

To Kari, Kathy said, "You okay? Can we get you anything?"

Kari, whose sobs had settled down to sniffles, said, "I'm okay."

"Okay, well, I'm just about finished with what I'm working on, and I hope to have answers soon. If you folks need anything…."

"Sheriff Cole and I are here," Bill said. "We'll keep an eye on things."

"Thanks, Bill," Kathy said, and headed back to the office.

Bill moved off to check on the others around the room, and once again Kari was left to wait with Cicely.

"I don't think I can do this," she said to Cicely. "I can't take it anymore."

"I know," Cicely said. "I imagine it's natural in this situation."

Immediately alarmed, Kari's head snapped in the older woman's direction. Cicely looked at her questioningly.

"Is it you?" Kari whispered. "Are you really you?"

"Sugar," Cicely said, patting her hand. "It's me. Really, it's me."

"Okay," Kari answered, but it took a long time for the tension in her chest to uncoil.

* * * *

Kathy had just packed up her files and her laptop when there was a knock on the office door.

"Come in," she called.

The door opened and Bill leaned in. "You have to come see this," he said, breathless.

She came around the desk and followed him out the door.

In the main area, the crowd was buzzing anxiously near the door, which Sheriff Cole stood blocking. Next to him was a young man in a sheriff's department uniform, breathing heavily and bleeding from a gash on his forehead. Ted was arguing with them about something.

"We have the right to know!" he was shouting.

Sheriff Cole held up a hand. "Easy does it. No one's going out there until we know what we're dealing with."

"You can't keep us here indefinitely," someone shouted.

"Is it them?" a voice in the crowd asked. "Are they trying to get in?"

"They took three of your officers," Rob Sherman said. He was a nice-looking man, well-built and well-dressed, though a little too polished for Kathy. His voice, though soft-spoken, struck her as having the kind of confidence built from being used only when the man had something to say. "We just want to know what we're up against. We're just looking for information, that's all."

Sheriff Cole spotted Kathy and Bill and waved them over.

"What happened?" Kathy asked as she reached the edge of the crowd.

With a glance at the others, the sheriff said to her, "We want you to come take a look at something. Outside." To the rest of the crowd, he said, "Yes, they took three of our deputies. That means they have moved past only attacking people who have used the Door. For the listening-challenged, that means every single person in this room is in danger if we go out there. So please, allow us to consult with Ms. Ryan about the situation before you leave this room, okay?"

There was some grumbling, mostly from Ted's corner of the crowd, and some worried chatter, but ultimately, the crowd stepped back to let Kathy and Bill by.

"Stay here," Sheriff Cole told the crowd in that voice that did not invite comment, and then turned and led Kathy and Bill upstairs.

They moved through three rooms of shadowed interior where exhibits like old photographs, old books and ledgers, letters under glass, paintings, architectural artifacts from the homes and businesses of prominent families, pamphlets, and gift shop memorabilia were displayed in cases or on the walls. There was even a painting of the Door, though it offered no other explanation or description other than the title *Gods and Monsters*. There were no photographs of the Door, which didn't strike Kathy as particularly odd. Often, such interdimensional oddities negatively affected digital and film media.

They moved out into the lobby, a spacious foyer-style room with large front windows. The heavy wooden double doors at the front of the building were closed. One of them was horribly scratched…on the inside. It looked to Kathy like someone or something had been clawing at it before being dragged or drawn back outside.

Sheriff Cole led them to one of the windows. "Here. Look outside."

Kathy did so, but saw nothing stranger than she'd seen upon coming in. The front lawn, which separated the building from the street, hadn't changed. Its modern art sculptures, primarily arabesques and asymmetrical geometries made of brass and copper, continued to line the walkway. What she could see of the parking lot and the cars in it didn't strike her as anything unusual, either.

"What am I looking at? I don't see anything."

"Keep looking," Bill said.

Kathy scanned the full panorama visible from the window. The night seemed cloying, almost tangible, as it had even back at the Kilmeisters' house, but—

Then she saw it. The motion lights on the lawn had been triggered, and the play of light and shadow on the sculptures had changed. As her eyes adjusted to the discovery, that chiaroscuro resolved itself into the beginnings of faces, yawning mouths and closed eyes. Kathy even thought she saw them breathing.

"The sculptures," she said. She turned to Cole. "They attacked your deputies?"

"Carried off Franks, Morgan, and the rookie kid, McCoy. They're gone." Sheriff Cole looked genuinely worried, and rightfully so. If his men were with those things out there, it was likely they were dead already.

As if noticing the trio watching them from inside, there was a blur of coppery skin and a thump against the window that made them all jump. Before them, with just inches of glass between them, was a face, a shrieking mask of agony that sank into the mottled mass that suspended it above the ground. Another face surfaced, growling and glaring at them with unadulterated hatred before sinking back into the body again. They watched the mass twist and stretch and snap back, forming tentacles that slapped the glass. One of those, Kathy thought, might make a good show of noise, but a few of them might be able to crack the glass. The whole lot of them could break it down.

"Franks told me something." Cole watched the sculptures as he spoke. "He said he thought those things could cause mutations if they wanted to. Like that thing in your toolbox, maybe. I think it's how they kill people, or one way, at least."

"It's possible," Kathy said.

"They're strong," Bill said as one tentacle rattled the glass in front of him. "Do you...do you think those deputies are already...uh...?"

Kathy didn't want to say what she thought, and Cole really didn't need to hear it. Instead, she asked, "How's the surviving deputy?"

"Pretty shaken up," Cole said. "I left him downstairs with the others. He's a tough kid and he knows his training, but he's still pretty new to all this. Hell, we all are, except you." He turned on Kathy. "They're right, you know. Those people downstairs. We can't keep them here forever. You know as well as I do that it's just a matter of time before those things out there get in here. We need to do something. I will not watch these things pick off everyone I know."

"I know," Kathy said. She knew Cole was feeling responsible for those officers and their families, and therefore probably both angry and sad. She also suspected Cole was not a man easily in touch with such feelings. He wanted answers and he wanted action. She said, "I have a solution. It's not one you're going to want to hear, but it's the only answer."

"The only answer you could come up with?"

"The only answer that will work."

"So let's hear it."

"I'd prefer to tell everyone at once."

Cole considered that, then walked away, back toward the basement. Bill and Kathy exchanged glances, then hurried to catch up to Cole. He said nothing as he led the way through each of the rooms and down the stairs. When he reached the basement, however, he shouted, "Everyone, listen up. Kathy Ryan has something to say."

The nervous crowd, who had been milling about the basement trying to walk off or talk out their nervous energy, gathered around Kathy.

She cleared her throat. "Okay, well, here is the situation. I'm not going to lie and I'm not going to sugarcoat things. This is what we're dealing with. First, one of your fellow townspeople had an artifact from the other side of the Door."

This was met with astonished murmurs from the crowd.

"What is it?" Kari asked.

"Is it here? In the room with us?" Cicely looked around.

"It's secured in this building, yes," Kathy said. "Now, listen. This artifact had an inscription. Most of what I was trying to figure out was the translation of that inscription, and then further, how to properly pronounce it. And after some study and consultation with a few people I know, we've come to the conclusion that it is, in fact, an incantation, and we are in agreement on how it should be pronounced. Also, the object, we believe, is a key. Together, both the object and the inscription can be used to force the creatures from beyond the Door back where they came from, and to relock the Door so that this doesn't happen again."

"Okay, so what are you waiting for?" Ted asked. "Say the inscription or whatever and get rid of these things."

"It's not that simple," Kathy said. "And here's the bad news. For starters, we need to take this key out to the Door and perform the incantation there."

"What? Are you crazy? Go out there? With those things?" someone shouted.

"Didn't the sheriff say there were a bunch of them outside?" the alien abduction woman asked. "How will we get past them?"

"There are a number of those creatures out there—creatures that have already taken three deputies, yes. I believe we can hold them at bay with weapons, but we will need to move quickly."

"Why do you keep saying 'we'?" Ted asked, his face a pudgy grimace of suspicion. "Don't you mean *you*?"

"No," Kathy said. "That's the other piece of bad news. To complete this reversal incantation, I'll need eight other people. I need a circle. I'll need volunteers."

"Obviously, I'm going," Bill said, and Sheriff Cole chimed in, "Me too."

"What about the rest of us?" the girl's mother asked. "Where will we go?"

"I think the creatures will be more interested in following us," Kathy said, "than in bothering the rest of you in here. Even if a few stay behind, the nine of us can do what we have to, I believe, before the lot of them can work their way in here. Yes, it's a risk, but it's a calculated risk, and my expert opinion is that the rest of you are better off here."

"Edmundson," Cole said, "you stay here. Guard these people as best you can. Keep them together, keep them calm, and keep them busy, you hear?"

"Yessir," Edmundson said.

"So who's going to go, then?" another man in the crowd asked. "Who's going to volunteer?"

"It's a suicide mission," Ted said, throwing up his hands. "You go out there and there's no way even nine of you are going to make it there."

"Shut up, Ted," Rob replied, rolling his eyes. "You're scaring people. Seriously, man. Just shut up."

"You shut up!" Ted replied. "This is crazy! You can go off and get yourself killed for some voodoo mumbo jumbo, but I'm not."

"Good, stay here. No one wants you along anyway."

"Oh, and you think they want you along? Whatcha gonna do, speak Latin at them? Fucking fa—"

"Enough!" Edmundson said. He looked close to breaking. "I've had a long night and I swear, man, if you don't knock it off, I will lay you out flat on your ass."

Ted must have sensed Edmundson would and could do just that, because he turned and wandered off, muttering curses under his breath.

"Sorry, ma'am," Edmundson said. "Go on."

Kathy suppressed a little smile. "Thanks. Now, I know it's asking a lot, but you're doing it for yourselves and for each other. You're doing it for your families and your community. Trust me, if there was a way I could do this alone, I would. But there isn't. I need eight of you, and the more varied the eight, the better. Men, women...even children."

"No!" the mother immediately said, pulling her little girl into a hug. "No. No way."

"I'm only asking for volunteers," Kathy said. "No one is obligated to go."

The silence that followed drew out uncomfortably. People cleared their throats and looked away, shuffled their feet and fidgeted.

Finally, a voice said, "I'll do it."

Kathy and the rest of the crowd turned to see who had broken the silence. It was Toby.

"I'll go," he said. "Just...just tell me what I need to do."

"So that's four of us," Bill said. "Five more to go."

"I'll go," Kari said.

"And me as well," Cicely added.

"Three more," Bill said.

"You can count me in," Rob said. "Variety for the win, right? Spice of life and all."

"Why do you need a varied group?" the mother of the little girl asked suddenly. "Why is that important?"

"It makes the incantation stronger," Kathy said. "Different voices, different energies, different experiences, all channeling one single purpose. It increases the chances of the incantation working, both quickly and completely."

"So…if Gracie and I go with you," the mother said slowly, "that would help…you know, make this spell or whatever, this incantation, strong enough to send these things back?"

"It would. I wish I could say otherwise. I'd never even suggest it under other circumstances."

"Can you promise, if we come along, that you'll do everything you can to protect her?"

Kathy looked at her, surprised. She gave Kathy a sheepish little smile. "She insists on going, but I won't let her go alone. I'm coming too. I'm sure Deputy Edmundson here is a fine police officer, but I'm thinking about my little girl, and I can't help feeling maybe she'd be safer with an expert in this stuff, a sheriff with a gun, and an ex-sheriff, right? Still…I want your word—your personal word, Ms. Ryan—that you'll do everything you can to keep her safe."

"You have it," Kathy said.

The mother let out a shuddery sigh. "Okay. Okay. We'll come too. I'm Louise, by the way."

"Louise, thank you."

A tear escaped Louise's eye. "Just please try to keep my baby safe," she said softly.

Kathy nodded. "Thank you. All of you, thank you."

"You'll need guns," Ted said from the back of the crowd. He cocked the pistol he was holding. "Still think this is bullshit, but can't no one say I didn't do my part." He handed the pistol to Rob, along with a set of keys. "My SUV is parked in the back. White Chevy Tahoe. Will fit all nine of you."

"Thank you, Ted," Kathy said, offering him a small but genuinely appreciative smile.

The alien abduction woman and the man with the baseball cap came forward. "Ellie and Bob," the woman said, gesturing at herself and her companion. "Take our guns as well." With a big grin, she added, "Don't worry. We have more."

Toby took one of the offered guns and Kari took the other.

"You're good folks, all of you," Kathy said. "And I'm going to do everything I can to fix this. Know that. Volunteers, take fifteen minutes, get yourselves and your things together, and we'll go. To everyone else, stay here and stay safe. Watch out for each other. And don't give Deputy Edmundson a hard time."

Little Gracie tugged on the hem of Kathy's blouse and she looked down. "Are we gonna kill the monsters, Ms. Ryan?"

"Yeah, sweetie, we're gonna sure as heck try."

Chapter 17

Twenty minutes later, Kathy and the eight volunteer members of her circle stood by the front doors of the Heritage Center, along with Ted, Ellie, and Bob. The latter three, led by Ellie, had grudgingly volunteered to provide a distraction at the windows if necessary so that the other nine could slip out the back door to Ted's SUV. The three of them were armed to the teeth, more so than the deputy downstairs or even the sheriff, which under other circumstances, Kathy might have found a bit unsettling. In this case, though, she was glad that Pennsylvania folks liked their guns and had thought to bring them.

They all stood looking out the window at the sculptures, assessing the situation. There were nine of those things out there, and they were no longer lining the walkway. They had essentially given up the pretense of blending in to their surroundings. Hovering, pulling, and stretching, they surged over the lawn, forming an uneven and constantly changing barrier between the doors and the parking lot. While no eyes surfaced from that nebulous mass of bodies, often several mouths appeared as they growled and nipped at each other. The lack of eyes could mean one of two things: Either their attention spans were short and their ability to sense humans based on proximity...or they were deliberately pretending to ignore the small group of people pressed up to the windows.

"Ugly fuckers, aren't they?" Ted said.

"Language," Louise muttered. She was clutching her wide-eyed little girl close. Both looked pretty terrified, and were probably having serious doubts about volunteering. Kathy didn't blame them.

"Pretty big too," Bob added. He chewed on the filtered end of an unlit cigarette—there was no smoking in the Heritage Center, and he wasn't about to step outside for a smoke—and frowned. He went to tap on the glass, but Cole grabbed his wrist.

"Not a good idea," Cole said and let go.

"Can they hear us?" Bob asked. "Or see us? Shit, they don't have ears or eyes or—"

"They can see," Kathy said, "and I'd guess they can either hear or smell us, or feel changes in the air akin to those senses." She shifted the toolbox to her other hand. The box inside was vibrating audibly now, and some of the others were glancing at it uncomfortably.

"So…if they look like they're leaving, heading around back or something, we make some noise here, right?" Ted asked. He had settled down considerably from the large, disgruntled man he'd been in the basement. Kathy had found that often, coming face-to-face (such as the face may be) with proof of interdimensional entities had that effect on people.

"Yes, but try to keep them outside and you inside at all times, if possible," Cole said. "If they do break in or you have to go out, shoot them in the mouth. We don't know if it hurts them, but they sure don't like it. Makes 'em fold up and disappear."

"And if they break through the glass?" Ellie asked.

"Retreat to the basement. Hold down the fort," Bill answered. "We hope it won't come to that."

"So don't mess with them unless they mess with you or us," Bob said.

Kathy turned to him. "I'm counting on the three of you to keep cool heads. Don't fire unless you have to. Don't draw their attention unless you have to. And if you have to, shoot wisely. Get me?"

"Yes, ma'am," Bob replied. "Shoot smart, not hard."

"Exactly."

Bob went to the far end of the lobby and set himself up in a shadow by the window, his gun drawn. Ted took the other side and Ellie took watch by the doors.

"Good luck," Ellie said to Kathy. "Be safe."

"Do what you gotta do and do it quick," Ted added.

"Thanks," Kathy said, and to Cole, "Lead the way."

Cole led them back through all the rooms to a small hallway, past the offices of Historical Society members and then on past storage rooms to a small metal door. Kathy handed Cole the keys that Mrs. Pulaski had given her, and Cole unlocked the back door. It was the kind with a long metal push bar, and it groaned when Cole opened it. The nine of them waited a moment, listening for the keening or growling sounds of possible nearby creatures. When they were satisfied that the dense darkness was empty, they filed quietly out, one at a time, into the open air.

The back parking lot of the Heritage Center was thankfully empty, with the exception of two sedans and Ted's Tahoe. His keys had a fob dangling from the key ring that would automatically open the doors, but the accompanying noise was too much of a risk. They'd have to open the doors manually.

They crept across the lot, sticking close together and keeping little Gracie in the middle. They were acutely aware of their surroundings, flinching at every little sound, shivering at the slightest shifts of the breeze.

They had just reached the Tahoe when the first of the screeches sounded over the top of the building.

"Cole," Kathy warned. She was on the passenger side of the van, waiting for Cole, on the driver's side, to unlock the door. The toolbox trembled in excitement.

"On it," Cole said tensely.

A dark shape soared upward against the sky, its outlines glowing faintly. Its newly formed wings made a terrible buzzing sound, despite the slow flap of their movement.

Next to Kathy, Bill said, "Stick close to the truck, folks."

Cole got the driver's-side door open and pushed the button to unlock the other doors. Another screech zigzagged through the air, followed by a gunshot, and then another.

The others opened their doors, piling in to the Tahoe. Kathy hopped into the passenger seat and at the satisfying sound of doors slamming, Kathy let go of the breath she had been holding. She turned in her seat and quickly counted seven people, plus Cole and herself.

"Everybody in," she said, putting the toolbox on her lap. "Everyone okay?"

"We're fine," Bill said. "Let's go."

Cole fired up the engine and took off. As he turned the corner, Kathy could see Ted on the front lawn, firing wildly. Inside the open doors, Ellie and Bob were trying to help without compromising the security of the building, but it was a losing battle. The creatures swarmed Ted like a black, slightly iridescent fog, and his screams followed the van as it pulled out onto the road.

Louise clutched her daughter close, trying to cover her eyes and ears. Toby watched out the back window. The others looked worried.

No one spoke during the ten-minute drive to the edge of the woods.

When Cole parked the truck, they all looked to Kathy. She knew they wanted instruction and leadership. Even more than that, she knew they wanted to hear that everything would be okay.

She could at least provide the former.

"We need to stay together going through the woods. It's about an hour's hike in, but the path is fairly clear and the terrain is easy. Still, *stay together.* Hold hands if you want—I don't care. Just make sure you don't get lost, okay? I don't know what's in there, but I can only assume that the closer we get to the Door, the more desperate those things will be to keep us from it."

"Kathy," Cicely said, "are we going to die?"

"Was Ted right?" Kari added. "Is this really a suicide mission?"

Kathy paused, knowing full well that each second that ticked by that she didn't answer them was going to erode their confidence. Finally, she said, "Not necessarily. It's dangerous. You all know that. But if you do what I tell you, we have the best odds of surviving. Once I begin the incantation, the only thing you need to do is hold hands, close your eyes, and concentrate. That's it. They won't be able to touch you then. We just have to get ourselves there and set up. That's the real tricky part."

"Let's go then," Toby said quietly.

The others agreed.

"If you're ready…." Kathy said.

"Ready as we'll ever be," Rob replied.

"Okay, then. Let's get to it."

* * * *

The nine of them made their way through the woods, led by Bill and Cole, then Kathy, carrying the toolbox. She had been partly joking when she'd suggested holding hands, but they did, forming a sort of chain that began with Gracie tightly gripping both Kathy's free hand and one of her mother's, then Rob, Kari, and Cicely, and ending with Toby. Since cell phones had ceased to work some hours ago, the density of the night possibly interfering not just with their reception, but even with the functioning of things like the flashlight app, Cole was using the utility light that he kept clipped to his belt. Bill had found another flashlight under one of Ted's car seats, and between the two of them, the illusion of safe passage was created. The group spoke little, and when they did, it was of superficial observations. Toby told a joke that elicited smiles, if not laughter, and Bill told a hunting story about the time a herd of deer pushed him into a lake.

Kathy smiled to herself. It never ceased to amaze her how adaptable human beings were to situations of intense fear. Soldiers did it. Trauma victims did it. Their methods varied from shutting down to cracking wise, from innuendo and physical contact to complete avoidance, but as a species, humans were survivors. In her lifetime, Kathy had found little reason to have faith in the better parts of humanity, but their resilience and their occasional acts of thoughtless bravery were why she kept doing what she did best. People surprised her in their will to find the best and bravest aspects of their character sometimes.

The increasing volume of their laughter and talk suggested that for the time being, they had forced the fear from their minds. It was, in part, due to the fact that the majority of the trip through the woods had been uneventful. The occasional crackling of a branch or the crunch of leaves that echoed in just such a way as to suggest something "out there" made them flinch, but in each case, it had proved to be nothing. They were starting to feel confident, allowing themselves the possibility that everything really would be okay.

Kathy hoped they were right.

They were close, maybe five minutes or so away, when Kathy saw the eyes. First, it was a pair, shark-like and faintly glowing, from a clump of shrubs. Then another pair lit up nearby, and another, and another.

The laughter trickled off quickly and the chatter ground to a halt. The others had noticed. Bill and Cole had slowed considerably, so that the entire line crept stealthily now, afraid sudden or swift movement would incite the things behind those predatory eyes to attack.

"Kathy, what do we do?" Toby asked from the far end of the line.

"Hold onto each other. Don't run unless they attack. If they do, head for the clearing up there. We're close."

All around them, a low hum almost like words closed in on them.

They kept moving. Occasionally a tentacle would snap out at them, making Kari or Louise cry out. Cicely half-whispered prayers.

When one of the creatures leaned out and roared in Toby's face, he fired three bullets into its mouth. It shrieked and snapped back into the darkness. Another lunged at Kari, but Kathy pulled the gun from the other woman's pocket and fired until that shrieking mouth jerked back into the gloom.

Bill and Cole broke through to the clearing and Kathy shouted, "Go! Go!" The others, still holding onto each other, half-ran and half-stumbled into the clearing.

The runes around the doorframe glowed. In the space beneath the Door itself, bluish mist roiled out and into the air. The oaks, distorted by the alien light and the encroaching dark, seemed to shrink even further away from the groaning and bowing boards of the Door. Whatever was on the other side—maybe the true gods behind the Door—couldn't slip underneath, and Kathy was glad for that. But the way the planks were bending against the strain, it would be a miracle if those gods didn't find a way to break straight through.

"Quick, everyone! Form a circle." Kathy stood before the Door and the others joined hands in a circle around her. She looked at each in turn—Kari to Cicely to Rob to Toby to Gracie and Louise, then to Bill and Cole. Then she opened the toolbox and took out the wooden box within. It glowed so brightly that for a moment, its bluish light was all she could see. It also trembled violently in her hands, and it took a good deal of her strength just to hold onto it.

She'd written phonetic notes for the incantation on the inside of her left arm, and as she held the box out toward the Door, she began to speak.

The hum of the Door, in response, grew louder, punctuated by a loud bang and then another from the other side. The darkness had swallowed the woods in all directions, flowing toward the ring of oaks, toward the circle of people and the Door.

A cry from Toby grew her glance in his direction, but she kept speaking. She caught a glimpse of the gash on the back of his shoulder, issued from a tentacle withdrawing into that encroaching dark. He was clearly in pain, but he held onto the hands of Gracie and Rob. Kari cried out next, though she too kept the circle unbroken, despite the blood running down her leg. Kathy kept going. The wood in her hands was splintering as the contents rattled violently against it, and her shoulder burned with white-hot pain, but she held on.

The creatures hadn't rushed them in the woods because the humans could have scattered and fled, but here, in front of the Door, they were fish in a barrel. Kathy's time was running out. She wasn't sure how long the eight of them surrounding her could hold onto each other.

"Hold on!" Bill shouted. "Don't break the circle." He stumbled forward from a blow to the back by another tentacle, but held fast to Cole's and Kari's hands.

Kathy spoke the words louder and faster. She wasn't sure what would happen once the incantation began to work, but she knew that around the ninth iteration, she would begin to see the change. She hoped the others could hold on, both figuratively and literally, for that long.

When Gracie cried out, she closed her eyes. The best she could do for these people was complete the incantation, so she kept saying the words. A burning in her hands had begun to travel up her wrists and down from her injured shoulder, but she focused the pain into speaking louder and louder. The hum, matching her volume, had increased to a roar and then a howl.

When she opened her eyes, she saw splintered fragments of wood sticking out of her palms. The wooden box had disintegrated completely, and in her hands, she clutched a bluish-green disc whose sharp edges bit into the inside bends of her fingers. There was something like a face in the center, and it screamed along with the howling from behind the Door. She held it higher, just over Gracie's head and toward the Door.

She entered into the ninth repetition of the incantation and the blue glow travelled farther up her arms. Bluish mist poured out from around all sides of the Door. The howl was deafening now, and the pain in her hands and wrists was threatening to cause the muscles in her arms to seize. All around her, the circle remained unbroken, but she could see from their terrified faces that their strength was ebbing.

Kathy finished the words, and suddenly the Door blew inward.

The disc in her hands flew over Gracie's head and through the opening, which Kathy stared at in awe. Beyond the neat, rectangular edges of this dimension was a storming black sky with angry purplish-gray clouds. Bright blue lightning flashed, striking quicksilver waves that spit their spray and foam against a far-off island. On the island, as Kari had described, was an immense tower, glowing faintly blue.

"Oh my God," Kathy breathed, but her words were lost in the din.

A series of shrieks preceded first one blur, then another and another, as the creatures were sucked out of the darkness. They narrowly missed the members of the circle as they were pulled through the open space. All eight of them, too terrified to move, gaped at the opening or watched the creatures zipping by them. The opening was sucking in everything: the thick darkness, stretched to plumes like smoke, which had made the night so opaque, the hums and howls and screams, the blue mist.

A creature whizzed past Kathy and over Gracie's little head, but before it could be funneled into the storm on the other side, a tentacle smacked the wood of the Door and held fast. Another wrapped around Gracie's arm and yanked her free of the circle, pulling her into the opening and dangling her over the water. Louise screamed. The tentacle holding onto the Door let go, but Gracie remained.

Toby was holding the girl's arm with one hand; the other had the gun pointed at the creature holding onto her. A number of mouths bloomed suddenly in its flesh and Toby began to fire. The gun made no sound, but the bullets flew…and found their mark. The creature let go of Gracie and Toby pulled her back through the opening, shoving her toward Louise, who scooped her up and held her tightly.

Another creature flew by, wrapping a tentacle around Toby's wrist and wrenching the gun free. It fell down and disappeared in the monstrous waves. The creature yanked him through the opening before letting go, but he grabbed at the planks of the Door. Bill dove for his hand and held on. Kathy ran to hold onto Bill, Kari and Cicely held onto her, and Cole held onto them. Rob held Louise and Gracie, moving them away from the pull of the wind.

"Toby!" Kathy cried out.

The Door began to close.

"Pull!" Bill shouted. The group pulled, but Bill slid forward. The force of the incantation threatened to flush them all through the Door and slam it shut.

"The Door's closing!" Rob called out.

"Pull!" Bill shouted again and the group pulled, but Toby was on the other side now, buffeted by the storm winds that Kathy had created.

The Door slid even further closed.

Toby glanced at Kathy and then fixed his gaze on Bill. "Let go," he said, and although his voice should have been swallowed by the storm, Kathy could still hear him.

"What? Toby, no," Bill said.

"You'll die!" Kari cried. "You can't!"

They tried again to pull him through, but the storm was getting stronger. Having reclaimed the remains of that other dimension, the Door was ready to close. It swung forward a few more inches. Now the edge of it was close to Bill's shoulder.

Toby, who looked scared enough, shook his head. "The Door's closing. You have to, or the whole lot of you will get sucked in too. We don't have time to argue. Just let me go."

"Don't do this, Tobias," Cicely said. "You don't have to do this."

Toby smiled at them, but his eyes were sad. To Kari, he said, "I'm so sorry." Then, to the others he said, "It's okay. Let me go. It's okay."

The Door bumped up against Bill's shoulder. The older man looked sad, but he knew Toby was right.

"I'm sorry," he said softly.

"Don't be. I'm ready."

With a final, pained look, Bill nodded, then let Toby go. Toby fell backward toward the silver water and disappeared under the waves. Kathy saw him surface once, wave and even smile, before another wave washed him under for good.

Bill pushed back with some force, shoving the group behind him onto their rears, but out of the way just as the Door slammed shut. The other world disappeared, cutting off the storm, the mists, the dark, and that terrible howl, fading to a scream, then to a hum, and finally to utter silence.

For several minutes, the eight of them gathered before the Door held each other. Some cried, some laughed, and some did both at once. Others remained shocked into silence, staring at the Door.

"Did we do it?" little Gracie asked. She looked dazed, her little pink cheeks streaked with tears and dirt. "Did we make all the monsters go away?"

"We sure did, sweetie," Kathy said. "We sure did."

Epilogue

Kathy stayed another three days or so in Zarephath, helping the sheriff and Bill tie up loose ends, process paperwork, and clean up some of the damage. The morning following their closing and locking of the Door, she was pleased to see that despite the damage to the lawn and the front of the Heritage Center building, Deputy Edmundson and the rest of the assembled townspeople had managed to stay safe the rest of the night. Ellie and Bob, looking a little bedraggled but otherwise not seriously hurt, were proudly flanking the deputy, whose splinted leg had been broken while assisting them with the two creatures who had made it into the lobby of the building. Edmundson was checked over, but he was holding up okay. Mostly, he was pleased by Cole's approval, which he received in the form of a smile and a hearty clap on the shoulder.

Over those three and a half days, Kathy checked in with Reece, who was relieved to hear she was safe and looking forward to seeing her when she got home. She was looking forward to it too. He had a way of soothing her even when she didn't realize she needed soothing, and in bringing normalcy back to the places in her that she worried might be permanently hollowed out by the strangeness of her job. She had her files and laptop packed and in the car. Her wounds had been checked out by the county hospital, which issued her some new bandages on her shoulder, wrists, and palms, and an otherwise clean bill of health. She saw to it that her circle was treated and cleared by doctors as well, and then moved on to the rest of the injured townsfolk. She determined to her satisfaction that there was no contagion from the other world, and readings on the Door left her confident that both the entities that had slipped through and those that had tried to break in had receded back to that silvery ocean, the island, and the tower.

Kathy was particularly interested in making sure no lingering effects or entities from the world behind the Door remained. She observed, with the help of the townspeople, that while the contents of their letters had been negated across the board, they were no longer being haunted by them in any way. Kathy knew it would take a long time, maybe years, to really feel safe in their homes and familiar hometown places, but they were a resilient people, stoic like the generations before them, and despite their being given a skeleton key to another world, it was far less likely that going forward, they would use it.

There were things worth surviving rather than changing, and there were things for which surviving was the option. Kathy knew that, and so did most of the population of Zarephath.

As Kathy drove away from Zarephath, she passed the far edge of the woods. She thought of Carl Dietrich, Ed Richter, and the Kilmeisters, and finally, of Toby. She remembered telling Bill that heaven and hell were just other dimensions, other planes of existence, and she did believe that, but she hoped that where the dead of Zarephath had gone was a place where the flaw of being human, all across the spectrum, was forgiven and they were at peace.

Lastly, she wondered about the tower she had seen. It was a place of significance and import; she could feel that radiating outward all the way from the island to her spot in the woods of her own dimension. It worried her a little, because it confirmed her belief that in those dimensions between heaven and hell, there was immense power, and with it, truly godlike sentience capable of tapping into that power.

Kathy began to hum along with the radio, then caught herself and stopped. She could do without humming for a while.

She left Zarephath comfortably in the rearview and headed home.

About the Author

Mary SanGiovanni, author of the Kathy Ryan series, is also the author of *Chills*, *Savage Woods*, and the Bram Stoker–nominated novel, *The Hollower* and its sequels *Found You* and *The Triumvirate*, *Thrall*, and *Chaos*. She is also the author of several other novels and numerous short stories. She has been writing fiction for over a decade, has a master's in writing popular fiction from Seton Hill University, and is a member of the Authors Guild, Penn Writers, and International Thriller Writers.

Her website is marysangiovanni.com.

Chills

If you enjoyed *Behind the Door*, be sure not to miss
Kathy Ryan's first appearance!

It begins with a freak snowstorm in May. Hit hardest is the rural town of
Colby, Connecticut. Schools and businesses are closed, power lines are
down, and police detective Jack Glazier has found a body in the snow. It
appears to be the victim of a bizarre ritual murder. It won't be the last. As
the snow piles up, so do the sacrifices. Cut off from the rest of the world,
Glazier teams up with an occult crime specialist to uncover a secret society
hiding in their midst.

The gods they worship are unthinkable. The powers they summon are
unstoppable. And the things they will do to the good people of Colby are
utterly, horribly unspeakable . . .

Read on for a special excerpt!

A Lyrical Underground e-book on sale now.

Chapter 1

Jack Glazier had worked Colby Township Homicide for going on nine long New England winters, but he had never seen blood freeze quite like that.

It certainly had been cold the last few nights; it was the kind of weather that cast phantom outlines of frost over everything. That hoary white made grass, tree branches, cars, even houses look fragile, like they might crack and shatter beneath the lightest touch. An icy wind that stabbed beneath the clothes and skin had been grating across the town of Colby for days now, and the place was raw.

Jack hated the cold. He hated it even more when his profession brought him out on brittle early mornings like this one, where the feeble sunlight did little even to suggest the idea of heat.

He had caught a murder case—a middle-aged John Doe found hanging upside down from the lowest branch of a massive oak tree at the northeastern edge of Edison Park. The body had been strung up off the ground by the right leg with some type of as-yet-unidentified rope. A crude hexagon had been dug roughly in the torn-up grass beneath the body. Scattered in those narrow trenches, he'd been told, the responding officers had found what they believed to be the contents of the man's pockets, which had been bagged as a potential starting point for identification.

Jack glanced up at the silver dome of sky with its gathering clouds of darker gray and listened for a moment to the low wail of the wind slicing at the men gathered near the body. They worked silently, their minimal conversation encased in tiny breath-puffs of white. The air carried a faint smell of freezer-burned meat that agitated Jack in a way the smell of dead bodies never really did. It made him think of lost things, things forgotten way in the back of dark, cold places and left to rot slowly. There was no closure and no dignity in it.

Of course, he supposed that closure and whatever little dignity he could scrape together for the victims of murder was part of *his* job.

It took an effort to focus on the body again, to duck under the strung-up lines of police tape and move toward it. He found that the closer he got to a decade of dealing with dead, clouded eyes, gelid, mutilated flesh, and distraught loved ones, the more energy it took to give himself over to getting cases started. He wanted them solved—that drive had propelled him to the rank of detective lieutenant and it made him good at what he did—but it was the *starting* of the investigations he had lost the taste for. It was getting harder and harder to stare the next few months of brooding and nightmares in the face.

As for the body itself, the throat looked like it had been cut—bitten, really—and there were lacerations on the naked torso, shoulders, bare arms, and face. Jack, who did his best to suppress his morbidly imaginative streak in these situations yet frequently failed, could imagine the John Doe dangling in the glacial night air, wracked with shivers as his blood poured from his wounds, cooling the fire of life in his body until there was no movement, no feeling. He was an end scene, frozen before the roll of the credits, his screen time cut suddenly short.

All of the John Doe's blood had formed, drop by drop, fringes of crimson icicles from the lowest-hanging parts of his body, as if every part, every tissue of the man had struggled to escape that branch and its pain and death. The overall effect stripped the humanity from the corpse, leaving it a gross caricature of what it once had been.

A uniformed officer whose name slipped Jack's mind—Morano or Moreno, something like that—nodded at him as he made his way up to the crime scene. Crouched beneath the body a foot or so from the outline of overturned grass clumps, Colby's thin, bald, and bespectacled coroner, Terrence Cordwell, was packing up his kit.

"They're calling for about eight to ten inches of snow, starting around midnight. Can you believe that? Probably keep up most of tomorrow," Cordwell was saying to Dave Brenner, his assistant, who had switched from the digital camera to the film. Dave was documenting the churned-dirt hexagon and the body with another series of close-up photos. Both men nodded to Jack as he joined them.

Brenner stepped carefully into the hexagon's center and took a close-up photo of the body's neck wound, a gaping tear like a second frown across his neck, then stepped outside the core of the crime scene, around to the back of the torso. He whistled, holding up his pocket ruler beneath the body's shoulder blades, and took another couple of photos. "Hey, Glazier. Where's Morris?"

Jack crouched and peered closer at the neck wound. It looked deep and uneven, like several serrated sharp objects had torn and gouged at the neck at once. It reminded him again of a bite. "Nephew's baptism. He's the godfather, I think."

"Poor kid. Hey, shit weather, huh? Too cold for May."

"Cold, yeah. Not unheard of, though, I guess."

"No," Brenner offered grudgingly over his shoulder, and Jack heard the whir and snap of the camera taking another picture. "Up north, maybe. But still awful late in the season for more snow around here. It's a sign that the planet is fucked, if you ask me. Global warming and shit."

Jack didn't answer. He wasn't particularly fond of Brenner; the guy always seemed to have one more thing to say than Jack had the patience to hear.

Instead, Jack rose and turned to Cordwell. "So what's the deal with this guy?"

The coroner peeled off his rubber gloves. "No ID, no wallet—but he's got teeth and fingertips, so if he's in the system, we should be able to find him. Dead eight, maybe nine hours. With the cold, it's hard to say for sure until we get him back to the cave. What I can tell you is that he froze to death before he had a chance to bleed out, although the hypothermia was likely accelerated by the blood loss. These lacerations and that neck wound were meant, I'm guessing, to speed up the process. They're animal, most of them. Not certain what kind yet, but we bagged and tagged what I'm pretty sure is a tooth."

"Animal bites? So what, someone fed him to something and then strung up what was left?"

Cordwell shrugged. "More likely, it happened the other way around. Someone strung this guy up and left him to . . . whatever did that to him."

Jack frowned, moving slowly as he examined the body. One of the hands was missing. When he pointed it out, Cordwell shook his head; they hadn't found it. The leg from which the John Doe was strung up was virtually untouched. Jack imagined a man would know that it would have to be kept intact to support the weight of the body, but how the animal or animals managed to avoid it, Jack could only guess. Likely, it was simply too high for them to reach. The other leg was mangled, but not nearly as badly as the head, arms, and torso. Those wounds alternated between slashes Jack figured for a knife and more of those ragged tears, right down to the bone in a lot of places. Jack shook his head at the brutality of it and moved around to the back of the body.

Then he saw the brand. In the entire space between the shoulder blades, ugly, angry pink swells of skin formed a large kind of symbol Jack didn't recognize, featuring asymmetric swirls crossed with an irregular lattice of lines. It looked deliberate; in fact, it surprised Jack that the design was as clearly and intricately formed as it was.

"Hey, Brennan, you get a picture of this?"

"The burn marks? Yeah. Creepy shit. Occult?"

"Maybe. Looks pretty new."

"You know," Brenner said with a careful, measured tone, "if this is some kinda devil-worshiping thing, they'll probably want to bring Ryan in on this."

Jack frowned, glancing at the younger man. "Don't think we'll need Ryan, necessarily."

Brenner shrugged. "Maybe not. Maybe the brand doesn't mean anything at all, other than deluded satanist fantasies of some nut job thinking he's some grand high wizard or something. But you know, if it's not—"

Jack turned the full attention of his gaze on Brenner and the rest of the sentence dropped off.

It wasn't that Jack didn't like Ryan; they'd worked very closely a few years back busting a child sex ring that had strong connections to a radical Golden Dawn sect working out of Newport. She'd also been called in to work with him on collaring a big-name drug dealer in Boston whose specialty product, in addition to persuasive pulpit revelations delivered in an abandoned Russian Orthodox church, was a powder rumored to make devoted users both see and attempt to kill demons. Occult practices, ancient grimoires, devil worship, blood sacrifices, and rites to archaic gods and monsters—that was Ryan's thing, her specialty. She'd worked all over the country as a private consultant to law enforcement evaluating occult involvement and assessing risk, and was known to be efficient and discreet. She also was apparently able, through resourcefulness or mystery connections, to skirt a lot of red tape and paperwork regarding freedom of religious pursuit that usually hung up other investigations. Jack thought she was brilliant, aloof, and intense, but the kind of woman one was dismayed to be inexorably drawn to.

Ryan was good at what she did, although to say she was popular with the people she worked for or with might be pushing it. How she'd come into her line of work or developed a reputation for being one of the country's leading experts in it was something she guarded closely. Jack suspected it contributed to what made her eyes dark and her smile fleeting, and any true attempt at getting close to her impossible. Her experiences formed the ghosts of truly haunted expressions beneath those she offered the world. And Jack thought she was a bottle of vodka and a .38 away from blowing all that she'd seen and learned about the fringes of the world out the back of her head.

Cordwell clapped him on the shoulder, jarring him from his thoughts. "I'll have a prelim report for you in a day or two. Stay warm."

Jack nodded as the men moved away, ducking under the police tape. He saw Cordwell motion to one of the technicians, say something, and then gesture in his direction. Jack assumed the tech had been told the body was ready for transport.

He stood a few moments, his eyes drawing over the details of the body, the contorted features of the face, the wounds already starting to take on that freezer-burn-like quality to match that smell that, when the wind shifted, found its way inside his nose on the back of the cold, dry air. He made his way over to the small blue tent top that had been set up over a folding table, designated as the detectives' safe area. He figured Detective Reece Teagan would already be there, getting a jump start on examining the items Cordwell said had been found in the dirt.

And so he was—Teagan's scuffed sneakers were propped up on the corner of the evidence table as he leaned back in a metal folding chair. He was squinting intently at the contents of a plastic evidence bag with a red label, an unlit Camel cigarette hanging out of his mouth. With his free hand, he absently ran his fingers through his hair, a quirky little habit that sent it up into dirty-blond spikes. When he noticed Jack's approach, he nodded a hello, which sent those spikes drifting back, more or less into place. Jack noticed for the first time that some of those spikes had the occasional strand of gray—not nearly as much as Jack had seen mixed in his own black hair the last year or so, but enough to remind him again just how many cases had come and gone for him with Teagan, Morris, Cordwell, and their winters in Colby.

"Jack. You seen these yet? Right feckin' warped."

Teagan had grown up in Westport and Inistioge in Ireland before going to Oxford and then working as a detective sergeant, and although he'd been almost ten years in the States, his brogue was still strong. It seemed a continuing source of amusement to him that American women swooned and giggled when he spoke to them, calling them "love." His accent and accompanying rakish grin never ceased to earn him confidences, phone numbers, and, when need be, forgiveness from the "birds" he occasionally dated. That he was a pretty good-looking guy beneath the facial scruff, with a lean, strong build to boot, didn't hurt his cause, either.

"How's that?" Jack pulled up a folding chair next to him and leaned in toward the evidence table. Nodding at Teagan's light jacket, he said, "Aren't you cold?"

"Fresh air, mate. Take a look at this stuff." Teagan gestured at the evidence bags. Jack examined the contents of the first few, taking note of some change (thirty-four cents), a key ring with car keys (although the Toyota they belonged to was conspicuously absent), and a receipt for chips and coffee from the nearby convenience store.

"Not sure what I'm supposed to be seeing here. Looks like the stuff on the floor of my car."

"Not those," Teagan said. "These." He slid a few bags over to Jack. The first bag contained what looked to Jack like a chunk of splintered wood about six inches long and three inches wide. He held it up by the bag and turned it over, then saw what Teagan meant. The back side of the wood was flat and smooth, and into it was burned or carved a series of runic marks that formed neat lines across the whole surface. Jack looked at Teagan questioningly, and the other man shrugged.

"Cordwell says this one's a tooth." He handed Jack another bag with a slightly curved bit of ivory substance about five or six inches long. One end held the remains of a rough kind of root while the other tapered to a very sharp point.

"What the hell has teeth like this around here? Is he serious?"

"Damned if I know," Teagan said. He slid another bag toward Jack. "And there's this card, here."

It was the size of a business card, although it was entirely black and there was no writing on it on either side. Jack studied the matte finish on both sides for signs of fingerprints but couldn't even find a smudge.

"Calling card, maybe? Business card?" Jack asked.

"No idea. Though, whoever it belongs to might want to be rethinking their business plan."

Jack handed it back. "Maybe they can get something off it. Or off that piece of wood there. Cordwell seems pretty sure this was some kind of orchestrated animal attack."

There was a pause. "Cordwell's saying they might call Kathy in on this," Teagan said, his gaze fixed on the piece of wood.

"Yeah, Brennan said the same thing to me," Jack replied. "For her sake, I hope all this black-magic bullshit is coincidental. Last I heard, she could use a break from it."

"Her input couldn't hurt," Teagan said thoughtfully, handling the bag with the wood sliver. "Even if she only identifies this . . . language, or whatever it is."

"You know superficial involvement, at least in cases, isn't how she operates."

Teagan reined in a small smile. "Yeah, I know."

Jack prided himself in thinking he understood the thoughts, feelings, and motivations below the surface—the ones others wore in their eyes and their smiles and nowhere else. He was fairly certain Teagan was in love with Kathy. The way he looked at her, the softness that crept into his voice when he said her name—it wasn't an investigative stretch to see his longing for her, however smooth and subtle he thought he was. Kathy, though, likely had no clue. In spite of their individual eccentricities, or maybe because of them, Teagan and Kathy were probably soul mates, but knowing her as Jack did, he was pretty sure she never allowed herself to entertain the thought. And Teagan . . . he approached his job with the relentless instinct and perseverance of someone resigned to giving up anything like a normal life. To Teagan, there were dead folks and the folks who killed them, the psychology behind how and why, and not much else.

"Well, I'm off. Could eat the ass of a low-flyin' duck," Teagan said suddenly. "We on this thing together, yeah?"

"Yeah, looks like," Jack said, leaning an elbow on the table. "You, me, and Morris. Tomorrow, nine a.m. My office."

Teagan nodded and jogged off to his car. Jack watched him go, then turned his attention back to the chunk of wood in the bag. He took a deep breath, frigid in his nose and throat, and let it out in little white puffs. It was time, he knew, to start the job.

Savage Woods

**Bram Stoker award-nominated author Mary SanGiovanni returns
with a terrifying tale of madness, murder, and mind-shattering evil...**
Nilhollow—six-hundred-plus acres of haunted woods in New Jersey's Pine
Barrens—is the stuff of urban legend. Amid tales of tree spirits and all-
powerful forest gods are frightening accounts of hikers who went insane
right before taking their own lives. It is here that Julia Russo flees when
her violent ex-boyfriend runs her off the road . . . here that she vanishes
without a trace.

State Trooper Peter Grainger has witnessed unspeakable things that have
broken other men.

But he has to find Julia and can't turn back now. Every step takes him
closer to an ugliness that won't be appeased—a centuries-old, devouring
hatred rising up to eviscerate humankind. Waiting, feeding, surviving.
It's unstoppable. And its time has come.

Printed in the United States
by Baker & Taylor Publisher Services